Instructions for the Working Day

JOANNA CAMPBELL

Fairlight Books

First published by Fairlight Books 2022
This paperback edition first published by Fairlight Books 2023

Fairlight Books
Summertown Pavilion, 18–24 Middle Way, Oxford, OX2 7LG

A CIP catalogue record for this book is available from the
British Library

1 2 3 4 5 6 7 8 9 10

ISBN 978-1-914148-24-8

www.fairlightbooks.com

Printed and bound in Great Britain

Designed by Jack Smyth

This is a work of fiction. Names, characters and businesses are
the products of the author's imagination. Any resemblance to
actual persons, living or dead is purely coincidental.

To my family

Shall we never, never get rid of this Past? ... It lies upon the Present like a giant's dead body!

—Nathaniel Hawthorne, *The House of the Seven Gables*

Chapter One

Neil Fischer drives with his window down, the warm air lifting the hairs on his arms. Dust blows in, making his eyes water. The sun shimmers on the tarmac, softening it enough to melt. His car could sink without anyone noticing.

The last time he was on this road, his father was driving. Neil was twelve. He sat in the back seat with his little sister, Kersten. Their mother sat in the front, wearing a pink straw hat. The moment she wound her window down, it was whipped away. Neil watched it cartwheeling out of sight.

A girl in a white T-shirt and jeans wide enough to waft in the breeze is standing by the roadside, holding her thumb out. Neil has never picked anyone up before. When he slows down, the car feels even warmer.

It was about here, shortly after his mother lost her hat, that his father spotted an agitated man wanting a lift. He pulled up and told Neil's mother to squeeze into the back with the children. The man bounced about in the front seat, shot it backwards into Neil's knees and unfolded a ventriloquist's dummy from his holdall. Kersten crawled onto their mother's lap. The man twisted round and made the dummy say thank you. It had a varnished face with startled eyes and only spoke German. It talked for the entire hour the man was in the car. Neil thought it might be telling jokes, because his father kept laughing. Their mother cried into his sister's hair.

Neil's father changed their plans. He decided they would spend the night at a guesthouse the dummy had recommended. It was beside a small lake with an artificial beach. Neil imagined plastic shells and wondered if Kersten would be allowed to pick them up for her collection. They might be glued in place, or perhaps you would have to pay. His mother clutched her handbag and stared ahead, letting her eyes brim over, as if she wanted everything to blur and soften.

The guesthouse was expensive. They had to share a room with two single beds. His father made them lie down in different combinations. The best fit was for Kersten to sleep with him, Neil with his mother. In the restaurant, the fresh trout was out of the question because it cost too much. They had to order small bowls of chips and cucumber salad. Kersten let the white dressing drip off her spoon onto the tablecloth. Their father frowned. Beneath the table he rapped her knee with the spoon, while their mother dabbed the stain with her serviette.

When the fruit salad arrived, their father managed to smile. He recalled the years when oranges and bananas were hard to come by in East Germany. Fruit was still a treat for him, he said three times. Neil's mother said he should help himself to as much as he liked. They were all too full of chips, she told him. Neil would have liked a few cherries, but he did not mention it. Kersten gripped the tablecloth draping over her lap. She bunched it in her hands. Her eyelashes were wet. She looked up when their father said they would be going to the beach straight away.

'But it's the evening,' their mother said.

'Indeed it is. How observant of you.'

Back in the room, Neil's mother unpacked their towels. She said it would take a minute to find everyone's swimming costumes. She pointed out that both Kersten and Neil were yawning.

'This place is for families,' Neil's father told her. 'There are children younger than four out there. And what big boy of twelve needs his bed at eight o'clock?'

They were all going to stay up for sunset, for the mauve and apricot sky. They must hurry. The little beach was filling up. They would not need swimming costumes anyway. Everyone here was naked.

The girl in the white T-shirt crouches to smile at Neil, her hands flat on the passenger window. He opens it for her.

'Berlin?' she says.

Berlin is out of his way, but he can take her about fifty kilometres closer. She shrugs off her backpack and slides into the seat. Her long hair swings, brushing his bare arm. Her soft, doughy cheeks remind him of Kersten, who is twenty now. He has not seen her for years, not since she moved to Birmingham. She is studying to be a dental nurse. He imagines her marrying a dentist and settling in the Midlands.

'So good to be out of the sun,' the girl says.

'It burnt my arm,' Neil tells her. 'I had to close my window.'

'You should always keep your window closed.'

She takes a packet of biscuits out of her backpack and offers him one. He shakes his head. He hears crumbs scattering over his gearstick.

'I'm Gudrun. Are you on holiday?'

'Not really. It's more of a visit. I've inherited a village. I'm going to see it for the first time.'

Her packet rustles. 'A village?'

Her English is good, but she pronounces it 'willage'.

'Yes. It's pretty dilapidated, I believe. Falling apart.'

'It is dying?'

'In a way. All the houses were owned by a coal factory, but it closed down.'

She twists the open end of the packet and ties it with a rubber band from her wrist. 'It sounds like a sad place.'

Neil drives over a bump. His toolbox rattles in the boot.

'I'm going to do some repairs. Then it will be fine.'

'Will you live there?'

'Maybe.'

'Are the houses empty?'

'Some are. All the young people left after reunification. Too many local industries closed down. There were no prospects left. Only a few older people live there now.'

'I wonder: will they like an Englishman owning their village?'

'My father was German. He lived there when he was a child.'

The sun disappears. Neil glances at Gudrun's pale arms resting on her backpack, at the golden hairs rising.

'Close your window if you're cold.'

'I have.'

She piles up her hair and winds it into a knot, securing it with a pencil from behind her ear. 'I'm going to a museum,' she says. 'It used to be a prison in East Berlin, for those who tried to leave.'

'Do you always hitch-hike?'

'Sometimes. I like trains best. It's better being between places. Not here and not there. No one can expect anything from you.'

'And are you a student? Are you studying the Cold War or something?'

'I am always studying.'

Neil is not sure if her English is slipping or if she is being deliberately vague. She kicks off her sandals and rests her feet on the dashboard. One of her big toenails is bruised.

'You don't mind, do you?' she asks.

Her head rests against the window and she falls asleep. The sky darkens and it begins to spit with rain. After a few minutes it turns torrential. Neil switches on the wipers, quickly tapping the lever from intermittent to full pelt. He turns up the air conditioning to clear the mist climbing up the windscreen. It struggles to fully evaporate. Gudrun's mouth hangs open, her breath clinging to the glass.

Neil sits forward, peering into the downpour. He needs to decide where to let her out. He has to leave this road soon. He has booked a cheap hotel for the night. He whispers her name, but she barely stirs.

His junction is coming up. He lifts his foot off the accelerator and indicates. He takes the turning smoothly and her eyes stay closed. Her short eyelashes cast violet smudges on her face.

After another kilometre she stretches her arms and yawns, her jaw clicking. She takes a small tin of mints out of her pocket and perforates the cellophane coating with her fingernail. Neil considers turning back to the main road and pretending he is lost. He is being no help to her at all. By the time he reaches his hotel, she will be no closer to her destination than she was when he picked her up. She might be further away.

The rain eases and he slows the wipers to normal speed. He has a raging thirst and his head aches.

A ring pull snaps. The car fills with effervescence and a synthetic citrus scent. A can touches his arm.

'Lemonade?'

The drink is not cold. Something sticky and cherry-flavoured is clinging to the rim, but Neil takes a few sips and feels better.

'Are we on a different road?'

'Yes. Yes, I had to turn off. I didn't know what to do. I didn't like to wake you. I imagine you've been on the road for a while.'

'You are so polite. The English are famous for three things. Their bacon and eggs for breakfast, their perfect grasses – what is the word... lawns? – and their good manners.'

'I have Weetabix, actually, and my garden is mostly nettles. Look, I can turn round and drive you back.'

She takes a plaster out of her pack, peels off the protective backing and smoothes it over a blister on her heel. The daylight changes, turning yellowish and filmy, before darkening again.

'Shall we keep going?' Neil asks. 'You'll get soaked otherwise.'

She sighs and curls up, facing him. The edge of his seatbelt is chafing his neck and he untucks one arm to stop the friction.

'You are not safe,' Gudrun says.

He hesitates for a minute, then replaces the seatbelt. He takes one hand off the steering wheel to hold it away from his skin.

'Here,' she says, passing him a soft, folded handkerchief. It smells of artificial fruit flavours. 'Put it between your neck and the belt.'

She fails to answer his question about turning round. He ought to ask her again. But if she wants him to turn, he will lose so much time. He has reserved a table for seven o'clock and needs a shower first.

'Will you have to make notes at the museum?' he asks after a few minutes of silence, a few minutes of her watching him.

'Probably not,' she says. 'I will want to listen.'

'Will there be a guided tour?'

'I believe so.'

'Quite depressing, a tour of a prison.'

'But I can walk out whenever I like.'

'I see what you're saying—'

'What am I saying?'

'You're saying it's not depressing to look round a prison when you're not a prisoner.'

'No, it is still depressing to realise ordinary people were locked up for daring to be free. It is important to never forget.'

'I agree with you.'

'But you said it would be depressing. You think I should change my mind. Have fun in a bar or a nightclub. Young girl on her own, you say to yourself. She is surely in the big city for a good time.'

They fall silent again. Neil is unsure whether he has followed her logic. The handkerchief falls out and he eases off his seatbelt again.

Gudrun glances at him. 'You are not safe.'

He doesn't respond, staring ahead as if the rain is too loud for him to hear her, concentrating on what he can see of the road, barely more than a few metres. He has memorised the directions to the hotel. Soon there should be a right-hand turn, partly concealed.

He drives as fast as he dares, conscious of the time, the conditions, the girl beside him so far from where she needs to be. Eventually, he raises his voice. 'Where are you staying in Berlin?'

'I am planning to read.'

'Pardon?' He takes one hand off the wheel and cups it round his ear.

She leans towards him and speaks deeply into his eardrum. 'I am going to read all night. In a library. In the quietest corner.'

'You make it sound pleasant.'

'It is pleasant. I do not make it so.'

She laughs, sitting back in her seat again and tugging a jacket out of her pack. When she shakes it out, the fur trim touches his neck. She straps her sandals on and zips her backpack shut. There is not far to go.

'Look, it's much too late to leave you on the roads. But this hotel I've booked... I don't know if they'll have any spare rooms or if—'

'I will sleep here, in this car.'

'But that will be uncomfortable. It gets cold late at night.'

It will feel awkward if he tries to deter her any more than that. It will give her the wrong idea.

'I like to sleep in cars.'

'I'll leave you with my coat.'

'No, keep it for yourself. You never know.'

Neil has missed the right turn. He thought he saw it, but couldn't tell for sure, could not commit to it. It was easier to keep going.

'You have no satnav?'

'I prefer maps. My father showed me how to read them when I was a child.'

The day after Neil turned eleven, his father drove him into the countryside. Neil spotted the name of a shopping centre on a signpost and thought they were going there to spend his birthday money. He thought perhaps there was an envelope in the glove compartment, the cash folded inside. He settled back because it was still twenty miles away and considered buying a new model aeroplane kit.

After a few minutes, his father parked by a gritty, yellow path at the edge of a wood.

'It leads back home,' he said, reaching across to open the passenger door and handing Neil a small backpack before driving off. It was raining as hard as it is now.

Neil feels too far from home. He pulls into a lay-by. He will be all right in a minute. Driving on the wrong side of the road is a strain. He ought to turn round. This time he will definitely not miss the turning. He will see it coming.

The car smells sickly sweet. In the chill from the fan, he feels skinned, his heart weak and bleeding. He has felt like this before, when he was fifteen and his mother came into his room and sat next to him on the bed.

She had a broken finger at the time. He remembers the bandage, grey-edged by then, the large safety pin which held it together appearing to pierce the soft flesh at the base of her thumb. An optical illusion, he supposed.

She spoke to him about a house on a new estate. She wished they could all live in it together, but she had tried for too long and it was impossible.

'I've had enough,' she said. 'I've had it up to here.'

This was not the way she usually spoke. Perhaps it was an expression she had heard on the bus or at the hairdresser's. She sounded nothing like his mother at all. She sounded like someone who was learning to speak English and trying out a new idiom.

She waited for Neil to say something, but he was too happy. He was overcome with relief at the brand-new future opening up. If he spoke, he would burst. He might even cry.

She was not smiling when she took his hand and said, 'I know who you'd rather live with. But there's no point offering you the choice. You do understand, don't you?'

He laughed, as if she had told him a joke. If his father had been a different man, it would have been one of those impossible dilemmas people gave you at school: whether you would rather die in boiling lava or quicksand. But as he did not have a different father, there was no need to say anything.

He knew it was not a joke. There was no need to answer the question. It was not even a question. His hand throbbed, as if his mother were holding his heart.

A bee was battering the window, desperate to be let out. It was too dozy to realise a smaller window was open. Neil's mother let go of his hand and flapped a magazine to encourage the bee towards the gap.

When the bee had flown out, he said, 'I'll leave it up to you, then, shall I?'

The words clotted in his throat before they struggled out, thicker than phlegm. He swallowed hard and smiled to show her he was fine with whatever she decided.

Two weeks later, he was sure he would be living in the new house, because his mother took him and Kersten to visit the show home on the estate. It had views of the river and the hills beyond. The furnishings blended, their patterns gentle. The kitchen gleamed, reflecting a softer version of his face in every surface. There were three bedrooms, with large windows and white quilts. He noticed the golden keys in the locks on the bathroom and cloakroom doors. The house reminded him of a clean sheet of paper before he messed it up with his terrible handwriting.

Kersten skipped between the bedrooms, changing her mind about which one she wanted. She was only seven. It was impossible for her to understand that this particular house was for show only. It would not be theirs. While they waited for her to finish exploring, their mother explained to Neil that not all the houses were built yet. There would be an assortment, several different sizes, some with smart, red bricks and some painted over. In time, the development would resemble a village which had always been there.

The houses had grand-sounding names: The Hemingway, The Chapters, The Chesterton. Not all of them could share the countryside view. Some would look out on the old biscuit factory, which was quite a pretty building in its way. The show home was a Hemingway. The one his mother had reserved was called The Lewis. It was the smallest type. It would not have the picture window or the utility room.

When they were leaving the show home, they paused in the dining room for his mother to speak to the saleswoman. She wore a blue uniform with a red silk scarf tied round her neck. She handed their mother a leaflet printed with artists' impressions of the finished estate and a detailed plan of the site. On the cover she wrote *Plot 33* with her red felt pen.

'Have a wander if you like and see where your Lewis will eventually be,' she said, her tongue flicking a crumb of lipstick from her front teeth. She looked down at their sandals and added, 'Watch where you tread.'

Neil asked if he could hold the leaflet and lead the way. His mother looked relieved, as if she had not expected him to be this interested. Neil held Kersten's hand and tried to keep her out of the mud, but her white socks were soon splashed and stained.

His finger traced the pathways marked on the plan, but it was difficult to follow roads which did not yet exist.

'It's here, I think,' he said when they had walked far away from the earthmovers and the stacks of bricks, the tarpaulins snapping in the breeze.

'Where?' his mother said, looking round.

'According to the map, this is definitely it.'

There was nothing to see. His mother asked a builder with a wheelbarrow if he could help and discovered they had passed their Lewis. They should have taken a turning fairly close to where they started. They would have to double back and keep their eyes peeled on the way.

Neil kept looking, but it was Kersten who spotted the sign which said *Plot 33*. The foundations were already laid, the walls begun.

'I still can't see the house,' Kersten said, scratching inside her wet sock.

'Not yet,' their mother said. 'But these are its beginnings.'

Neil thought it looked narrow, sandwiched between several other Lewises.

Their mother took a picture and they walked away. Near the show home, the saleswoman was showing a couple the plot designated for their Hemingway. All three were kitted out with red and blue wellingtons.

In the months that followed, Neil tried to find out which day they would be moving. The builders were behind schedule, his mother kept saying. She could not be certain yet.

'When will you tell Dad?' he asked in the hospital when they were waiting to find out if her finger had healed.

'He knows. I told him last night.'

'I didn't hear anything.'

'He was too shocked. Quite broken. I've never seen him like that.' She toyed with the safety pin. It was beginning to rust. 'You know, Neil, I'm not sure how well he'll manage alone.'

She was called into the cubicle. Through the plastic curtain, Neil heard the nurse say the finger had not yet mended.

His father had made them play football in the garden one Sunday morning. He put Neil's mother in goal and tested her with a penalty kick. When she reached out to save it, her finger was bent right back. She played down the pain, but her eyes looked bluer than usual and too bright. She couldn't use her hand. Neil's father said she could take a pie out of the freezer for dinner and keep the pork for the following Sunday.

Neil wondered when she had started allowing him to control her. It couldn't always have been like this. They met when she was teaching English for a year in West Berlin. The Wall came down while she was there. Neil's father had been trapped behind it for almost thirty years. He was among the many who crossed the border that night. She was in the crowd and he fought his way through to her. He asked her to have a drink with him and she paid with her West German Deutschmarks, which he noticed were thicker and more solid than his East German coins.

When she was packing to go back to England, he proposed. He wanted out of Berlin, out of Germany. He was still suffering from Wall sickness. Over the years, it had crept inside people's heads, like an infection. It made the sufferer feel hemmed in, bone-weary, sometimes severely depressed. His father had a cousin who lived in a Berlin suburb where the boundary between East and West zigged and zagged all around. There was a photograph of her smiling in her back garden, a watchtower looming behind her. Everywhere she went, the Wall followed. Every corner she turned, it turned with her. When his cousin was diagnosed with the sickness, Neil's father recognised the symptoms in himself.

When they bought the house in England, he was unable to tolerate internal doors being closed. Wedges jammed them all open. The front and back doors had to have clear glass panels inserted. He unscrewed the locks on the bathroom and toilet doors and threw them away.

Once, when Kersten was playing with the rubber wedge, the wind slammed a bedroom door shut. Their father opened it, took hold of her hands and shoved her fingers into the gap beneath. She had to sit there all morning, keeping it open.

Many allowances had to be made. His father was not naturally obsessive, Neil's mother told him. He had an untreatable illness.

'When the Wall came down, it unclogged a lot of emotions,' she whispered on Neil's thirteenth birthday, after the celebrations were ruined. 'And he can't cope with them. He doesn't understand how to live a normal life.'

'But it's been years,' Neil said, picking up fragments of china.

'He misses having a barrier,' she said, scraping birthday cake from the kitchen wall. 'He was afraid of what might be beyond it. And when it fell, he was exposed to his fears. It isn't his fault. It was how they were made to feel over there.'

'Are you all right?' Gudrun asks him. 'We are not moving.'

Neil always knows which direction he is facing. He can work it out by instinct, without a compass. Whenever he sets out, he is aware of where north is. He registers the changes by intuition. But here, in the small lay-by with cars and lorries shooting past, he is lost.

Gudrun applies balm to her lips from a stick she keeps in her sleeve. 'If you get into the right position,' she says, clicking the cap back on, 'I can tell you when is a good time.'

Neil manoeuvres the car. It is tricky in the shallow space, but at last he is at the correct angle. After a minute Gudrun says, '*Now*,' and he rejoins the traffic.

Soon after The Lewis was ready, Neil came home from school to suitcases in the hall. He ran up to his room to check his drawers and wardrobe were empty, to see if his model planes had been taken down from the wires suspending them from the ceiling. He was too old for them, really, but he didn't want them left behind.

They were still there, the wings thick with dust. Maybe they had to stay. They would disintegrate as soon as they were touched.

All his things were still in place: his clothes and books, his lava lamp and illuminated globe, all his seaside pebbles on the windowsill. The leaflet had made it clear that The Lewis only had two bedrooms. He sat on the bed, listening to the wheels of the suitcases bumping over the gravel to the taxi.

His mother left him a New Address card from the packet she had bought for relatives. Neil had posted them for her. His card was on his chest of drawers, underneath the recipe book they had made together.

Her brief note in the card was faint, as if the pen was drying out. She wrote that the situation was temporary. She could not be selfish and take both children away at once. It helped her no end to know his father had company during this difficult time. She asked Neil to take good care of the chickens. She had left them a mountain of grain.

During the first week, Neil spent most of the time in his room. Up there, it was easier to believe his mother was in the kitchen, his sister dancing and singing all over the house. In any case, his father was destroying everything his mother had left behind: crockery and photographs, the piano.

His father became obsessed with The Lewis, with finding the leaflet. He turned out cupboards and drawers until the house looked burgled. They never did find it and nothing was put back properly. He became fixated on Neil having a key for his mother's house. Could he not ask her? If she said no, Neil should slip her spare key into his pocket when he visited.

'I can have a duplicate cut,' his father kept saying. 'Once you have a copy, you can take hers back. She will never know it was missing.'

Neil had to keep explaining he could not visit yet. His mother wanted to settle in first. She had curtains to make and there were carpets still to be fitted. The Lewis would be new and bare, full of echoes.

The subject was dropped when his father developed a new obsession: cooking meals for Neil and watching him eat, ladling second helpings onto his plate before he had waded through the first. He cooked the food of his East German childhood: boiled pork knuckle served with mountains of cabbage and a blood-filled sausage he called Dead Grandma. There was a vanilla pudding he wanted to perfect.

'How did my mother do it?' he kept saying. 'Maybe less sugar.'

He stayed up late at night, making batches of pudding. Neil would step in them the next morning.

One Saturday lunchtime, he said to Neil, 'I don't feel well. I have a bad stomach. Will you make me a plain omelette?'

He looked pitifully thankful when Neil shrugged and said, 'Okay.' He pulled a chair across to the work surface to watch. When Neil picked up the eggs, they all felt light in his hand. The slightest pressure from his thumb made the shells cave in.

'What the...?'

Every single egg in the box was hollow, blown out.

His father was laughing so hard he had to keep wiping his eyes.

'What the actual...?'

'Your face,' his father said. 'Your *face*.'

'You look worried,' Gudrun says, as Neil watches for the turning.

'I really don't like losing my bearings.'

'Wait, is this it?'

'Where?'

'Here.'

He has to make a sharp turn. The hotel is large and white and welcoming. He parks in a corner overhung by trees, pulls up the handbrake with relief and turns to Gudrun. She is looking at her phone.

'I'll bring you something to eat.'

'Cool. Thank you. I will call my boyfriend's mother and then read.'

The hotel is less impressive inside. Neil's room is boxy and the carpet worn. The mattress has no more give than a block of foam rubber. He slips the free duo-pack of coffee-flavoured biscuits into his pocket for Gudrun. There are fifteen minutes until dinner, but he goes down to the restaurant anyway. It smells of stale cooking fat. His name is written on a piece of paper on the table next to the kitchen. He sits down, the high-backed chair forcing him too upright. He is used to eating from a bowl on his lap, bringing the fork to his mouth while he watches television. He rarely eats out, not since his ex-girlfriend said waiters might spit in your food.

The waiter brings the menu, but points out that Neil is early.

'I know,' he says in German. 'But I have nothing else to do.'

The waiter says, 'No problem,' in English.

Neil dislikes the expression. It suggests he is an obstacle to the restaurant's routine, but this fact is going to be overlooked as a special favour. He is disappointed the waiter did not continue the conversation in German. He hides behind the menu and searches for something which would show the spit. Schnitzel perhaps, with boiled potatoes and undressed salad.

He waits for three quarters of an hour. When it finally arrives, at least the schnitzel is large. He cuts a third off and wraps it in a serviette with a potato and all the greenery. There is an unexpected dollop of egg mayonnaise among the lettuce leaves and he distrusts it. He finishes the meal quickly and goes straight out to the car.

Gudrun is rubbing her eyes with the heels of her hands.

'Are you all right?'

'Not exactly. I can't find out if my boyfriend is still alive.'

'Oh God, I'm sorry. Is he in hospital?'

'I don't know where he is. He ended it with me yesterday.'

'I'm sorry. But in that case, shouldn't he be worried about you?'

'No, I am fine. But I was angry last night. I made a model of him from clay. It was pretty good. I put the spikes in his hair and made the fat little belly.'

'That won't kill him.'

'I stuck pins in it.'

'Pins?'

'Last time I did that, the boyfriend I had then drove his car into a tree.'

'Christ.'

'Last night I was hoping it would work. Now I am praying it does not.'

Neil hands her the biscuits, then grapples with the slimy serviette in his pocket. The batter is breaking through the thin paper. Gudrun shakes her head. She can't face it, she tells him.

'There's some lettuce. And a potato as well.'

She frowns for a moment, then says, 'Okay, give me that.'

His hands are greasy now. He drops the parcel on the dashboard and searches for a tissue, but has to lick his fingers. Gudrun breaks off small pieces of potato and drops them onto a magazine from her backpack. She squashes the remaining potato into a shape which she says is a reasonable likeness of her boyfriend.

'There. If I stick no pins in this, he will be safe.'

'You sound sure.'

'Of course.'

Neil has to resort to wiping his hands on his shirt. Gudrun places her boyfriend in the cupholder. 'He must stay upright, I think.'

'Why did you change your mind about him?'

'I did not change my mind. I am still mad with him. But I don't want to be... what is the word... responsible? Yes, responsible for his death. It did not feel nice the last time.'

'It can't possibly be your fault that someone hit a tree.'

Gudrun closes the magazine, trapping the fallen scraps of potato inside. 'You are too certain, Neil. You can never be sure what is your fault. You don't know what danger you bring to someone, or to yourself.'

Chapter Two

Silke gets up at five and goes outside to feed the chickens. The grass is cold beneath her bare feet and still damp from the rain. Early in the morning, the log stack smells sweeter and the chicken coop stronger. She tries to stop the bucket handle rattling. Her brother, Thomas, is still asleep. He was up until late, fretting about the man, Neil Fischer, who is expected later.

She has brought her breakfast outside: a slice of dark bread with cheese and a cup of black coffee. She has to sit on top of the coop to keep out of the cockerel's way. He is bad-tempered with her when he first wakes up. Her lower legs are scarred.

She tears up a crust and throws it as far as she can, watching the chickens scuttle and scatter. The cockerel spreads his wings and jogs after them. 'That's it,' she says. 'Give me a little peace.'

When it is safe to climb down, she goes out for a walk, to see the village through the eyes of the stranger who has taken ownership: eleven crumbling houses, an abandoned coal factory and one working farm. There is also the charred circle of grass where they light the Friday bonfire, the shop – with its bleached sign – that is no longer a shop and the empty school, which is leaning. Paying close attention to it all makes the familiar seem suddenly strange; the way, perhaps, Herr Fischer will see it.

She has never thought about the deterioration: the rendering that has flaked away from the bricks, the missing roof tiles, the fallen gutters, the rubble and debris. Perhaps it has been too gradual to notice. The decay has its own beauty: dusty-red bricks exposed by broken cladding, a tarpaulin bandage quivering on a fractured roof, a magpie drinking water from a dished windowsill.

The farm dog is barking. Somewhere apples are stewing. The sky is veined with lavender and salmon-pink, day growing out of night.

Last time she saw the village as a stranger might see it was thirty-one years ago, when she returned from East Berlin in 1988. Six years before that, when she was eighteen, she had gone to university to study zoology. She was a student for less than a term.

The Stasi were watching her from the start. They took away the notes she made in lectures, the essay on the robber crab she was halfway through, a few poems she wrote for her boyfriend. She has nothing to show she was ever there. She has not left the village since her return.

Thomas drives to the town twice a week to do the shopping – mostly tinned food and chilled goods, beer and wine. The village still provides its own vegetables and some meat. Her chickens provide the eggs. Thomas chops wood and charges too much for his logs. He also works at the farm in exchange for beef.

Silke recently gave up meat. She developed a distaste for it after a fox forced open the coop and attacked the hens. She came out at dawn to gleaming white neck bones, blood and feathers in the grass, and small hearts. She wants to stick to it because Thomas refuses to believe you can live on pulses. He sometimes pinches the flesh on her hips and wants to know how she will keep it. Last week he told her there were no tinned beans in the shops. She would have to share his meat, he said, lumping the joint onto the table. She opted for scrambled eggs and watched him poke his fork at the bleeding pork their unpredictable oven had failed to cook. It surprised her, how good and rich the eggs tasted.

Yesterday she booked herself a day-return ticket to Berlin. Every time she looks at the confirmation email, her stomach folds over.

For decades she has ached to go back. Hopefully, Herr Fischer will be the kind of man who will drive her to the station. She will travel on Thursday, when Thomas is at the farm all day.

As she walks home, the last smudge of dawn colour evaporates. She must make sure the spare room is ready for Herr Fischer. She has shared Thomas's bedroom since their parents died. Not only because the ceiling in hers has collapsed, but because Thomas finds it hard to sleep alone. Thank goodness they have Herr Fischer to do the replastering. And since he is staying with her and Thomas, theirs will be the first house to be mended.

Thomas keeps reminding her that the Englishman is not coming to be an odd-job man or a decorator. He's coming to take advantage of their hospitality and sneer at their country ways. He will walk along their lanes, his smart shoes getting splashed, taking pictures to entertain his friends and show off his eccentricity.

She tells Thomas she is not envisaging smooth paint and white fencing and English roses climbing round the door. Herr Fischer is a property developer. He is in the trade. He will understand how to fix things so they never fall apart again. Her ceiling, for example. She has tried without success to patch the new cracks with a tube of filler from the internet. He will know how to look beneath the surface. He will see if there are deeper problems.

Maybe he will encourage professionals to move into the village. There used to be a doctor, but he died last month. The dentist has long gone, like some of her teeth. And he might pacify their temperamental plumbing. Thomas insists it is only rats, but there is genuine rage in those pipes. Sometimes Silke believes she hears herself howling inside them.

She arrives home and hurries up to the spare room and stands in the doorway to take in Herr Fischer's first view. In the far corner, a foamy patch of mushroom-like growth is spreading over the wall and up to the ceiling. The paint has peeled off the metal window frame and condensation is rotting the sill. The furniture is dark and gloomy, but she has polished it for him with a lemon-scented spray to mask the smell of mildew. She wishes she had bought a shade for the ceiling light. The mattress is decent enough because she dragged her own across the landing yesterday when Thomas was out. She took the thin, floppy one back to her room and rearranged the fallen plaster over it.

She sits on the bed, wincing at the shriek from the rusty springs, and looks out of the window at the view across the fields. It still astonishes her that there is no longer a border, that she can go wherever she likes, that a man from England is driving here – through west and east – to stay in her home.

She looks round. Thomas, in his vest and pants, is standing in the doorway.

'Why can't he stay in one of the empty houses?' he says, shaking his can of lemon-and-lime shaving cream.

'Because they have no door and no windows.'

'It's summer. No rain forecast. No one here is a burglar.'

'Because they are infested.'

'Well, he owns the place now. He can invite the rat man to pay a visit.'

'It's up to him where he stays, Thomas. This is his village now.'

'If he's our guest, then this house is not his.'

'Technically, it is. He calls himself our guest to be polite. He could flatten every single building if he wants, destroy the whole village, obliterate it all. He could build a theme park if he wants.'

Thomas strides across to her and pumps shaving cream in her face. He walks out, his rough heels rasping on the splintered floor. He goes into the bathroom and starts filling the bath. It will take an hour. He comes back and wipes her face, replacing the citrus tang with the stench of damp flannel.

'I'm worried about this man,' he says, rubbing her cheek. 'Everyone is. Why aren't you worried?'

'Is that what makes you angry? That I don't worry about him?'

Thomas shrugs. He lets the flannel drop to the floor and lowers his head. The hot water pipes are grumbling. Soon they will judder, then bellow.

'What in this world is there left for me to worry about?' she asks. 'The worst has already happened.'

Thomas picks up the flannel and hurls it at the window. It clings for a second before sliding down the glass, leaving a smeary trail. Thomas wipes it dry with the embroidered mat that Silke has placed on the dressing table for Herr Fischer's brush and comb.

'All this trouble you're taking,' Thomas says, leaving the crumpled mat on the sill. 'All this for Herr Fischer.'

She understands what he means: all this trouble, when all the man will notice is decay.

She goes down to make him coffee and brings his cup to the bath. He is sitting in two inches of tepid water, waiting for it to rise. She places his clean, folded clothes on the bathroom stool. He shampoos his hair and Silke scoops what she can from the shallow water into a brass jug and rinses it for him.

'The steam will help,' she tells him.

'There isn't any.'

'It will come. It's getting hotter.'

Thomas broke his nose a long time ago and the shattered pieces are still inside. He struggles to breathe, but refuses an operation. He is a big man. He does not trust the anaesthetic to knock him out. Growths have formed inside his nostrils: fleshy, purple polyps. Silke imagines they are like the mushrooms on the bedroom wall, relishing darkness and dankness, swelling and bloating until they fill all the space.

'By the way, Fischer's not going to be interested in you,' Thomas says.

'How do you know he won't?'

'Because the mayor told me he's twenty-eight – half your age.'

'Not quite. Not by a year.'

'You think a year makes a difference? You're long past your best.'

She pours the water over his head without warning him to close his eyes. She goes to the bedroom and perches on the end of their bed. From the upturned turnip crate which serves as a bedside table, she picks up her lipstick. It has worn down to a stub. She opens the compact mirror that belonged to her mother. It catches the sun, creating a dot of light she can make bounce from wall to wall.

The lipstick is dark and crumbly, and makes her look old. She smears Vaseline on top and pats powder on her nose. Most of it flies up. It would have coated the big, black-spotted mirror on the wall, but Thomas has hung towels over it. He cannot bear to see himself.

Chapter Three

In the morning, Neil brings two bread rolls and a pat of butter to Gudrun. The car smells stale. He lets all the windows down, then immediately closes them in case it offends her.

'Come to Berlin with me,' she says, pulling on a jumper over her T-shirt. 'I will pay for the petrol.'

'I can't. I've made my plans.'

She picks up the potato. Her boyfriend's curves and edges are already discoloured. She pushes it back into the cupholder.

'Where shall I drop you?' he asks.

'Wherever I need to be.'

'Well, I know I'm not going your way. Tell you what, I could take you to the main road. You'll be safe in daylight.'

'It's not me I'm worried about.'

'Why not phone your boyfriend – or ex, whatever he is – and let him reassure you he's alive and kicking?'

She breaks open a roll, the crusty top splintering over the dashboard. 'I already have,' she says, posting half the roll into her mouth, followed by the entire pat of butter.

'And?'

She shakes her head and he waits for her to swallow. An official from the hotel knocks on the window and says Neil's space is needed for a new guest. Neil explains he wants to take the car rubbish to the bin first, but apparently there is no time.

The traffic is already bad and he has to concentrate. Gudrun finishes her breakfast and rubs toothpaste onto her teeth. She drinks water from a bottle, then pours some into her cupped hand and splashes her face.

'I might have some wet wipes,' Neil says.

'Water is enough.'

When she brushes her hair, loose strands float across, settling on his trousers. She applies her lip balm and offers it to him. He shakes his head.

'You need it,' she says.

'I don't like the taste of cherry.'

'You mustn't taste it. That's the point. It stops you licking your lips.'

'Why do they bother making it fruity, then?'

'Because it smells good. You don't taste cut grass or new-laid roads, do you?'

'Okay,' he says, paying attention to the busy junction.

'It's for protection,' she tells him.

'I don't need it.'

She screws on the cap and says, 'I'll leave it here for you.'

She draws up one leg to pull on her sandal. An expanse of bare knee protrudes from a huge hole in her jeans. He was thinking about her last night when he was trying to sleep. He almost went to the car and invited her to his room for coffee. For an hour or two, he wanted to pretend she was Kersten, to imagine they were the kind of brother and sister who meet for a catch-up.

He is not looking forward to letting Gudrun out. He wishes he could go to Berlin with her. But it would be like sheltering under a stranger's umbrella. At some point you have to let them go their own way, even if the rain is still bucketing down. In any case, he has learnt to be careful about wishes.

*

When he was five, Neil wished for a train set. On his sixth birthday, his presents were piled at the end of the dining table. He watched them during breakfast, while he demolished the plateful of Scotch pancakes his mother had made especially for him. He guessed from the size and shape which one could be the train set.

'Pace yourself,' his father warned. 'You will be sick.'

Afterwards, he sat on his father's lap, which was where he always opened his presents. He saved the train set until last. The blood in his head was pounding like an express train.

As he unwrapped handkerchiefs from his aunt and a money box from his grandparents, his father piled up the discarded gift-wrap on the arm of the chair. Neil's excitement swelled like rising dough. It was the size of a farmhouse loaf by the time he tore the paper off the largest present.

'Are you all right?' his mother asked when he was prising off the lid.

He stared at the red Night Mail locomotive, at the coach which could gather and deliver mail bags as it passed the pick-up point and receiving bin. It was everything he had hoped for and more. It was too much, too perfect.

His father was watching him, waiting to be thanked. The loaf rose higher and Neil was violently sick. The vomit poured over every item in the box, streamed into every crevice.

'Oh my God, why in the box?' his father said. 'Why did you not turn away?'

He lifted Neil off his lap, held him at arm's length, then drew him close and threw him at his mother.

'You must have known what was coming,' he shouted. 'Look, here is paper. All this wrapping paper here. Look at it, ready to throw away. You could have done it in this paper. You had enough time to turn.'

After wiping Neil's face and wrapping him in a blanket, his mother filled a bucket with hot water and squirted in washing-up liquid. By the time she was ready to immerse the train set, his father had put the box with all its contents into a plastic bag and dumped it in the dustbin. It was collected the next day.

His mother bought him another train set, but it was not the Night Mail and he had to keep it a secret from his father, covered with an old dressing gown in the back of his wardrobe. The following year, Neil was careful not to wish for anything.

'Wait,' Gudrun says. 'I know where we are now. My uncle lives near here.'

Neil has turned onto the main road, but it looks different from yesterday. He is still struggling to work out which direction he is facing. And today it is even harder to remember to drive on the right-hand side. There is a large roundabout ahead, but he turns off, unable to cope with circling anticlockwise.

On a quieter road bordered by farmland, he loses concentration and veers to the left. A tractor towing a trailer full of animal feed is coming towards them. Neil eases off the accelerator, but his hands will not move.

Gudrun looks up from her phone and grabs the steering wheel, twisting it to the right in the nick of time.

'You are asking for trouble,' she says.

'I'm just tired. I couldn't sleep.'

'What was the problem?'

'No idea.'

'Why not take me to my uncle's house and have coffee with us?'

Neil agrees. Gudrun tells him what to look out for at the next signpost. It is a relief to be guided. She is good at telling him what to expect up ahead. She gives him plenty of warning.

Half an hour later, Neil parks outside a grey, prefabricated apartment block.

'I didn't take much notice of where we were going,' he says. 'I won't know what to do when I leave here.'

'You will,' Gudrun says, picking up her backpack from between her feet. 'You'll know because I will tell you.'

The apartment is tiny and all muted colours. The furniture is plain and functional, the shelf units cheap and plasticky, the yellow wallpaper glued directly onto the concrete walls. Its loud, circular pattern clashes with the floral lino. The doors seem to be made from cardboard.

Gudrun's uncle is elderly and bent double. He cranes his neck to look up, his eyes enormous behind thick, reflective glasses. He seems unsure who Gudrun is at first, but delighted to see them both.

'This is Neil Fischer,' Gudrun says. 'His father grew up in the DDR.'

Uncle asks them to make themselves at home and to please excuse him for a few minutes.

'We will make coffee,' Gudrun calls after him.

When the coffee is dripping through the filter, it smells strong and rich.

'There is whipped cream in the fridge,' Gudrun says. 'In an orange melamine bowl.'

Gudrun fetches three slices of cake from the freezer. She defrosts them in the microwave and puts them on mushroom-coloured plates. Neil adds the orange bowl to the tray and carries it into the lounge. He sets it on a rickety cane side-table. Uncle comes back in. He has changed out of his brown trousers and checked shirt into a dark suit, white shirt and tie. He shakes Neil's hand and says they should be drinking champagne.

'He thinks we are married,' Gudrun whispers. 'Don't tell him you own a village, for God's sake.'

Neil wishes they were married. He wishes he could drive back to England with her after the coffee and cake. He could forget the village and enjoy his normal working day with Gudrun to come home to.

Uncle gets up again and fetches his album of wedding photographs. Then he hobbles off to look for a bottle of wine. It seems impossible to pin him down. Neil would like him to stay in one place.

Neil keeps trying to eat his cake. He is famished, but it would be impolite to start without Uncle. Eventually, the old man sits down and picks up his fork.

'Eat, eat,' he cries.

There is a layer of stewed apple beneath the dense sponge and a crisp, sugary topping. The whipped cream is slightly sweetened and ice-cold. Neil has never tasted anything this good.

'Did you make this yourself?' he asks Uncle.

Uncle has difficulty understanding Neil's German. When he asks in English, the old man laughs and says, 'No, my wife.'

As he scrapes up the last of the cream, his fork screeching on the thin plate, Neil turns to Gudrun and whispers, 'I thought he was a widower.'

'He is. Before she died, she filled two freezers with cake, so he would not forget her.'

'Why does he think we're married?'

'I told him.'

'Why?'

'So he lets you stay here.'

Uncle gets up again and gently tugs Neil's sleeve, wanting to show him his dog. They go into the bedroom where a rough-haired mongrel is lying on a towel spread over the bed. His eyes are clouded. Neil pats his surprisingly soft head and the dog seems to look straight at him.

'He wants to know who is in his house,' Uncle says.

Neil strokes the dog, but he lets out a long growl.

'He doesn't like me,' Neil says, withdrawing his hand.

'Not true,' Gudrun says from the doorway. 'He is trying to tell you something.'

'Yes, yes,' says Uncle. 'He wants you to listen.'

Neil goes over to Gudrun. 'I can't stay here,' he says under his breath. 'I have to be on my way.'

'There are two beds,' she says. 'Uncle will make us push them together, but we can pull them apart.'

'Why have you lied to him?'

'It is a story, not a lie. Uncle loves stories.'

'There's quite a difference.'

'Yes, but does it matter?'

Uncle asks them to help make lunch. It is schnitzel again, made the old East German way, with a thick slice of sausage instead of veal. Gudrun dips it in beaten egg and Neil coats it in breadcrumbs. They fry the schnitzel until it turns golden. They boil pasta spirals. Uncle makes a sauce with tinned tomatoes and tomato ketchup.

'You like things the old way?' Neil asks Uncle when they sit at the kitchen table to eat.

'I like what is good for me. I have no complaints about how things were.'

'My father went through phases of cooking the old way. But he didn't use the authentic ingredients, so it was a bit of a sham, really.'

Uncle shakes his head. Gudrun taps Neil's arm and says Uncle has no idea what 'sham' means. Neil pushes his fork into the pasta and decides not to explain. Instead, he says, 'My father told me life was hard in East Germany. A fifteen-year wait for a car. Shortages, empty shelves in the shops, long queues.'

Uncle cuts into his schnitzel. 'True, but we stored things when we had them. And we preserved. God, so much preserve. To prepare for the bad times.'

'My father probably made it sound worse than it was.'

'Maybe it depends on the individual. I felt safe. My family were happy. We had work. We had a good health service, low rents, good friends. Women could go out to work and have free childcare. It was always enough.'

'But could you trust people? What about the Stasi informers? Didn't you look at your friends and think one of you could be one of them? Didn't even husbands and wives tell tales about each other? And the smallest, most ridiculous thing that was even vaguely anti-communist could get you arrested.'

'I lived correctly,' Uncle says. 'In the safe world they built for us.'

Uncle eats at a snail's pace. Neil forces himself to slow down. The food is good, tastier than last night's. From his seat he can see into Uncle's bedroom. The dog's milky eyes are staring at him. When he gets up to pour Uncle a glass of water, the dog whines as if in pain.

They all make a dessert together at the table. It reminds Neil of trifle: a glass bowl of cake scraps soaked in rum, onto which Gudrun tips a tin of fruit cocktail. Uncle makes a vanilla milk pudding from a packet and ladles it on top. When Neil dollops the trifle into everyone's dishes, the serving spoon makes a satisfying squelch.

'How do I know how much?' he whispers to Gudrun.

'We will be happy with whatever you give us.'

It is still a relief when no one complains about their portion.

'I definitely think my father felt nostalgic for the old days,' he says after he has passed Uncle and Gudrun their dishes.

'I have no nostalgia,' Uncle says. 'Why dwell on the past, or question it?'

Neil tracks the tip of his spoon through the vanilla pudding and pushes aside some unidentifiable pieces of fruit. 'Do you never think about being watched? The Stasi going through your house when you were out, trying to find evidence that you were not a good citizen?'

Gudrun taps his arm with her spoon. 'You go too far, Neil.'

'I didn't mean your uncle personally. When I say "you", I mean people in general.'

Uncle is staring into his pudding. He looks up at Neil again and pushes his heavy glasses higher up his nose. The lenses are opaque with mist. 'Yesterday the Stasi,' he says. 'And today the internet. All the world is being watched.'

'And for better or worse,' Gudrun says, 'all the world is watching.'

Uncle excuses himself from the table.

Neil turns to Gudrun. 'Did I do something wrong?'

Gudrun sighs and pours more wine. 'Try to understand,' she says. 'My uncle watched himself constantly. Inside his own head, of course he distrusted the system, but the only way to survive was to pretend to tolerate it. Even now, he says nothing against the regime. How else could he have managed?'

'Do you think he wished he could get away?'

'Wishing was dangerous. You could be arrested just for being friends or neighbours with someone planning to escape. While parents were being interrogated in prison, their children were given away, adopted by strangers.'

Neil puts his hand over his wine glass. 'I have to keep driving. I'm behind schedule.'

Gudrun sips her wine and says, 'Honestly, my uncle was not unhappy. He accepted how he had to live.'

'Don't you think he might be toning it down to maintain his dignity?'

'Defending his own life, you mean? Aren't we all doing that? We preserve our image and declare our achievements all the time. We do it every day.'

Neil glances at his watch and pushes back his chair.

'You will disappoint us if you leave. What will Uncle think?'

'You can tell him we had second thoughts.'

'And do you care about what *I* think?'

'I can't afford to. I have my plans.'

'Perhaps I am part of your plans.'

Neil once had dinner with a woman he had been seeing for a few weeks. While the waiter was boxing up the pizza slices Neil had left for his lunch the next day, he decided to tell her he was in love with her. She was already putting her coat on and saying she had to rush off. To keep her there, Neil said they should look at the dessert menu. She rolled her eyes and sat back down. With reluctance, she agreed to a small coffee. While he ate his pudding, she stared into her cup. She pushed it aside in the end and asked if he would mind her being honest. He told her to go ahead and she said, 'I don't like you very much.'

When he tried to discuss who would be paying for what, she said she had seen the waiter spit in Neil's tiramisu. After she left, he sat alone, his hands around her cold coffee cup, trying to work out what he would do with all that love, where it would go.

He knows now that the love stayed with him. He could easily give it to Gudrun. But he would disappoint her. He would be hurt again.

Uncle comes back, wiping his glasses on his tie. Neil gets up and thanks him for his hospitality.

'You are leaving?'

'I must. I have plans.'

Mist slowly rises over Uncle's lenses again.

Neil glances at Gudrun. She looks unfazed. 'Sorry, Uncle,' she says. 'We will come back to visit you soon.'

In the car, Neil watches her clip on her seatbelt. The backpack, fatter now she has the wine and the rest of the sausage, slides down between her legs into the footwell.

'I can't take you any further,' he says, switching on the engine.

'You need directions.'

'Okay. I will follow your directions until I know where I am. Then we must say our goodbyes.'

He drives on. A young deer runs in front of the car. His flank brushes the wing. Neil swerves across the road, onto the verge. The driver of an oncoming van blasts his horn.

'He's fine,' Gudrun says, releasing her seatbelt. 'He ran into the wood.'

'I hit him, though.'

'Yes, but he didn't fall.'

'But I hit him. There was a knocking sound.'

'It was only a touch.'

He is still holding the steering wheel, as if to keep the car steady while the traffic rushes by. Gudrun tells him to let go. He sits back and closes his eyes. He is not used to a big lunch and wine in the middle of the day. He must have gone briefly mad, letting Gudrun talk him into her story.

When his father left him at the entrance to the woods, Neil's first instinct was to walk home along the main road. He took one step and stopped. His father would catch sight of him in the rear-view mirror. He would point his finger out of the car window, indicating the direction of the yellow path.

Neil turned back and went into the wood. The rain eased to a drizzle. He unzipped the backpack, imagining a map and a compass, but finding a bottle of water, a ham sandwich and a rather grizzled apple.

The clouds drifted away and pale sunlight darted between branches, then disappeared. After half an hour, he took his glasses off to clean them and they slipped out of his hands. All he could see without them were blurred colours, spots of brightness, fuzzy shapes.

He crouched and felt about. He knelt on the rough ground, spreading his fingers wider, patting twigs and stones and wet leaves. At last he touched his glasses, but his flailing hands batted them further away. He heard them skating across the gritty path.

When Neil opens his eyes, he senses where north is at last.

'Shall I get out here?' Gudrun asks, watching him.

'Good a place as any. You should have no problem getting a lift.'

'And you are sure?'

'Yes, you won't be waiting long.'

'I don't mean my lift.'

'I'm sure.'

She gets out quickly and turns round to face the way they have driven. He glances in the wing mirror, but she is not visible there. He wants to see her go. He can't get out his side because of the traffic. He slides across to her seat, which is awkward because he is tall and long limbed. He catches the tail of his shirt on the gearstick. When he is finally outside, there is no sign of Gudrun. Someone must have picked her up straight away.

He climbs in and threads the car back into the traffic. The road is straight all the way to the unnamed side-road which leads to his village. The map shows the tight turning, but he is still taken by surprise. He can't work out how to negotiate it. He continues on. He loses his bearings and finds himself on a complicated round-about. He circles it three times and eventually chooses a vehicle to follow, copying its exit.

He feels as if he has left his car. He is a stranger driving on the tail of another. His stomach is a full bag of water, the brown kind that falters from the tap after the supply has been interrupted. After fifteen minutes or so, a sense of familiarity returns, a notion that the next turn on the right is the one for the village. He would rather keep shadowing the car in front, braking when it brakes, turning when it turns, stopping at the same red lights.

He takes the turn. It would be madness to let it go again. His plan was to arrive in the early afternoon and it is already four o'clock. His stomach still feels spongy and bloated. He has let himself get in a state. Now he is nearly there, it will settle down.

The track taking him into the heart of the village keeps narrowing. It peters out. Trees crowd in, their branches whipping the car. This must be wrong. It has lured him into a field or something. There is no sign declaring he has arrived in Marschwald.

His instructions mentioned the coal factory and he watches out for it. He passes a wrecked car, a cluster of battered bikes and a decrepit leather chair, its seat encrusted with moss. A grimy building with a tall, defiant chimney rises at last from wasteland; a rusting steam engine, which must have once pulled wagons filled with coal briquettes, is tethered by weeds to its rails. He is overcome with relief.

Chapter Four

People have been knocking on the door all day, asking if Herr Fischer has arrived. Silke's lipstick has diminished to a few stubborn specks. Her hair is escaping its elastic band.

'Where is he?' Thomas asks, coming into the kitchen. Wood shavings cling to his clothes. He has brought in his axe. It needs oiling, he says. Still wiping his boots on the mat at the door, he hurls it onto the table. Silke's wooden spoon drops into the soup.

'No idea,' she says, turning from the cooker to face him.

'So when's he coming?'

She shrugs. 'When he gets here.'

'He was meant to phone.'

'If he's close, he has no signal. Not if he left it too late.'

The bread basket is on the table, with the water jug and glasses. A seed cake sits at the far end under a plastic dome.

'He was meant to be here for a late lunch.'

'It looks like it will be an even later one now.'

'So this will be our evening meal? There will be no lunch?'

'It's nearly four, Thomas. So yes, probably. You demolished a whole packet of biscuits to stop you fainting.'

She sets the table and groups a few old beer mats together in the middle for the soup tureen to stand on. She doesn't know why she bothers. The table is scarred with scorches from hot pans and rings from wet glasses. They make a pattern that is part of the grain. The familiar chaos of streaks and circles was a welcome sight when she came back from Berlin. There were new marks, but the old ones were still there.

As she slides the tureen into the oven to keep warm, she hears a car. Thomas stops her opening the door.

'Let him make his own way.'

The three knocks are hesitant. Thomas holds her arm. The next three are slightly louder, further apart. Thomas lets her go and she opens the door.

Herr Fischer has to stoop to fit under the lintel. He has long arms and legs, but his upper body is surprisingly short for his height. He is pigeon-chested. He says his name is Neil Fischer and that he is pleased to meet them. He is silent for a moment, then asks if he has the right house.

'Yes, I am Silke and this is Thomas.'

Thomas has told her to make the introductions, but not to appear too friendly.

'Come and eat,' Silke says in English. She finds his German awkward, hard to follow.

They all sit down and Herr Fischer says, 'I hope I haven't kept the meal waiting.'

'No, you have kept us waiting,' Thomas says.

Silke quickly points out it is only soup, which improves with standing. Thomas kicks her ankle under the table for being too nice. He slices the bread and pours the water. He slides a glass towards Herr Fischer, not within easy reach. His axe is still there, between the bread and the butter.

Silke ladles the soup into two bowls. 'It is goulash soup,' she says. 'You eat meat?'

'It looks delicious,' says Herr Fischer. 'Yes, I eat meat. Not every day. I try to go meat-free a couple of times a week. It's a thing now, isn't it? For health and that. Not that... not that meat isn't healthy... This looks amazing.'

Silke cannot understand all he says, but she likes the way his smile comes and goes, and his pale schoolboy's fingers.

'Who cooks for you?' she asks.

'I manage it myself. Sort of. My mother and I once wrote a recipe book. Mostly cakes, but there was a grain mix we made up for our chickens. It looked good enough for humans.'

'Your soup will be cold, Herr Fischer,' Thomas says, reaching for the bread.

'Oh, call me Neil. Don't let's stand on ceremony.'

Silke concentrates on eating a slice of bread and butter, aware of Thomas watching her.

After they have eaten the cake, Herr Fischer tries to extricate a seed from between his teeth. He is still struggling with it when he goes out to his car. He comes back with a red box of English shortbread and waves it awkwardly about. It is unclear if this is a gift for her or for Thomas. She thanks him, but does not reach out for the box, which seems the best compromise. He has to put it on the table. Thomas remains silent, but he does make the coffee.

The last time Thomas made coffee for her, they were students. He is two years older, but eighteen months of national service meant they started university together. They travelled to East Berlin by train with a dozen cushions Silke had made from scraps and stuffed into plastic bags. They took up so much space they made a few passengers glare. Others asked if they could use them as pillows. Silke had never had so much attention. Thomas rolled his eyes and pretended not to know her.

They were allocated a flat in one of the many high-rise blocks. It was a shock for Silke: the nearness of the West, the height of the Wall.

Six weeks after they moved in, she woke up with flu and couldn't get out of bed. Her bones ached. The roots of her hair were hurting. She knew she would be horribly ill for days, maybe longer, but she needed to contact her friends. Andreas and Martin came from the town twenty kilometres from Marschwald. As children, they were all in the Young Pioneers together. She had met the others in the group only a few days ago. Although she trusted Thomas to take a message, it would make them uneasy. It was not worth the risk.

After Thomas left for his morning lecture, she dragged herself down fifteen flights of concrete stairs and had to rest before she staggered to the bus stop. She missed the bus by a minute and had to walk the six kilometres to Café Danika for the ten o'clock meet-up. How she put one foot in front of the other she would never know. She could only stay for an hour because Thomas would be back at the flat by lunchtime, expecting her to still be in bed.

Beneath the table, Martin scribbled on a paper serviette. He wiped his hands with it and crumpled it onto his plate. To anyone watching, there was nothing suspicious. They were eating greasy fried potatoes. She could only pick at hers, but pretended her hands needed wiping. Martin shook his serviette out and offered it to her. She made a show of accepting it with a mock grimace, but it was easy to hold it to her face, taste his salt and grease on her lips. She was in love with Martin.

She balled the serviette in her hand and let it fall into her bag on the floor, between her feet. When she stood up to leave, her legs would barely support her. Andreas and Martin helped her to the door. One of the others had a car, but said he could not give her a lift. She understood.

She thought she would have to crawl back, but Martin saw a bus coming and ran out to make sure it stopped. She turned to say goodbye to Andreas and froze. Thomas was in the café.

He must have come in when she was getting up to leave. He had not sat down yet. He was leaning on a table, talking to a bearded man in a short raincoat, who was already in the café when she arrived. Silke had made a point of noticing him. Ill though she was, she had to notice everyone: where they sat, what they ate and drank, who they spoke to, what time they arrived and left.

Thomas looked up and frowned, then gave her a puzzled smile. She went over to him. Andreas melted away. Thomas hugged her while she explained she had felt well enough to go out, but now she was exhausted and must catch the bus home. She said hello to the man in the short coat and Thomas said they were on the same course. They were discussing a project they were working on together.

She caught the bus with a second to spare and her legs gave way. An old man took her arm and helped her to a seat. She sank onto it, clutching her bag on her lap. She was damp with sweat, but smiled with relief that she had kept her appointment at the café. They needed to know she would never let them down.

She glanced at the other passengers and put her hand into her bag. No, she couldn't risk looking at the serviette. Not until she was back in the flat.

Thomas came home a minute after she had toiled up the stairs. He had begged a lift from a lecturer, he said, because he was worried about her. He had never worried about her before. He made coffee and brought a cup to her bedside. She was so grateful and weak, she almost confided in him. She smiled instead and insisted he should go to his afternoon lectures. She pretended to fall asleep.

The coffee turned cold while she listened to him make a sandwich, go to the toilet, pick up his coat and his keys. She waited for the self-closing door to groan, waited for the long, metal lever to swing it shut.

*

Silke shows Herr Fischer his room. He has no time to look at it properly because Thomas calls up to say the mayor is at the door. As Herr Fischer hurries down, he crosses Thomas on the stairs, bringing up his suitcase and holdall. Herr Fischer thanks him as they pass each other, but Thomas is not being helpful.

In the room, he unzips the holdall and pulls out Herr Fischer's things.

'No,' Silke hisses. 'Put them back.'

Thomas releases the catches on the suitcase. He rummages through the clothes and shoes, pokes at holes in the lining.

'Stop now,' Silke says.

He is holding something grey and oblong. It is stiff with a rounded end, like a tongue from a shoe.

'Put it back.'

From the kitchen comes a metallic scraping. Silke clutches Thomas.

'It's only the chair,' he says. 'The one that lost the pads on its feet. Fischer or the mayor is pulling it out from the table.'

It shrieks again and Silke grips his sleeve harder.

'Now one of them is pulling it into the table,' Thomas says, making her sit on the bed.

'It's still in my head.'

'It will go soon. It is only an echo now.'

'An echo,' she whispers.

Thomas unfolds her fingers from his sleeve and thunders down, the stairs creaking under his weight. He will make sure the chair does not scrape again. Silke stays on the edge of the bed, sweat rolling down her spine. Thomas has not replaced the tongue in Neil Fischer's bag.

Chapter Five

Neil cannot sleep. He has read that you can breathe in spores from mould. He imagines them flaking off, microscopically small, floating into his mouth and nostrils while he sleeps. He gets up and goes to the bathroom. The walls are grey-green, like the ring around the yolk of a hard-boiled egg. The floorboards slope and sink a little under his feet. When he washes his hands, he closes his eyes to the spots of spat-out toothpaste, the water pooling around the base of the taps, the damp flannels and towels hanging on rubber hooks suctioned to the off-white tiles. The rubber is perishing. Dirt has collected in the cracks.

Back in the bedroom, he switches on the lightbulb dangling from the ceiling and begins unpacking. His holdall must have rolled about in the boot of the car. Nothing is tidy anymore. He refolds his clothes and puts them in the musty drawers. There was no need to have bought new shirts and jeans. He hangs his suit in the wardrobe and it embarrasses him to see it there. He leaves his tie rolled up in the holdall, with his aftershave and cufflinks.

He was not expecting luxury or anything formal. He was aware the village was rundown. But you never know. He could be invited to visit some of the other houses and people might still dress for dinner. He is afraid of being caught out, wrong-footed. All those years ago in the car, as soon as his father parked beside the woods, Neil knew the day had tipped out of kilter. He had no idea what was wrong, only that something had been displaced. It reminded him of the party game where you have to study a tray of objects, then be blindfolded while one is removed. When the blindfold is taken off, you have to work out what is missing by its absence.

He has no clue what time Silke will serve breakfast because, after the mayor left, she did not come back downstairs. As lunch was at four-ish and supper not at all, the next meal is anyone's guess. Thomas has also vanished, after pounding downstairs to make Neil stand up slowly, without moving the chair. Apparently, there was something wrong with it. Thomas carried it to a corner and Neil had to sit on another one.

It makes him think of Musical Chairs, the most unsettling party game of all. You know there is one chair fewer than the number of people needing to sit down. If that is not daunting enough, every other chair in the line has its back to you. You have to keep circling. You try to use stealth, but the person behind you is using it too, forcing you to move faster. They refuse to let you linger by the chairs facing you. You have no idea when the music will stop. No wonder children grow up full of fear.

Neil takes out his cassette player, checking the cassette inside has fully rewound. He places it on the rough, wooden crate beside the bed. He pulls out his suitcase from under the bed and releases the two catches. Everything looks muddled in there. The elasticated straps he clipped together to keep order are lying slack over the contents. Perhaps they came undone because they are old. His father bought the case in East Berlin, in the Cold War. It is plain cardboard, primitive by today's standards, the cheap lining worn out.

Neil rearranges things into their correct positions. He crosses and clips the straps. He examines the items for half an hour, but cannot fathom what is missing. Extra underwear still in packets, a pair of long-sleeved pyjamas, two thick jerseys, four paperbacks, the recipe book he compiled with his mother, a spare toothbrush, a compass, a water bottle, a white hair ribbon Kersten had left behind, a ball of string, a letter from his father, a bag of fun-size Milky Way and a pack of blank tapes wrapped in cellophane. He detaches the straps again and inspects the block of cassettes. The tapes tumble out, clattering on the floor.

At dawn he gives up trying to sleep and gets out of bed again. He pushes back the blue towel on a wire which serves as a curtain. He has a view of the yard in front of the house. A chicken coop stands on a square of mossy grass. Logs are stacked high against the wall.

After a struggle with the latch, he pushes open the window. He can smell the salt marsh. He was expecting it to be like the sea, fresh and tangy. But it stinks of bad eggs. He has looked up a few facts about salt marshes and knows they flood with the tides and are spongy underfoot.

When he was twelve, he cycled to a disused quarry. He knew from listening to conversations at school that a group of boys larked about there on Saturdays. They saw him arrive and watched him chain his bike to the fence. They lit cigarettes and mumbled to one another. They took no further notice of him. He was disappointed, but felt it would help to look at his diary in the future and see: *Went to the quarry and had a laugh with the lads.*

He stood back at first and observed. They ran down the gravelly slopes, shouting to make echoes, then climbed back up. They flung stones about. They were quick and sure-footed. They knew what to leap over, which parts to dodge. They stripped to their under-pants and splashed about in a shallow lake, ducking one another.

Neil worried about joining in. The water looked cold and dirty. He knew the quarry was an unstable place. But he wanted to be part of the shouting and laughter. He struggled down the slope and took off his clothes, but by the time he had folded them, the other boys were out again and climbing back up. He quickly got dressed, but they had already disappeared.

He could hear them whooping. Maybe they trusted him to work out how to find them. He was treading carefully, following their sound, when it felt as if the sandy ground had lost all its strength.

The panic came from being alone. The harder he fought to pull himself out, the lower he sank. He shouted for the boys, his voice echoing through the pit, but they were too far away to hear him. When he was waist-deep and could see them in the distance, climbing back onto their bikes, he gave up. He waited to be buried, suddenly calm.

The surrender saved him. The sand settled and felt more solid. It was supporting him now. He tried making small, subtle movements, shifting gradually onto his back rather than flailing, until at last he extricated himself.

Cycling home afterwards, he knew he would recover from the shock of sinking, now that he understood how to survive. Avoiding gravel pits was probably the most important lesson learnt, followed closely by the value of keeping calm. He also knew he would not recover so easily from the knowledge that when he gave up, he felt no fear.

He tiptoes to the bathroom, brushes his teeth and wipes the basin with toilet paper. It is the hard kind. One side is glossy. Which is he meant to use? He tries both, but neither has the absorbency of the soft sort. It surprises him that you can still buy communist products. He uses the toilet, but does not dare flush it. He remembers it being noisy last night. They might be one of those households with rules about not flushing while people are asleep.

The shower is over the bath. He steps in and rattles the plastic curtain along, making sure he keeps it inside. It takes a while to discover how to make the water emerge from the showerhead rather than the taps. It trickles in fits and starts. He squirts a large blob of his foaming shower mousse into his hand and massages it over his body. The water is soft and it takes ages to rinse off the lather. A white mountain of it stays in the bath.

Someone might be knocking on the door, but it is hard to tell with the water pipes making such a racket. He scoops the froth up in his arms and dumps it in the toilet. He has to flush it then, the noise drowned out by a spasm of futile gurgling from the shower drain. The bath mat is wet, the floor saturated. He must have done something wrong. No one warned him. If he had invited someone to stay in his house, he would have let them know about any hostile appliances.

He tries to mop the floor with toilet paper, but it disintegrates, the shreds clinging to his hands. The knocking is now a constant volley. When he opens the door, Thomas is standing there in a grey vest and pants.

'Silke cannot wait,' he says.

'Of course, of course. Sorry to take so long. I had a bit of trouble with the shower.'

'The shower is broken.'

Silke hurries in and Neil vacates the bathroom. He sits down on his bed, touching his face, aware it is burning. He has never had a way with people. They rarely warm to him. He can make conversation, but either it sounds flat or he puts his foot in it. He might have made a decent enough impression on Gudrun. She tolerated his company well enough. Probably because she was on the make, though. He should not have left his suitcase in the car. He wishes he could work out what is missing. On the drive home, he could try to find Uncle's apartment and ask for her address. He remembers they are supposed to be married. It might not be fair to subject Uncle to so much confusion.

He takes a pair of boxers and a shirt out of their packets and gets dressed. In the mildewy room, the clothes don't feel new against his skin. After he has taken time combing his hair and soothing his hot face with witch hazel, he makes the bed and pushes his case and holdall underneath. His armpits are already damp. He pulls his shirt off over his head and rubs his deodorant stick back and forth, pushing it hard into the flesh until the hairs glue together. Once his shirt is back on, he is ready. He is not entirely sure what he is ready for.

In the kitchen, Thomas is wading about in rubber boots. Water is pouring through the ceiling from the bathroom floor. Neil recognises the peach smell of his mousse.

'Shower is broken,' Thomas repeats.

'I realise that now. I couldn't have known, though. No one said. Anyway, let me mop up.'

'Silke will do that. She is outside with the chickens.'

'I could give her a hand. I've fed chickens before.'

'Silke likes to do it herself.'

They stand either side of the table. The flood soon drenches Neil's new slippers and finds its way into the turn-ups of his jeans.

'I'd like to have a look at the village this morning,' he says, lifting one foot out of the water. 'Would you be able to show me round?'

'I am working.'

'Ah. Of course. No problem.'

The door opens, bringing sunlight and the sulphurous waft of the marsh. Silke comes in. Her hair is coiled into a bun with wisps of straw caught in it. She keeps on her wellingtons, and takes a mop and bucket out of a recess with a curtain across it. Most of the cupboards have curtains instead of doors. Neil's father would have approved.

'Good morning,' Neil says. 'I'm sorry about the flood.'

'Sit, sit,' Silke says, smiling up at him. She indicates a chair at the table, but he will get in the way.

'Do you have another mop?'

'No, only one.'

'What about a broom? I could sweep some outside.'

She looks at Thomas, who folds his arms. 'No, just sit down. Then I will make breakfast.'

Thomas follows her round the kitchen with the bucket. Each time she fills it, he empties it down the sink. Neil wishes he could go outside and sit in his car. Once the floor is less swamped, Silke quickly fills a plate with sliced cheese and ham. She puts it on the table with a pot of cherry jam, the butter and the rest of last night's dark bread and cake. In a grill pan reeking of old lard, she makes toast from a sliced milk-loaf which, judging by the shy smile she gives him, was bought especially for the English visitor.

'Boiled eggs?' she says.

'We don't need them as well,' Thomas mutters to her. He throws a tea towel over the basket of eggs on the draining board. 'We have more than enough.'

'Yes, this is plenty,' Neil assures her. 'I only have a bowl of Weetabix at home.'

It is unclear whether he is expected to make a sandwich with the ham and cheese. He takes his time arranging everything on his plate, waiting to see how Silke and Thomas eat theirs. The window is behind him, the sun warming his back until he is nauseous and prickling with heat. He cannot look up. His limbs keep twitching. His feet slosh inside his slippers.

'Here,' Silke says. 'English toast with butter and marmalade.'

It is jam rather than marmalade, but Neil does not correct her. He picks it up in both hands to keep it steady. The grill-pan fat has seeped in and it tastes comforting. It is the taste of early childhood.

Silke says he can walk around the village in about fifteen minutes. Thomas corrects this to ten and asks if he has any boots.

'The weather seems fine,' Neil says, twisting to look out of the window.

'Everywhere is wet.'

Neil has small feet for a tall man – small enough to wear the slippers his mother left behind. Silke looks at them under the table and says he can borrow her boots.

Thomas gets up and says, 'What tools do you have?'

'I have a toolbox in the car.'

'No machinery coming? No plans for the sinking?'

'The subsidence, you mean? That's something I must have a think about.'

Thomas goes out. Silke smiles and shrugs. 'He is not used to visitors,' she says.

She stands up and starts clearing the table. Neil picks up the bread basket and the jam.

'No,' she says, her hands over his. 'Not necessary. You own us now. You are in charge here.'

'I don't own anyone.'

'You own this village. All our houses and land. We must pay you the rent now.'

'But it's still yours. I don't intend to make any sweeping changes. A few running repairs, maybe—'

'Then why buy us?'

'No one bought *you*. The village is a prospect. It's what I do. I'm a property developer. Admittedly, this is quite different from renovating a modern house, but—'

'A prospect? What do you mean by that? An impulse? A craze? A dream?'

'Sort of. That's not to say I don't take it seriously. And remember *I* didn't buy it. My father did. He left it to me in his will.'

'And why did your father buy our village?'

'I don't really know. I didn't get the chance to talk to him about it. I guess he wanted to reconnect with it. He left me a letter, but I'd like to sort things out myself first.'

'And then open the letter to discover you have done what he wanted?'

'That's right. I want to predict whatever he had in mind.'

'And if you fail?'

Neil stacks the plates without answering.

'Please, this is my job,' Silke says. 'Go outside and face your kingdom before it rains again.'

'All right, but I'm always happy to help. I'm grateful to you for letting me stay.'

Silke pauses on her way to the sink. 'There is something you can do.'

'Anything.'

'I am travelling to Berlin on Thursday. Can you drive me to the station?'

'Of course.'

'And please say nothing to Thomas.'

'I wouldn't dream of it.'

She smiles at him. 'You and your dreams.'

She fills the kettle for the washing-up bowl. Neil has used all the hot water for his shower.

He peels off his slippers and socks, and places them on top of the kitchen radiator. It is stone cold, but there is no airing cupboard, nowhere logical to put them.

The wellington boots are too large. Rubbering across the yard makes the chickens scatter in all directions. Thomas is piling logs onto his truck and does not look up as Neil wanders about. After a minute he shuffles to the gate. It refuses to open. When he arrived yesterday, he had to climb over it. Thomas strides over and, without a word, unties a complex tangle of string. Neil walks out to his car on the track and takes out his toolbox, but the gate is already tied shut again. He has to reach over and drop the toolbox onto the ground. It lands with a tinny rattle.

The track leads to the old school building near the patch of scorched grass. Neil pauses to take in its scabbed walls, sagging roof and rotting window frames before he notices how badly it leans. It is sinking. He has never taken on a house with subsidence. He knows nothing about it. He imagines the gradual movement in the soil, unseen. The school could hold on for years, or fall down as he watches.

He only buys houses with surface flaws. He is competent with sandpaper, a wallpaper scraper, paintbrushes and rollers. He owns a cordless drill. He has watched television programmes and YouTube videos which show you how to keep the redecoration process neutral and cheap. His ex-girlfriend keeps some decent furniture in storage and for a reasonable charge – cheaper than rental from a company – she lets him borrow it to kit out each house until it is sold. His favourite part of the process is dressing the rooms. He keeps it minimal – a small sofa and one armchair, no pictures, a single clock on the mantelpiece – to maximise the space. He calls it the art of illusion.

After his first purchase turned out to be a haven for rafter-munching beetles, he discovered it was not always easy to detect signs of deeper problems. He has steered clear of older places ever since. So far, he has managed to avoid any more hidden surprises.

The track takes him around the back of the tilting school to an area of wasteland with a pond – or huge puddle, perhaps – surrounded by flinty soil. It reminds him of the artificial lake at the guesthouse, the place where everyone was naked.

His mother was crying in the twin-bedded room. Her voice jerking, she told his father she wished he wouldn't spring things on her. She did not let the children see her without clothes on. He told her she was narrow-minded. She was holding her children back, stunting their development. Nudity would feel natural to them if she stopped twisting it into something distasteful. He had lived so much of his life longing for freedom. Did she want to keep denying him the opportunity to enjoy it?

When she said she would be too embarrassed, he said, 'And you think everyone will be busy looking at *you*?'

'Of course they won't,' she managed to say. 'This isn't about them. It's about you. About you having ideas we have to fall in with, whether we like it or not.'

He sat on the bed, refusing to speak. An hour passed and he was still there. Neil's mother managed to tuck Kersten under the duvet without disturbing him. In the morning, his father was not there. They packed their things and went downstairs. There was no sign of him in the dining room.

'No, thank you,' Neil's mother said to the waiter who approached them. 'We're looking for my husband.'

'Mum, let's have breakfast,' Neil said, reaching for her hand when she turned away. 'Please. We're starving.'

'We can't without Dad.'

'But we *can*.'

Neil looked back at the smiling waiter in the doorway. The smell of fresh bread was drifting towards them.

'Mum, let's be normal,' he whispered. 'We're hungry. Break-fast's included in the price. The waiter has a table for us. And Dad will find us if he wants to.'

Kersten wailed, 'Please, Mummy, please.'

His mother kept walking. 'We have to find out where he's gone.'

It dawned on Neil that she was scared he had driven off without them. He hurried outside to check. The car was still there. They trooped back up to the room. His father's clothes were still there with his toothbrush, but none of the essentials. His wallet had gone. He kept all the traveller's cheques and cash in there with the ferry tickets. He also had the car keys, the house keys, the travel sweets.

They went outside and walked all the way around the guesthouse to the back. Neil had to help Kersten down the steep, grassy slope. The sun was shining, but had not reached the lake. A few people were taking an early morning swim, their dark heads bobbing up and down.

Neil's father was sitting erect on a sunbed, reading a newspaper. He looked up and beckoned them over.

'I don't feel like driving today,' he said. 'I've booked us lunch here. Come on, you must swim.'

Neil's mother said she would have to go back for towels and sun lotion. Neil offered to go with her and help carry everything. Kersten was too excited about the water to leave it. His father moved aside a little, patting the sunbed, and she perched on the edge. There was a bruise on her kneecap from being rapped with the spoon.

'Be quick,' she said.

Back in the room, Neil found the sun lotion. His mother knelt on the floor and slowly unfolded the towels from the suitcase. She had to fold them up again to fit them into a carrier bag. She pushed one towel inside, then stopped.

'Neil, I don't want to.'

'Then don't. I still think we should have breakfast.'

'I wouldn't be able to eat anything. We don't know how he'll be, do we? He's so set on this.'

'That doesn't mean *we* have to be.'

'But if we don't go along with what he wants, he'll make the rest of the holiday unbearable. He'll never let me forget it.'

Other people's sandals kept slapping happily along the corridor. The doors at the end squeaked open and shut. The room darkened.

'He'll be furious if the sun goes before we get there.'

'Okay,' Neil said. 'I know what we'll do. We'll stay in the water the whole time.'

'What about walking down there?'

'We'll need to wear our clothes for that.'

'But then we'll have to take them off by the lake. Everyone will be looking.'

'They might not. They'll either be swimming or flat on their backs sunbathing.'

'What if the sun doesn't last? They'll all be sitting up, playing Rummy and peering over their cards at us. Kersten will be noisy. She'll keep attracting attention.'

'Okay, let's stay in our clothes. He can't exactly make us take them off.'

'No, we'll stand out even more. They'll think we're prudes.'

'Well, we are, aren't we?'

In the end they walked down to the lake wearing their swimming gear under their clothes. They had to sit on the grass because there were no sunbeds left.

'I couldn't keep one for you,' Neil's father said. 'You took too long. You should go straight in the water now.'

They stood up quickly, stripped off their outerwear and hurried to the water's edge, Neil in his trunks and his mother in her striped swimming costume. Kersten was playing in the shallows with a large group of children.

'We got away with it,' Neil mumbled out of the side of his mouth.

'Don't count your chickens,' said his mother as they waded in.

The lake was cold, but it warmed up once they were immersed. While his mother floated on her back, Neil kept vigil, sculling on the spot to stay upright. She had not slept well. He was worried she might nod off and drown. He kept an eye on Kersten and also watched his father chatting to people on the other sunbeds. They looked normal enough like that, but when they stood up and wandered about, it was a bit unsettling. Not so much because things were uncovered. More because they were not contained. They were free to waggle and bounce, as if they had a life of their own. It was difficult not to stare, especially at the variety of shapes and sizes.. Hard to believe that nature had endowed one person with something so modest and the next with something so extravagant. Some breasts were tiny and pointed like Iced Gems; others were pancakes sliding down a wall. One set were as round as tennis balls. There were some teenage girls with brand-new-looking ones and he felt ashamed to be looking at those. They seemed more private than the older pairs. They all moved in different ways. Some sprang up and down; others shifted from side to side. Bottoms were similar, although most of those fell into the swaying category.

When his father beckoned them back, Neil guessed it must be lunchtime. He and his mother waded out.

'Definitely got away with it,' they both said.

While they dried off, Neil's father stayed on his sunbed. A line of waiters appeared on the slope, carrying tables and chairs, parasols, serviettes and cutlery. There was a paved area further along where they set everything up. People hurried to take their seats.

'I will get us a table,' Neil's father said, 'while you quickly get undressed.'

'But it seems so silly, doesn't it?' Neil's mother said. 'Taking our clothes off to eat.'

'People will feel insulted if you do not. They will think you are judging them.'

He sprinted off to the lunch area. He kept himself lean and fit. His bottom was the springy kind. Kersten followed, calling for him. She had to run to catch up.

Neil and his mother looked at each other.

'We'll have to now, Mum. Honestly, I feel like I'm standing out too much in my trunks.'

He peeled them off. They splatted onto the grass. He wrung them out and considered wrapping a towel around his waist, just to walk across. But his father would frown at him, maybe snatch it away. Possibly even fling it so hard it landed in the lake.

'Let's go over together, Mum,' he said.

She eased the straps off her shoulders as if she had sunburn. Neil looked away. He heard the weight of the water as her costume dropped next to his trunks, then her towel patting her skin dry, shielding her body for a final few seconds.

Neil didn't mind being at the table. With his chair pulled right in, everything private remained unseen. The metal slats dug into the backs of his thighs, but he was so famished he could only think about his hollow stomach. When the waiter brought the menu, Neil saw how ill-at-ease his mother was and he wanted to run back, fetch her cardigan and drape it round her. But it was too much of a risk. Not because of his self-consciousness, or the prospect of his father's disapproval, but because of the spotlight it would throw on his mother.

The sun bloomed again. She was sitting in its full glare. Her hair was short, so she couldn't even arrange that to cover herself. Her breasts, he could not help noticing, were the shape of large Williams pears, well-ripened ones. They were not the worst there. They were probably among the most presentable, although the thought made him feel gross, a bit of a pervert. Her chair was on rough ground and kept wobbling. When she tried to adjust its position, he noticed that her breasts belonged to the sprightly type. He flushed when his father told him he was supposed to be focusing on the menu. He was still dithering when the waiter's pencil was poised and in the end his father ordered on his behalf. It turned out to be a bowl of enormous, pale meatballs and potato dumplings, and Neil fitted them all into the substantial category, bordering on hefty.

Neil walks beyond the inhabited part of the village and past a scattering of abandoned, doorless houses with shattered windows. After a few minutes he reaches the edge of the marsh. The sun has faded and the sky seems full of milk, the soggy ground like fog. It is impossible to work out where to tread. There is no ground as such, only long grasses which he pokes with the toe of his boot. As far as he can tell, there is nothing solid beneath. He looks for a path, but imagines they never last long.

A heron watches him from the mudflats, tall and hunched like an old man in a grey raincoat. Neil senses life teeming in the undergrowth, in the sludge and under the water: insects and birds, frogs and fish. The air is thick with humming and twitching, a constant vibration, and also the fetid smell of putrefaction. He is caught between high energy and extreme stillness.

When Neil was nine, there was a holiday in America. He and his father took a trip to an oyster reef. It was evening and overcast. The sky was like an old cobweb. Seabirds had almost finished smashing shells for the day.

The reef turned silver and rocked in the swell. When the water stirred, the oyster shells clicked together. Neil sat down with the guidebook and flicked on his torch. His father asked him to read out any interesting facts. Neil told him the reef had made the sea between tides a hideout for barnacles and hooked mussels. They gripped the oysters, keeping them safely housed in the nooks between them, well hidden from croakers and catfish slithering just beneath the surface.

His father said, 'I can feel the suction keeping them there.' He was a little breathless, as if moved by their organisational skills, by the hierarchy.

Neil nodded and kept reading. His father made no further comments, but Neil could feel him caught up in the words, imagining the lively world below the sea.

An old man in a checked shirt stopped to listen. He told them he had lived by the coast all his life.

'My pa and me tried to catch the weakfish, but they live up to their name most times. Their mouth muscles are so damn slack, the hook rips clean out soon as it catches on. We reckon we're damn near about to take one, but they wrench free every damn time. Best thing was the silence late at night, when we listened to the fish dreaming.'

The man walked on and Neil finished reading out the information. It sounded flat now. When he closed the book, his father said again, 'I can feel the suction keeping them there.'

They stayed late into the night, until the shallows were creeping over the stones, until the long day's conversation was petering out – not into silence, but into a kind of peace.

When they returned to the hotel, Neil's mother was still awake, terrified of what might have happened.

'It's so late. I thought you'd drowned.'

Kersten was still up, exhausted and sobbing. Neil had looked forward to tiptoeing about, whispering goodnight to his father. He wanted to thank him. He already knew the trip to the oyster reef was the outing of his life.

The next morning, his father would not leave the hotel room.

'You will take the children out,' he said to Neil's mother. 'Since I am not to be trusted.'

'I never said I didn't trust you. I was just worried. You were so much later than I was expecting.'

'You thought I could not prevent our son from drowning.'

'No, I didn't know what to think.'

'You should know what to think.'

Neil had to help his mother find the bus stop. Their schedule for that day was to visit an aquarium and have lunch in a restaurant, then go to the beach. Kersten was still in nappies. There had to be so many stops. She was prone to tantrums as well, and you couldn't schedule those. You only knew they would happen. Some of them never really stopped. It made Neil's mother tense when people stared. She could never think straight in public.

'We don't have to go to the aquarium if you don't want to,' Neil said when they were waiting for the bus. 'It's probably boring.'

He had planned to learn about the life of the hermit crab. He was going to write about it for a school project.

'We'll have to,' said his mother. 'Your father will want to know all about it. And when we tell him, he'll cheer up.'

On the bus, Kersten was quieter than Neil had expected. He realised that his mother was discreetly breastfeeding, a cardigan draped over her front. She was meant to have given up. It was a great relief, though. Maybe Kersten could be plugged in every time she wailed.

He missed his father at the aquarium. There was so much to point out, so many things you could only marvel at with someone else. His mother was too busy trying to make Kersten stay in the pushchair. She had to keep it moving the whole time. If she paused, Kersten strained against the straps and screamed to get out. When she was cross, her fat, wobbly face turned a brilliant red. It rivalled the colours of the more flamboyant sea creatures.

Neil savoured the hermit crab facts to share later with his father. It fascinated him that they formed a vacancy chain. He already knew they lived in shells vacated by other species and moved into a larger one as they grew. Now he discovered that when a new, vacant shell is too large, the crab waits patiently beside it until others turn up. They take a look at the shell and if it is too big for them as well, they form an orderly queue from largest to smallest. Once a crab who fits the shell comes along, he gives up his old one and everyone in the queue can swap, each one going up a size.

Neil made copious notes. He was anxious not to forget any of the details. He wrote them down in the burger restaurant while Kersten was busy nuzzling his mother under the cardigan. They went to the beach afterwards, but by the time they had found toilets and somewhere suitable to change Kersten's nappy, and manoeuvred the pushchair down the steps, there was only about twenty minutes before their bus was due. Neil quickly collected some interesting pebbles. He held onto the pushchair while his mother and Kersten had a paddle. He carried Kersten up the steps while his mother carried everything else. He found the right stop for their bus in the nick of time. His mother sat down, exhausted and sunburnt. She said she would never have managed without him. Neil was glad he had turned her punishment into a day she might remember in a good way.

Back at the hotel, his father was impressed with the hermit crabs' orderliness and the good sense of it all. He was glad that Neil had taken charge. The two of them ate together in the hotel restaurant and talked about the sea. Neil's father was surprised by how little his son knew about tides.

Neil's mother had said she wasn't hungry and, in any case, she had to settle Kersten, who was dropping with fatigue. Neil missed her at dinner. She never had many expectations of him. She was the kind of mum who let you get on with your food.

With his father in a better mood and the day so successful, Neil went to bed feeling less nervous than he usually did on holiday. He thought about the crabs as he drifted off to sleep. He decided the most reassuring thing about the shell exchange sequence was that it was perpetual.

Leaving the marsh, he finds a ramshackle seat in a field with a rusty swing and slide. He takes out his phone and makes a list of jobs he can do in the village. When he started property developing, he made a pact with himself never to stray from budget. His aim is to achieve all he reasonably can within his parameters and no more. He doesn't mind painting and decorating, but he never touches roofs. He told the mayor that last night.

He has the feeling the mayor was expecting more. Like Thomas, he asked about machinery. He pointed out there are no local trades in the village anymore. He asked if Neil had a team. Neil explained he often uses a kitchen fitter, an electrician and a plumber, but none of them could come all this way. He would have to pay their travel expenses and provide meals and find them somewhere decent to stay. Costs would quickly get out of hand.

The mayor said he was setting up a village meeting for Neil to speak about his plans and answer questions. Neil was not sure about being put on show. He told the mayor he had done plenty of research online. He was aware of other rural villages in the east, many of them semi-abandoned and left to decline. He understood why younger residents were attracted to a more prosperous life in the West and why the older ones preferred to stay. It was a sad fact that some of these villages would not be saved. But at least he was giving this one a chance. His father had left him an incredible gift and he was taking it seriously.

The mayor listened patiently, then repeated the date and time of the meeting. 'Have your speech ready,' he said. 'The village deserves to meet you formally and hear your plans.'

Neil wanted to say that, as the owner, he would decide himself if a meeting were necessary. But the mayor was a reasonable man with soft jowls and sad eyes. He looked at Neil as if he believed Herr Fischer held all the answers.

Neil looks at his list. He has typed *sanding/repainting*. He adds *save the sinking school*.

He walks back to it and looks up at the substantial tree nearby. Its trunk is gnarled and massive. He gives it a tentative rub, as if daring to touch a wild creature he was hoping to tame. It must be sapping moisture from the soil, forcing it to shrink and collapse. Most of the men here would be too elderly to help him fell it, but Thomas would surely be willing. It would produce a year's supply of logs for the village, maybe more.

The drains might need checking. If they are in a bad state, the soil could be waterlogged, even washed away. He once cleared a blockage by poking about with a length of thin wire. He prefers uncomplicated equipment. He was inspired by a woman in a television programme, who renovated an entire, tumbledown house without any tools apart from a wallpaper scraper.

He gives the tree a confident pat. The school is in bad shape, but he would prefer not to lose it. Thomas will definitely help. He must be well into his fifties, but strong and fit. He has colossal biceps. Between them, they can lick the place into shape and become friends in the process.

Neil walks briskly back to the house. The sun is lighting up the silvery logs, the clean sheets pegged to the rope stretched across the yard, the grass encrusted with chicken droppings.

Thomas is still chopping and does not look up. Neil watches him. He can see something of his father in him. Not his physical appearance or mannerisms. His father was lean, his face animated; Thomas is stocky and expressionless. Neil struggles to locate the link. He almost has it. As Thomas raises his axe again, the connection breaks.

Chapter Six

Silke feels sick in the city. In the thirty-seven years since her arrest, Berlin has changed, yet not changed. The grey Soviet architecture is now lustrous glass and steel, although the bronze statues of Marx and Engels remain. It is a jolt to the heart, the point where the unfamiliar meets the familiar. People are jostling her. She is in their way and keeps apologising. She finds a coffee shop and sits at a table outside. A brightly lit bakery nearby is packed with new loaves, drifting the smell of hot yeast.

She has been planning the trip for a year and a half and has lived each stage of it in her mind, although she did not know she would be driven to the station until the other day. She had imagined stowing away in the milk lorry.

Herr Fischer said he could take her all the way to Berlin. For a split second she was tempted. She smiles now, despite the nausea. Still in his twenties, he makes her feel like a student again. Her own memories fail to distil the essence of those days – only this fresh-faced Englishman. So yes, she was tempted, but she had already bought her ticket and mapped out the forty-five-minute walk from the station. If she had been driven door to door, the intensity of the day would have been diluted. When she first arrived in Berlin as an eighteen-year-old, she took the city in her stride. She is going to take it in her stride again.

She sips her coffee. People pass by in sleeveless tops and shorts. Silke is wearing a dark-blue dress and jacket she bought on the internet, something cheap. Black tights and navy shoes as well. She had the parcel delivered to Renate at the farm. She told her it was a gift for Thomas, something she wanted to keep secret. There was also a jumper for his next birthday in the package, for the sake of honesty.

She is sitting in full sunlight. It is far too warm for her dark, scratchy outfit. She ironed it this morning, but the fabric wrinkles with every movement. The nylon lining crackles with static. Her stiff shoes press against the backs of her heels. The whole thing feels like a costume. When she left her first student flat for the last time, she was unsuitably dressed too. She was wearing a cotton nightdress that was far too short. The sleeves of her old dressing gown barely reached her elbows. It was midwinter and snowing hard.

During her first weeks at the university, Silke stayed up late at boisterous, sweaty parties. The city excited her, brought her out of her shell, and her liveliness made her seem more attractive than she was. Within days Martin became her unofficial boyfriend. Andreas used to put his arm round her and say he wished she had a twin. They were pale and dark-eyed. They always wore black, like popstars. It thrilled her to have their attention.

One afternoon she slumped into her seat at Café Danika and thumped her new ring-binder on the table.

'Hey, what's up?' asked Martin, lighting a cigarette.

'Apparently there are certain books in the library we are not allowed to borrow. They are there on the shelves, but we can't read them.'

Martin suggested they go for a stroll in the park. Walking with him was like flying. When he took her hand, her feet barely touched the ground. Once he was sure no one was nearby, he held her close. He told her about some friends he and Andreas had made, a group planning to escape through a tunnel under the Wall. Defectors already in the West had been quietly digging with trowels, their progress painfully slow, but ceaseless. They were close now.

'Come with us,' Martin whispered. 'You could go to a university where no books are banned. No one opening your post, eavesdropping on your phone calls, telling you what music you can listen to. You wouldn't be watched all the time.'

'I'm not aware of being watched.'

'Come on, there are eyes everywhere.'

'Not on me. I mean, I think about leaving all the time, but no one knows. Not even my family—'

'That's why you'd be ideal,' Martin said. 'If no one is watching...'

'I don't know what to say.'

His breath was hot in her ear. 'Say yes. I need you. I couldn't go without you.'

At the last few parties, she had slipped outside with Martin, late at night in the freezing cold. Last time, he wrapped his black overcoat around her and unfastened her blouse. He slotted his cold fingers into the dips between her ribs, as if they were the only warm places he would ever find.

Next day at the café, Silke was introduced to the group. They were older, no longer students, and lacked the vitality of Martin and Andreas. They looked at Silke as if she made them uneasy. Imagining the long crawl beneath the city in the dark nauseated her. She nudged Martin and said she wasn't sure anymore.

'It's not as if you'll be far away,' he said, stirring sugar into her coffee, forgetting she didn't take it. 'West or East, it's all Berlin.'

'I don't think I can leave Thomas. I could ask him to come with us, but our parents would be so unhappy if we both—'

'I've already asked him,' Andreas cut in, leaning across the table to light the cigarette Martin had placed between her lips, although she was not a regular smoker. 'He wants to stay here, but he wishes us well.'

'Don't tell him your plans, though,' Martin said. 'He seems protective of you. He'll talk you out of it.'

Silke laughed. 'I can't keep it from him. I'm his sister.'

'The fewer people who know, the better,' said one of the older men.

'Look, once we've gone, he will be interrogated,' Andreas said. 'What he doesn't know can't hurt him.'

Silke blew out the smoke, shaking her head. 'Surely it will hurt him more. They'll never believe he knows nothing about his sister's plans. They'll never leave him alone.'

Andreas frowned. 'Don't be dramatic. You're making people stare. We don't know who's listening, who's watching.'

'There's only one other person in here,' Silke said, glancing at a woman in an orange headscarf, who was reading a newspaper in the opposite corner.

One man complained that Silke was not reliable enough. The others nodded their agreement. Martin begged them to give her a chance. They all shrugged and turned back to their glasses of Vita Cola.

Later that night, Silke went to a park with Martin and wore nothing under her coat. He took out his pocket torch and shone it all over her body. It felt like a doctor's examination and she didn't like it much, but his surprise and happiness made her fall deeper in love.

He grew serious after a while and refastened her coat. He promised they would live in a flat together in West Berlin. The walls would be white, the carpets deep, the sofa covered in soft leather. No, she couldn't bring her horrible cushions.

He was supposed to share with Andreas, but now his future was with Silke. They would have fun all the time. Nothing like their drab, miserable life here, with all its shortages and queues and restrictions.

'You'll be safe with me,' he said, cupping her chin, his fingers pressing into her cheeks. 'But you have to leave before they start following you. I know you don't believe they are, but soon they'll be stepping on your shadow. I mean, who wouldn't want to look at you all the time?'

He eased her belt out of the buckle and warmed his hands inside her coat again. The excitement erased her fear. With Martin she was invincible.

'Please think about it,' he said. 'Think about us.'

Silke said she would, but gave it no thought at all. If Martin was going, she was going.

'I'll talk to the others,' he said. 'Convince them to trust you.'

Silke had to miss the next few meetings. Martin was either 'talking the others round' or 'discussing finer details'. 'The others' became a sinister phrase. She wished she and Martin could escape without them. When she was finally readmitted to the inner circle, they met at many different times of the day and in various locations. It was vital to avoid arousing suspicion. Sometimes she had to miss a lecture to be at the café for updates passed to her on serviettes and till receipts. She was too distracted to focus properly on her studies and Thomas kept asking when she was going to knuckle down.

The tunnel had taken three years of punishing work. It would soon reach the border area, the inner wall, the signal fence, the electrified wire with alarms, the spikes in the ground, the watchtowers, floodlights, anti-vehicle traps, armed guards on patrol, the death strip. The group would gain access through a hole which Martin and Andreas were digging in the basement of a house near the border. It would be terrifying and painful, crawling on their stomachs in the suffocating dark. But after less than fifteen minutes, they would be free. She did not need to know more.

They had given her lookout duties to carry out on the night and a coded message to deliver to everyone involved. Every chance she could get, she rehearsed. She was ready. Love had prepared her for anything.

It did not prepare her for the eight Stasi men who broke into the flat in the dead of night and surrounded her bed. She was allowed to put on her dressing gown and her slippers that were full of holes. Snow seeped in as she was walked to the little bakery van. It looked so innocent parked behind the block of flats.

At the prison, she was taken to a bare room and stripped of her nightclothes. She was made to stand with her arms outstretched and legs wide. Every part of her was searched with rubber-gloved hands. She could do nothing to stop the grunts of pain or the violent shivering. They told her repeatedly to stand still. They kept starting again. The search felt like an archaeological dig. Their fingers burrowed into her body for longer than it would have taken her to crawl through the tunnel.

She focused on her little pile of nightclothes in the corner. She could still smell the flat on them, the sliced potatoes and eggs she had fried that evening.

At the end of her forty-five-minute walk, Silke's feet are bleeding. She passes several chemists where she could buy plasters. On an ordinary day, she would attend to it. But she refuses to stop. She shuffles in an attempt to minimise the chafing.

When the building comes into view, she slows down. There is no one she can talk to about the outcome of her appointment. Thomas is adamant that, for her sake, the past must be forgotten. He pretends they share a bedroom because she is unable to sleep alone.

She has always known this would be a solitary mission, but had not realised it would be such a lonely one. She wishes Herr Fischer was with her. He would show a polite interest and keep it to himself. Perhaps she will tell him a little about it later, in the car. Sometimes you can trust strangers more than friends, or family.

It is time to go inside. She tries not to hobble into the Stasi Records Agency. Despite the pain, she reverts to her usual lengthy stride, her spine straight. The shoes are digging in badly, but she takes no notice.

She is handed her file and takes it with both hands. It is thicker than a block of marzipan. She carries it to a wood-effect table and sits down, but does not open it straight away. It has been a long thirty-seven years.

There is a picture of her on the cover. Her short, fair hair was spiky then, the roots dark. It needed a wash. There are grey smudges under her startled eyes. She should have remained startled. It would have given her something to feel.

Emotions were ground down in prison. She had no cellmate, nothing to read or listen to, no window. The bare lightbulb hanging from the ceiling was never switched off.

The guards watched her through a slot in the door. The metal covering shot back and the eyes appeared. She had to sit in a certain position, bolt upright with her hands at her sides, all day long. She was not permitted to exercise, not even to pace around the tiny cell. At night, she waited to be told when she was allowed to lie down on her bunk. Even then, the position was not her own choice. Hands had to remain outside the thin blanket. If she turned in her sleep, they woke her up.

She left the cell only for visits to the interrogation room. These happened without warning, often at night. She was not allowed to sleep the next day. She still had to sit on the hard stool in her cell. The metal plate in the door would shriek back, the eyes watching for her to doze off, waiting until her breaths slowed to the rhythm of deep sleep. Then she was ordered to wake up. Metallic noises terrify her, even now.

The interrogation room was the same as any living room in East Germany. Drab, yellow wallpaper, plain green curtains, beige furniture. It was designed to make you feel at home, or miss home. Either way, secrets were more likely to spill out.

She eases her heels out of the shoes and opens the file. The paper smells sour. There are hundreds of pages. She reads that a Stasi member code-named 'Schmetterling' observed her life in Berlin in microscopic detail. He watched her through binoculars from a kitchen window in the tower block opposite.

When she and Thomas were out, 'Schmetterling' let himself in with a skeleton key and took photographs. They were all pasted into the file: the contents of her drawers, the books on her shelf, the open packet of Gouda cheese sent by Martin's aunt in the West. He had brought it round as a gift for her and Thomas. A ruler had been placed beneath the cheese to demonstrate its size.

There is a photograph of the essay she was in the middle of writing, its pages spread out on her rumpled sheets where she had left them to dash out to a lecture. She remembers the day well. She met Martin later on and they went to a Goldbroiler café. She can still taste the juicy, golden chicken and feel Martin's tongue licking grease from her fingers.

Information about her involvement in the planned escape was reported in detail. There were photographs of her in the café, with Martin in the queue for chicken, in the university grounds. Also in the park, fastening the belt of her raincoat.

Facets of Silke's life were passed to the Stasi by an unofficial informer, code name 'Mustang'. She imagines everyone who views their file tries to guess the true identity of their betrayer. Sometimes a single detail gives it away. 'Mustang' knew many things about Silke. 'Mustang' knew things only one person could possibly have known.

Chapter Seven

Driving back to the village, Neil wishes he had taken Silke to Berlin. She was nervous, squeezing her hands together all the way to the station. It might have been his driving, of course. Narrow roads are new to him.

She stumbled out of the car in a pair of shoes that didn't suit her. He asked if she would be all right, but there was no reply. She looked different all dressed up, not like the Silke who throws corn, tossing it from her apron pockets with the chickens clustering round her. When Neil crosses the yard, they huddle in one corner and stare at him, cackling. If he isn't careful, the cockerel thrusts his chest out, struts along at breakneck pace and makes a beeline for his turn-ups.

He is looking forward to six o'clock, when he'll pick Silke up from the station. He likes having someone else to think about. Nine years ago, his father decided to live entirely downstairs. He said the upstairs was a self-contained unit for Neil.

Neil's bedroom and the bathroom stayed the same. His parents' old room became his lounge and Kersten's room his rather makeshift kitchen. Neil's mother asked if his father had made the division to keep Neil at arm's length, or to keep him at home. Neil knew the answer, but kept it to himself.

He has the run of the house now his father is dead, but still lives in his unit. He has tried sitting downstairs, but his father is always there. The huge Bavarian ashtray with its flugelhorn centrepiece is still full of his cigarette stubs. Neil feels uncomfortable every time he tries to clear anything up, but it is impossible to sit there surrounded by it. His mother suggested coming round to help toss everything out, as she put it. Neil turned her down.

The potato is wrinkling in the cupholder. Neil wishes Gudrun were sitting beside him, pulling oddments out of her backpack. He would like to show her around his manor. That is probably how he would describe it to his male friends, if he had any.

He ought to socialise again, now he is on his own. He used to worry about leaving his father alone towards the end. And it was awkward bringing anyone home. He had to warn them they would be going straight upstairs, otherwise girls he had only just met would feel wrong-footed.

He had brought two girls home. The first was a geography student with a cap of brown hair like an elderly mushroom. He got to know her on a Hunt Saboteurs coach trip. He had only joined it to meet people. She liked taping music onto cassettes and gave him everything Steely Dan had ever recorded. She thought all sabo-teurs should be vegetarians and was crestfallen to see him with a luncheon-meat sandwich. He pointed out that it had an awful lot of salad in it as well, but she still questioned how he could put flesh in his mouth. Even though her own tongue slithered in there while the coach was held up in Old Sodbury.

He invited her home afterwards and when he told her about going upstairs, she squealed, 'Oh, *you*,' as if he had said something hilarious. Nothing much happened. They sat on his bed and she put her tongue in his mouth a few more times. Mostly, she smoked menthol cigarettes, and talked about glacial moraine and trun-cated spurs.

He eventually lost his virginity to a depressed girl with low blood pressure. She had to go slowly up his stairs and be careful not to stand up too quickly in case she passed out. When he was puffing and panting on top of her, he worried that she might lose consciousness and they would have to be surgically de-suctioned. He imagined the paramedic attaching clamps and inserting spatulas. He thought about their damp skin being prised apart with a pitiful sound, like wet newspapers tearing.

At one point, such was the excitement, her glasses fell off. Without them she looked like someone lost underwater. He pretended to be asleep when she left. Which was a mistake, because she stole all his Steely Dan cassettes.

He used to have an occasional night out with Jack Claridge from the house on the corner. After sixth form, they went to college together to retake their A Levels. Jack was stocky, loud and confident. He had legions of friends and girls attached themselves to him like iron filings to a magnet. In all honesty, they were not actual nights out with Jack and his entourage. It was more a case of Neil listening to their plans in the canteen at lunchtime and tagging along. But once the evening was underway, and people were drinking and laughing, he felt part of things. Jack went away to London, eventually – able to move on in a way Neil could not.

The last time Neil had a night out with Jack was at the end of the autumn term. Jack was with his latest girlfriend, Jessie Lynch, and there was also a girl Neil had hoped to click with, but he struggled to find any common ground. She had never heard of a hunt saboteur. Neil had lost interest in all that anyway. He told her he liked playing chess against himself.

'There are no secrets, that's why. The absolute truth is always on the board. I quite often beat myself because the moment I make a move, the other me spots my mistakes.'

She had never played chess. She was into opera music. He had no experience of that, but was excited because it was unexpected. He wanted to understand new things and maybe try them himself.

She rolled her eyes, though, when he said that. As if he was trying to butter her up. She said she was going to be an artist, but she barely talked about that either and he didn't really believe her. He had looked her up online recently and discovered she was a success. She held exhibitions and people paid money for her still-life paintings. They were mostly vegetables and fruit, their colours soft and blurred, almost apologetic. If you can call artichokes and lemons apologetic.

On their way home, it was cold. Dry leaves were skating along the pavement in the wind. Neil reached out and caught a pure red one, but the girl didn't notice. She had dropped back to chat to the others. Jack was in the mood to impress. Sometimes he walked into people's gardens and picked flowers for the girls; sometimes he walked on walls. Whatever he did, the rest of them stopped and started accordingly, matching his pace. He pulled Neil's leg about the plastic mac he was wearing and cracked a few jokes about him having a German father. He swaggered into the middle of the road and did a backflip. He made Jessie dance the tango, sweeping her off her feet. She shrieked with laughter and told him he was mad.

Halfway home, they passed Jessie's ex-boyfriend, Davey Ashdown. He was walking alone on the pavement opposite, the hood of his quilted anorak flapping, hands deep in his pockets. Davey was under a streetlamp when he acknowledged Jessie. It was just a slight nod and a shy wave. Seconds later he was flat on the ground.

Neil stops the car outside the village. Driving sometimes makes him panic. It must be the power you have, the absolute control. At any moment there could be a mistake – a lapse of judgement, a fleeting loss of attention. You press your foot a fraction harder on the accelerator, steer a little wildly. In a split second, something changes inside you. You know you should wait longer at the junction, stay further back from the vehicle in front, turn off the road immediately. You know you shouldn't go out at all. But you still do it.

A tall woman with a thin dog walks past the car. She pauses and turns round. Neil smiles, as best he can during a panic attack. The look on her face makes him flinch. His father once gave him the same look. It was the night Neil was getting ready to go out with Jack and the others. He came into the hall when Neil was combing his hair in front of the mirror. He said nothing. He stood in front of the coats on the hooks by the door and refused to move out of the way, which was why Neil had to make do with the old plastic mac from the garage.

The panic is still rising. It has to reach a peak before it goes away. He tries the alternate nostril breathing he learnt from a yoga book his mother had left behind, but it gets worse. The woman with the dog walks on, clicking her tongue to bring him to heel.

Davey tried to get up. Jack punched him and he collapsed again. Everyone was silent. The girls were clutching each other. Neil crossed the road halfway. He told himself he didn't really know Davey anymore. He used to, back when they were at school. But he knew nothing about him now, nothing about what he might have done wrong.

The wind gusted. Leaves billowed over Davey. One tucked itself into his nylon hood. He groaned, but did not move. Jack stood still in the pool of light from the streetlamp, his fist slowly unclenching. He retained perfect balance, a kind of elegance, as he drew his leg back and kicked Davey in the stomach. Davey tried to curl up, but Jack kicked him again and again. He jumped up and stamped on him, the heels of his boots driving in hard. He had a reason, Neil was sure. Davey must have goaded him somehow. If not tonight, then some other time.

'Come on,' Jack said, crossing back.

'What did he do?' Neil asked as they walked on.

'Bloody nightmare, that one.'

'What was it?'

'Spreading shit around about Jess. Winding us both up. Got me narked, didn't he. Seriously narked.'

They kept going, their breath turning to steam. The only sound was the crackle of Neil's mac. After a while, the girls began chatting again, more subdued now. Jack danced about, like a boxer warming up.

'Do you think he'll be okay?' Neil asked.

'What?'

'Him. The one you...'

Jack was skipping with an imaginary rope, panting a little. 'Why wouldn't he?'

They went to the chip shop. Afterwards Jack steered Jessie into a doorway. They posted the opposite ends of a long chip into their mouths, biting along its length until they reached the middle and kissing with their mouths full.

'God, that was hot,' she said, fanning her face.

'Any time, darling,' said Jack.

'Not you, the bloody chip. Burnt my bloody tongue.'

She definitely thought Jack was hot. All the girls did. You could tell from the way she hung onto the kiss. She didn't lick her greasy lips afterwards. Neil wondered if they would do it again. He was quite good at appearing not to watch. He wanted to think about it when he was falling asleep. But Jessie went back into the shop for a can of shandy and Jack polished off the chips on his own.

'I checked,' he said, scrunching up the paper bag and booting it straight into the bin.

'Checked?' Neil said.

'That Davey git. Ran off home, didn't he.'

*

The panic refuses to shift. Neil gets out of the car and walks towards the village in the glare of the sun. His heartbeat is too fast. He catches up with the thin woman and wishes her a breathless good day in German.

'You are the new owner?' she says in English.

'Yes, Neil Fischer.' He holds out his hand and she barely shakes it, as though it is made of glass.

'I am Renate and this is my farm,' she tells him, pointing across a field. 'You want to see it?'

'Yes, I'd like to. I'm staying with Thomas. He's working here today, I believe.'

She stares at him and says, 'You will slip.'

'Slip?'

She points at his loafers. They are a decent leather pair that belonged to his mother – not badly worn, just a little tired.

'You can wear these shoes in the wet and the mud?'

'Yes, no problem.'

She raises her eyebrows. Her face is shrivelled like an apple that has lain all summer in the grass.

They walk across the mud-clogged field, the thin dog quivering between them. Several times he looks up at Neil, his dark eyes quizzical. The farm buildings are ramshackle. Rising high above them is a colossal silo: a thick cylinder tapering to a point, like a pencil stub belonging to a giant.

'Four metres tall,' Renate says. 'It is old, but does the job. I got it from eBay.'

They crane their necks, shading their eyes with their hands. The dented metal is glossy in the sun. A chill slams into Neil, the same chill he feels at the railway station when a freight train thunders through. He never goes there to travel, only to stand on the platform. He goes there for the shock of it.

He told a girl about it once and she said, 'Why the hell go there if it gives you the creeps?'

'It's the thrill of being close to something which scares you.'

'Well, make sure you stay behind the yellow line,' she said. 'Don't get carried away.'

Neil always stands with his toes touching the yellow line. 'The cold air blasts you,' he told the girl. 'Your entire body shudders.'

'What are you intending to change here?' Renate asks.

'Here? At your farm? Nothing. I don't know anything about farming.'

'You think I mean the farm? When I am fully operational and the only employer left?'

'No, carry on as you are, of course. I won't intervene.'

'And the village?'

'I'd like to save the school.'

'It is beyond help. The day after the Wall fell, attendance was less than half. Most families had travelled west overnight. Now there are no children at all. What plans do you have for our residents, for those who have stayed?'

'I'll be doing some repairs—'

'No plans?'

He shakes his head, still gazing up at the silo, at its brutal thrust, its domed head invading the sky. His heart is beating too hard.

'We are not seeking change,' Renate says, throwing a stick for the dog. 'We are hoping for safety. Is that not what everyone wants? You too, no?'

He looks at her and recoils again. She is fierce and probing, like teachers who know you have not been listening, but still demand answers. One of his feet is stuck in the mud. He battles to move it. He doesn't want her to know his shoes are letting him down. He concentrates on making tiny adjustments left and right, until it is free. He looks up at the silo again. His other shoe is stuck now. He does nothing about it.

Renate calls for the dog. He hares towards her, coils his skinny body around her legs and sits obediently at her feet.

'Look around if you like,' Renate says, staring at his sinking shoes. 'I have much to do. You must be busy yourself.'

She goes into the house and shuts the door. A metal latch clicks into place.

Neil stays with the silo for a long time before he walks away. The day is muggy now, the air stifling. The breeze has given up. When he returns to his car, the sunlight reflecting from the wing mirror briefly blinds him. Back in the driver's seat, the air conditioning blasts a cold surge of relief.

He drives to the town again. He has an urge to buy Silke something, although it is a long time since he gave anyone a present. He and his father never exchanged gifts. He sends cards to his mother and sister for their birthdays. The process of choosing them is agony. In the supermarket he stands for ages in front of the cards for Sister or Mother. He can never decide if they would prefer a picture of flowers, or clinking glasses of Prosecco, or cartoonish women in stilettos.

When he reads the sentiments printed inside, his eyes swim out of focus. *You mean so much... The moments spent with you... You're truly special in so many ways...* Eventually, he has to leave the shop. Another day – too late for the birthday itself – he buys an all-purpose card. It is the same one every time: a milky-grey pattern of maple leaves, as if you are seeing them through driving rain.

It rained heavily the night Davey Ashdown was lying on the ground. No one found him until morning. A man walking his dog spotted what he thought was a heap of old clothes covered in wet leaves. Davey was soaked through. He had not moved all night. The paramedics said he had died several hours before he was discovered. There were internal injuries. Didn't see much blood, the dog walker said, but you never know, do you, what could be happening inside?

Neil read the news online. He did nothing else all morning. He searched all the news sites and the same few facts were repeated. The police were asking for witnesses, for anyone in the area that night to come forward. Neil did nothing.

At lunchtime, the police knocked on the door. Jessie Lynch had come forward. All the girls had come forward, and most of the boys.

Neil was driven to the police station. He sat in a cold interview room with walls the colour of weak tea. He shivered on a plastic chair, unable to pick up the polystyrene cup of coffee.

'I was way back the whole time,' he kept saying. 'I was in the middle of the road.'

They asked for details of the assault. It sounded monstrous in words: the vicious blows, the final kick, all without a word from Neil to stop it.

'Yes, I could see clearly. But I was way back. And it was over so fast there wasn't time to understand it.'

What was there to understand?

'I don't know. That's sort of what I mean. I was confused.'

Too confused to know what a punch is, or a kick?

'I knew what they were, but I kind of turned to stone.'

Was he afraid he would be hurt too?

'I think so, yes. Maybe.'

Why did he cross to the middle of the road, then? For a ring-side seat?

'No. No, of course not.'

To help?

'I wanted to. I wasn't there to gawp. I was going across to reason with Jack, I suppose. Or to try.'

'But you didn't, did you? You didn't reason. You didn't try.'

'Because it was over so fast. Davey was on the ground and we were away.'

'You didn't think about checking if Davey Ashdown needed help? After several severe punches and kicks, after falling down and not moving?'

'No.' Neil could say nothing else. His throat was swollen, his heart in the room.

'You went for chips instead?'

He nodded once, looking at the floor.

'And then home to bed?'

And then home to bed?

And then home to bed?

He nodded again and was told to answer.

'Yes,' he whispered.

When it was over, he went out into the bright street. People were busy with their Saturday shopping, sitting on benches with burgers, hugging friends in the park. He put his cold hands in his pockets and the red leaf was there, still perfect. He knew it would be impossible to leave that night behind. He would always be in the middle of that road.

His father fired the same questions at him as the police had asked. He was repulsed by his son's failure to act. He followed Neil up to his room and filled the doorway.

'Faced with this cruelty, this undeserved cruelty, you do nothing?'

'I couldn't—'

'You cannot throw yourself on Jack Claridge, pin him down? You cannot knock on the nearest door? You cannot phone the police?'

'It was all over too quickly.'

'And when it is over, you cannot phone for an ambulance, stay with the dying young man, make a pillow for him with your coat?'

Neil turned away. His father left him alone in his room. It was the first time Neil had known him to close a door.

If Davey had spread vile rumours about Jessie Lynch on social media, it probably counted as slander. He must have come on to her. He had come on to her after their short relationship was long over, resentful she was with Jack. The truth would come up in court. Jack's defence would focus on the reason for the attack, how Davey had provoked him into using violence.

The next day, Neil's father told him there was a microwave, toaster and kettle in Kersten's old bedroom, plus a box containing a plate, a bowl, a mug, a knife, fork and spoon, and a bottle of Fairy liquid. Neil could wash up in the bath. Later on, he was given a mini fridge, an electric hotplate, a saucepan and frying pan. He kept groceries in a pink chest that used to contain Kersten's dressing-up clothes. A small sofa and coffee table from the second-hand shop and an old television appeared in his parents' room. The bed was shoved against one wall and the wardrobe shunted along to make space.

Alone in his bedroom, he whacked his shins with a boot, dropped to the carpet and pounded his fist into his stomach, banged his head against the wall. He dropped out of college, but pretended he was still going in. When his father was leaving for work in the mornings, Neil came hurrying down as if he were running late, a ring-binder under his arm.

Some evenings, Neil sat on the stairs, halfway down. He listened to his father's television programmes, the click of his lighter, the glue-stiffened pages of the holiday photograph album, creaking as they turned.

Neil parks in the town centre and walks down a quiet side-road to knock the dry mud off his shoes. He goes back to the main street and finds a department store. The lino floors buckle and slope. The lifts are out of order. Short staircases lead to passages full of echoes and more short staircases. The departments are not clear-cut. Garden Tools, for example, mingles with Toys. He loses his bearings. He worries about finding his way out.

A savoury aroma wafts from the restaurant. He follows it from Handbags to Shoes. It is even more appetising by the time he reaches Indoor Games. He has to pass a display of elaborate chess sets made of glass and porcelain. The wooden ones are in different colours from the usual black and white. He looks for traditional pieces on an ordinary board. Maybe no one makes them anymore.

When the police asked Neil if he knew the victim, he said, 'No. I maybe played chess with him once at school. But I didn't really know him.'

He and Davey played chess fourteen times. It was the winter term and there was a lunchtime craze for it at school. Davey mentioned that he went fishing on Saturdays. Neil unearthed the old tackle he had hardly ever used from the cupboard under the stairs. He bumped into Davey on the riverbank. He took along a tube of bitter-cherry boiled sweets which made Davey's breath tangy. The flavour had been discontinued, otherwise he would still buy them.

When Neil was pretending to dash out and catch the bus to college, he waited behind a hedge until his father had left for work. He went home again and got back into bed. He slept all morning. He heated a chicken jalfrezi ready-meal in his microwave for lunch, ate it from the carton and played computer games all afternoon. At weekends, he went fishing alone. If he caught anything, he threw it back in the water. When the weather was bad, he stayed in and watched YouTube. He stumbled across videos showing you how to maintain a house. He became addicted to them, addicted to writing down all the advice, word for word.

At sixteen, he had started working weekends at Starbucks. Since leaving college, he had taken on every shift available. With the money he had saved over the years, he bought a few tools. He damaged things in his unit so he could practise repairing them. He broke a small window and re-glazed it. He dug out the grouting from between the bathroom tiles and re-grouted. He pulled the sofa cover apart and sewed it back together with a curved upholstery needle. He bought cheap wallpaper, paint, a fat roller and a thin one, several paintbrushes.

He couldn't be bothered to move all the furniture out while he redecorated. He was not seeking the perfect home. He only wanted to see if he could get things right.

He papered around his parents' old bed and wardrobe. He chose plain first, to get the hang of it. Then he stripped it off to get the hang of that. He bought the fanciest pattern he could find, all peacocks and cherry blossom. He wasted quite a few lengths, but it didn't matter. Once he had papered the walls he could get to without shifting things aside, he felt he had mastered it. He painted the door and skirting with gloss. He painted over the peacock walls with half-price purple emulsion. He detached the washbasin fixed to the wall, then put it back in place. He re-tiled part of the splashback, removing five pale pink tiles and replacing them with five pale blue ones from a bargain bin. He took the washbasin out again, dumped it on the bed, and re-plastered the damaged wall.

He started working full-time for Starbucks and saved every penny. Frugality became his chief interest. He stopped buying ready meals and stocked up on off-brand cornflakes, tinned pulses, sardines, peanut butter and bread. He ate cornflakes for breakfast and snacks, sneaking milk from his father's fridge downstairs. He had a free sandwich for lunch at work. In the evenings he heated half a tin of kidney or cannellini beans with a couple of sardines on his hotplate. He served them on a slice of toast spread thinly with peanut butter. He stole the odd spoonful of coffee from downstairs and drank water from the bathroom tap.

The money piled up in his bank account. He sold his computer games, several boxes of books, his fishing tackle and his leather jacket. He worked every available shift. At Christmas, his total expenditure was nine pounds fifty on a seasonal bouquet from the supermarket. He left it on his mother's doorstep.

He walked to Davey's house every Christmas Eve and sat in the porch. Davey's parents were always away. They must have set a timer, because the same few lights were always on. At precisely eleven o'clock, they all went off. There were no decorations, no wreath on the door.

He had invited himself there once, on Davey's seventeenth birthday. The parents were kind and welcoming. They asked him about school and hobbies while Davey made everyone mugs of Cup a Soup because he disliked tea and coffee. The parents had switched to soup, they said, because it made sense. It kept Davey company.

They sat on high stools at the island in the kitchen to drink it. The steam fogged everyone's glasses and made them laugh. Afterwards, Davey and Neil played chess and chatted about television programmes. Neil had started watching *Breaking Bad*, which was Davey's favourite show or series, whatever you called it. Neil struggled to keep all the characters in his head. He was too busy writing down bits of the dialogue to quote when he next saw Davey. They listened to music, but Neil was unfamiliar with the bands Davey liked. He concentrated hard on the lyrics. When a track repeated, he was able to sing along here and there.

Later, Neil tried hunting down the soup. He had no idea of the brand or the flavour. The colour was whitish-green. Maybe cauliflower and something. He tried a few possibles, but they were not the same. It was probably discontinued.

There was a leavers' party for the sixth form. Neil wasn't keen on parties and he knew Davey felt the same. But Davey had not been available for a while – busy with revision, then busy with his family. He had given up fishing. Neil phoned to ask if he was bothering with the leaving do. When Davey said he might be going, Neil suggested they meet up first. There was a silence, then Davey said, 'Nah, probably see you there.'

'I can easily call for you,' Neil said.

Davey's breath filled the receiver, penetrating Neil's ear. Then he said, 'It's probably easier to go our separate ways.'

Neil didn't see why. He would have been more comfortable arriving with a friend. Gatherings made him awkward. Everyone else had a group they belonged to. Neil wasn't all that at chit-chat, at joking around.

He arrived at the party on time, but only a handful of students were already there, helping to set up with the teachers who had volunteered to supervise. Neil loitered just inside the hall at first, but he was in the way. More people started arriving in pairs or groups. He had to go further in.

Music blared from the speakers. The early arrivals had been waiting for it to begin. They were wildly excited, pulling each other into the middle of the floor. Neil did not have a clue how to dance. Everyone looked quite daft swaying their bodies about, waving their arms over their heads. He stepped back and stood against the wall, watching. He imagined them flinging themselves about like that without any music playing and it made him smile. He would remember to tell Davey. It would get him laughing.

The hall gradually filled up. Someone said Jack and his friends were not coming. It was too uncool for them. Neil heard the teachers give thanks to God. He kept watching the door, sweating in his new leather jacket. His mother had sent him the money for his eighteenth birthday. She had asked him over, but he said he had other plans.

Davey turned up an hour late. Neil began walking towards him, but he stopped. Davey was with Jessie Lynch. They were smiling and holding hands. Her hair was curled into little spirals which swung around her face. Her dress was cut so the top half of her breasts could swell out. A few girls left the dance floor and scuttled up to her. Jessie still held the long-jump record. She had the longest legs in the school. She was the kind of person who was never led by the crowd. She had dyed her hair spirals bright blue.

The girls jumped up and down with excitement, their high heels drilling dents in the floor. They squealed and clapped their hands to their mouths because Jessie and Davey were an item. Neil heard one of them say it had been a secret for two months.

One of Davey's favourite tracks was played, something happy. Davey and two other boys dashed into the middle of the dance floor. They must have got together and worked out some moves because they were in synch with the beat. People formed a circle around them, whistling and whooping. The teachers joined in, clapping the rhythm. They said Davey Ashdown was a dark horse. What a marvellous dancer. Who would have thought it? Who knew?

After an hour, the sixth-form captain and her cohort carried foil platters of sandwiches to the trestles at the far end of the hall. No one else noticed. They were busy with the music and dancing, with the new romance. People were saying they had seen it coming for ages. Some claimed they were in on the secret. Neil concentrated hard on the buffet coming together.

He went swiftly to one side of the hall and walked close to the wall, staying in the shadows. At the far end he moved quickly along the buffet table. There was a plastic carrier bag in his pocket. Inside it was a carefully folded T-shirt with a picture of Walter White on it. It was carefully wrapped in metallic gold paper. He peeled off the tape, emptied out the gift, kicked it under the trestles. He scooped vol-au-vents, crisps, sausages, miniature Scotch eggs, quiche slices, pizza wedges, cubes of cheese and pineapple on sticks, iced biscuits and cupcakes into the carrier bag.

He left by the side door. A sign on it said *No Exit – Use Main Doors Only*. He walked home, his jacket creaking in the quiet streets. It was a nuisance, the racket it made. He would not wear it again.

He walked slowly, so his father would be in bed when he got home. He went up to his room and ate all the food. It gave him a raging thirst. It tasted of school, of the desks and the labs and the changing rooms. It tasted of all his years there. It was all the salt and the sugar, all the artificial hormones they feed pigs, all the chemical flavourings, which made the tears come.

Once he had saved enough money for a deposit, Neil took out a mortgage on a cheap terraced house. It was a student rental, an ancient place. Fungus had weakened its oak joists. Deathwatch beetles had moved in and their larvae were munching through the core of the softening wood. Neil imagined them growing fatter in their dark tunnels.

He stayed there overnight a few times, listening to the adult males ticking. Six ticks followed by ten seconds of silence, then the rhythm began again. He googled it and discovered there was a superstition that the sound was a warning of imminent death. He checked again and settled for a different theory: the chief male was trying to attract a mate.

He injected an insecticide paste into the adults' exit holes. He didn't have enough to fill them all. The stuff was too expensive. He should have drilled larger holes and filled them to capacity. He could still hear the ticking. He looked it up again. This time he discovered it would grow louder during a night watch by the bedside of the dying.

He continued letting the house for two years, the income more than covering his mortgage repayments. Then he spent a summer doing it up, walking there after work to re-grout and repaint. It gave him pleasure to rip up the thin, stained carpets, to throw them into the tiny back garden. Years of dust flew up to be caught in the last of the day's sun. He watched YouTube to learn how to fit laminate boards together. The corners were troublesome. He couldn't make them neat. He hid them with furniture and pot plants. The roof had held out and no one complained about the ticking at night. Maybe only he could hear it.

It took a while to sell and he had to drop the price. In the end, he made a small profit to invest in the next house. He had enough paint and paper left over and it gave him pleasure to make it look exactly like the first.

By the time Neil was buying his fifth house, Jack had served eight years of his sentence for the manslaughter of Davey Ashdown. He texted Neil a few weeks after he was released. He said he was going away, starting again. His family were supporting him all the way. He did not mention Jessie at all. Someone in Starbucks had said she was waiting for Jack. Neil thought it was likely. Jack had gone to prison for defending her, after all.

Neil follows the aroma to the department-store restaurant: a zig-zag maze of buffets with counter after counter crammed with hot and cold food from every part of the world. He makes his way into the middle, but cannot make a decision. The place is packed with people who know exactly what they are doing and he gets in their way. He joins the queue for Chinese dishes, then changes his mind. People glare at him when he steps out of the line.

The Greek section is a little quieter because they have almost run out of food. He spies one last plate of moussaka and hurries to claim it. When he tries to pick it up, the plate is stuck fast to the counter. He pulls harder. There is a ripping sound. It has been fixed down with Velcro pads.

The serving man tells him to leave it alone. It is for display only. Neil must order the dish he wants and wait for it to be cooked.

Neil asks if he may have it without the exhibited tomato and mint salad, but is given a bewildering list of alternative side options, none of which include no side options.

He continues to look around. He wonders if anyone eventually eats the food that is only for display. Perhaps once the rush is over, you can buy it at half price. It ought to be free, smothered as it must be in coughs and sneezes and sighs. He decides to look only at the help-yourself counters and gather up a selection of dishes. Can you help yourself from all around the world or must you stick to one country?

He looks around for a helpful sign, but there are none. He asks another customer, but she shrugs and pulls a face. She only wants a two-egg omelette. He considers copying her, but it would be an anti-climax sitting down with something plain after all this. In the end, he plumps for the salad bar. It seems fairly cosmopolitan and you can help yourself to as many ladles of the different salads as you like. The pricing system is unclear, but as far as he can tell, it is irresistibly cheap.

Queuing at the till, he is glad he didn't choose anything hot. It would have been stone cold by the time he sits down. When at last he is told how much his meal comes to, he laughs. The cashier smiles doubtfully at first, but frowns with impatience when he makes no move to pay. She explains the system to him three times before he understands that her conveyor belt automatically weighs the salads. The prices he noticed are per hundred grams, not per ladle. It is the look on her face which embarrasses him, her disbelief that he is the only person in the restaurant who has misunderstood the system.

He turns to walk away. The cashier calls him back, her tone sharp. He has selected this food and brought it to her, she reminds him. Now he must pay for it.

The queue is angry with him. He has never been the kind of person to elicit sympathy. He feels the hostility growing behind him. He pays quickly with his contactless card and rushes off to find a corner table. The meal is good, but he struggles to enjoy it. He has spent almost an entire week's budget. He decides not to buy a present for Silke. He hasn't a clue what to get anyway.

Downstairs, the exit route takes him through Groceries and he spots a possible match for the cauliflower-and-something soup. He stares at the box of sachets, his eyes filling with tears. He tries to walk away, but bumps into a young woman in a mint-green dress.

'Watch where you're going,' she says.

She says it kindly, with concern, and briefly touches his arm. She is the image of Gudrun.

'Are you okay?' she asks.

He is deeply touched. People don't usually notice him.

'I'm fine,' he says. 'Is it... are you Gudrun?'

She smiles and goes on her way. He runs after her, weaving through the crowd. There is no sign of a woman in a mint-green dress. He goes back and buys the box of soup. It feels comforting in his pocket, the way a packet of cigarettes feels to a smoker.

When he collects Silke, she is subdued. Her floury face powder is patchy now, her smart dress crumpled.

'Did you have a good look round?'

'Something like that,' she says, closing her eyes.

She sleeps all the way back. Near the village, he takes the wrong road. It is ridiculously narrow and keeps winding.

'Silke,' he says. She does not answer.

He is close to the marsh, on a track which he realises might not be meant for cars.

Chapter Eight

When the car stops, Silke opens her eyes.

'I'm so sorry,' Herr Fischer says. 'I've taken a wrong turn somewhere.'

His hands are tight on the steering wheel. There is a tremor in his voice. Silke knows she will have to take over, but she has not driven for a long time. Until she left prison, she had not realised that everyday things require so much courage.

'I'm sorry,' says Herr Fischer. 'We're literally stuck. This is a disaster. We're sinking, literally sinking.'

She knows where they are. The first thing children used to learn here is where they could safely walk. There is no doubt that she and Herr Fischer are no longer on safe ground. They must reverse, but in a specific direction. The angle needs to be precise.

'Come,' she says. 'You have tools, don't you?'

'But are we safe?'

'You can drown here. In some parts, the long grasses deceive you. There is silt beneath them, so soft it increases the depth by another metre or so, if you sink.'

'In that case—'

'The ground can even feel firm when deep water is hiding under the soil.'

'I was stuck in quicksand once. I knew not to flail about. And not to lift one foot in case it placed too much weight on the other. I knew that could make me sink deeper.'

'Then you know a lot. You will know to tread carefully.'

She tells him to test with his foot before putting weight on it. He must dig around the tyres. He listens well. He responds well to instructions. He finds his shovel in the boot and sets obediently to work. She collects the rubber mats from the car and lays them underneath the tyres.

'Shall I try?' she asks him.

'Would you?'

He sits in the passenger seat. She guesses he has never sat there before. She puts the car into reverse and lets the engine rev gently. While she releases the handbrake, she visualises the car moving backwards. She knows how to create a clear picture, as if the event has already happened and she is remembering. It was how she manufactured 'memories' in prison.

The car refuses to budge. 'Stay here,' Silke says. She exaggerates her calmness. Herr Fischer's breathing has become erratic.

She removes the mats, then digs deeper and wider. She replaces the mats and tries again. Nothing happens. She applies a little less acceleration. When the car hesitates, she increases the pressure on the throttle gradually, until it moves back. She adjusts the steering wheel, coaxing the car towards firmer ground. Everything looks different in reverse.

She stops after a moment, her foot on the brake, trying to work out which way to turn the wheel. They are close to an expanse of tall, pale grasses. They conceal a deep pool of water beneath. Herr Fischer was lucky to have missed them. He is rigid with tension beside her. His breathing is quick and shallow. Its staccato rhythm reminds her of a section from her file.

Female object. Age: 18/19. Build: slim/medium. Height: 1.60cm. Hair: short, blonde spikes, black roots. Attire: denim jacket, blue trousers, white blouse, green sleeveless pullover.

13.00 hours: 'Schmetterling' takes up surveillance of object's kitchen from apartment opposite:

14.02 hours: object observed standing at kitchen window, eating bread.

14.30 hours: object leaves apartment.

14.31 hours: 'Schmetterling' telephones 'Engels'.

14.32 hours: 'Engels' takes up outside surveillance.

14.32 hours: object leaves building. Catches bus to city centre.

14.54 hours: object alights in Oderberger Strasse. Walks to Café Danika. Approaches corner table. Others already seated. 'Black Coat' and 'Sideburns' stand to greet object.

15.25 hours: object drinks black coffee.

17.00 hours: object eats apple cake.

17.14 hours: 'Sideburns' passes paper serviette to object. Object dabs mouth with serviette, transfers it from hand to hand, folds it into inside pocket of denim jacket.

17.18 hours: 'Black Coat' exits Café Danika with object close behind. They cross the road and walk to the park. They stand under trees in south-west corner. They kiss on the mouth. 'Black Coat' grasps object's buttocks.

17.31 hours: 'Black Coat' inserts right hand into waistband of object's trousers. Object presses willingly against 'Black Coat'. Kissing continues. 'Black Coat' transfers hand to front waistband area. Inserts hand. Object moves legs wider apart. Kissing continues.

17.34 hours: object and 'Black Coat' exit park. 'Black Coat' buys one large currywurst from kiosk at entrance. Object and 'Black Coat' walk in northerly direction. Take turns with currywurst.

17.38 hours: 'Black Coat' throws serviette wrapped around currywurst into litter bin outside fruit-and-vegetable shop. 'Black Coat' and object hold hands.

18.36 hours: object and 'Black Coat' arrive at object's apartment building. 'Black Coat' unfastens black coat, beckons object inside it. They embrace.

18.45 hours: object enters building alone, turns to wave three times. 'Black Coat' already moving on, in westerly direction. Now under separate surveillance.

18.46 hours: 'Schmetterling' resumes surveillance from apartment opposite:

18.48 hours: object appears in kitchen. Fills glass with water. Leaves kitchen.

18.51 hours: returns without jacket. Removes green sleeveless pullover. Puts it on table. Drinks from glass.

18.56 hours: leaves kitchen.

19.14 hours: returns. Breaks eggs into china bowl and beats with fork. Lights stove. Places pan on stove and pours eggs into pan. Slices omelette in half, serves onto two plates taken from draining board. Takes plates out of kitchen. Turns light off.

19.34 hours: surveillance terminated.

19.50 hours: 'Engel' meets 'Mustang' in cycle shed behind apartment block. Information obtained. Information attached.

'Wait here,' Silke says to Herr Fischer.

She gets out of the car and walks back the way they have come, towards the right. After each step, she tests the ground for sponginess beneath her foot. Her new shoes are soon waterlogged, but she will not wear them again. After a few minutes, she puts her right foot forward and is immediately soaked up to mid-calf. She retraces her route back to the car and tries another path, this time to the left. She stumbles immediately, one foot sinking, the other sliding. She clutches the long grass to pull herself up before she falls. She walks back again and this time treads in a straight line from the midpoint of the car, testing left and right, roughly a car's width. It feels stable enough. She believes she can trust it.

She returns to the car and turns on the engine.

'Are you sure?'

'Yes, Herr Fischer, I am as sure as possible.'

'Maybe we should call the garage in town to come and get us out safely.'

'I am as sure as possible.'

'Or we could abandon the car. Make our way out on foot. Go back to your house and phone from there.'

'No. I am sure.'

She starts the engine, twists round and appraises the path she has memorised. She pushes the gearstick into reverse, releases the clutch smoothly, applies gentle pressure on the accelerator.

She drives confidently, without haste. Herr Fischer keeps making suggestions which sound like instructions. She ignores them. When she knows she is on safe ground, she drives a little faster. It is not necessary, but she keeps it up. It amuses her that Herr Fischer is holding tight to the grab handle above his window.

When they rejoin the main road to the village, Herr Fischer lets out an extravagant sigh. After he has thanked her several times, Silke confesses she has not driven for decades. And even then, only a small tractor.

'Really? But you were a pro. You knew exactly what to do.'

'I understand the ground, where the danger lies.'

'So do you know why the school is sinking? Do you think it's subsidence?'

While she considers the question, a few spots of rain fall. 'Unsettled ground, I think,' she says, searching for the wiper switch.

'That's what subsidence is, really,' Neil says. 'That massive tree is causing it. Root damage is always the most likely cause. The roots are sapping all the moisture from the soil. Anyone round here got a chainsaw?'

Thomas has a chainsaw. He will refuse to lend it to Herr Fischer, but Silke can take it from the shed when Thomas is working at the farm. He might hear it growling in the distance, but if they wait until he is on the tractor, there is a chance they will get away with it.

After she left the Records Agency, Silke sat in the park where she and Martin used to kiss. It looked quite different. A double row of cobblestones in the ground indicated where the Wall used to cut through. She sat on a bench with fairy-tale proportions, so tall it made her feel like a child, her feet unable to touch the grass.

The bench was close to the trees. When the breeze whipped up, their branches stretched towards her. She saw herself walking hand in hand with Martin, into their shadows. Even if she had known Stasi officers were documenting every touch, she was too happy back then to have cared. Let the arrogant idiots watch her kissing if that was what turned them on. She could almost laugh at their pedantic note-taking, their painstaking surveillance, the gratification they derived from collating reams of useless facts.

Stasi antics do not shock her. Her distress comes from knowing who fed them extra information. Over the years, she had imagined it was a rogue member of the tunnel group. They all seemed committed to the escape, but the Stasi could wear anyone down. They would promise you a promotion at work, or a university place for your son or daughter, in return for information. And if you refused, there would never be a promotion or a university place. Every door of opportunity would slam shut in your face.

The Stasi watched 'Mustang' closely and eventually took him in for interrogation. When they had broken him, they said he could go free if he gathered information for them. 'Mustang' told them all he knew about Silke.

He told them she used to post letters to a BBC programme, which encouraged anonymous writers to describe their lives behind the Iron Curtain. Despite the BBC continually changing the postal address, the Stasi kept intercepting the letters. They tested the envelopes for fingerprints, also for saliva to determine blood group.

'Mustang' also revealed that Silke listened to forbidden Western radio stations, persevering until late at night in the hope of picking up a few minutes of crackly reception. She read the music magazines a friend's aunt sent over from the West, sliding them under her mattress. And she had developed a taste for Dutch cheese.

Only one person knew this information.

'Thomas has a chainsaw,' she tells Herr Fischer.

'Would he be inclined to lend it?'

'No, but I will.'

'Is that a good idea?'

'We never know, do we, if an idea is good? Not until we put it into action.'

'The thing is, I don't want to get on the wrong side of anyone. And I've never used a chainsaw before.'

'Between us we can work it out.'

Herr Fischer shifts in his seat, drumming his fingers on his knees.

'I have made you uncomfortable,' Silke says. 'May I tell you why I am willing to take the saw?'

'If that's all right with you.'

She stops the car and turns off the engine. 'I went to the Stasi Records Agency today, to read my file. I was involved with people planning to escape in a tunnel. Someone betrayed me. I was imprisoned without legal representation, without a trial.'

'Oh Christ, how long did you—'

'Four and a half years, but at the time I had no idea how long my sentence would be. Whenever I was interrogated, I was told my lack of cooperation would add more weeks. Sometimes it would be more months. Sometimes more years.'

'Did you know who betrayed you?'

'I do now. My brother.'

Herr Fischer's fingers are still and stiff on his knees. He says he doesn't know what to say.

'Please, there is no need to search for words. There are none. Thomas has been protective of me ever since my release. Protective in a furious, resentful way. I thought he was angry with me, or with the system. But no. Only with himself.'

'And how do you feel?'

'I feel something enormous. I think it is courage.'

'Maybe the courage comes from reading your file. It comes from knowledge.'

'Maybe. I will get us the chainsaw.'

She switches on the engine.

'Would you like me to take over?' Herr Fischer says. 'You must be terribly shaken up.'

Silke releases the handbrake. 'No, thank you. I am glad to sit in the driving seat.'

Chapter Nine

It is only Neil and Silke for dinner. Thomas is eating at the farm, staying late to play cards with Renate. While Silke heats a rabbit stew, Neil goes upstairs to wash his hands and face. He unfolds a hand towel from the pile he keeps in his room and sits on the bed to dry himself. He has brought up his toolbox. He puts it on his lap and tidies stray screwdrivers, spanners, packets of nails and screws into the correct compartments. He slides the toolbox under the bed.

He is uneasy about being here when Silke tells Thomas what she has found out. Perhaps Thomas was put under pressure to blow the whistle on his sister. People informed for the Stasi as a way of keeping safe from the Stasi. They might have kicked him out of university if he had refused to cooperate. Maybe he never finished his degree anyway. He might have felt safer coming back here to chop wood instead.

Neil searches his suitcase again, but is still baffled. One day he will work out what is missing. He folds his towel, places it on the chest of drawers and jogs downstairs. The atmosphere is easier without Thomas. Neil and Silke sit down and pass the bowl of vegetables back and forth. A strand of celery catches between two of Neil's back teeth. It feels like a serrated blade sawing his gum.

'Thanks again for rescuing us,' he says, reaching for another boiled potato. 'God knows where I'd be without you. Sunk without trace. Literally.'

She looks at him without smiling. Whenever he tries to be amusing, something seems to go missing in translation. Or maybe she is nervous about making friends. Who can she ever trust now she knows her own brother has let her down?

When he was alone in the woods, searching for his glasses, Neil was letting his father down badly. He kept scrambling blindly about, crawling in all directions, hating himself for whimpering. His father had told him many times: if you lose control, you lose yourself.

Neil sensed he was not all that far from the road. At some point he must have travelled in a circle or retraced his steps. But if he tried to follow the sound of the traffic, he would be even further away from his glasses. There was no pavement. He might step out and get run over. Or someone evil might force him into their car.

'You *see*,' he told himself, sitting on the ground to pick grit out of his knees. 'This is what happens when you panic.'

His father had given him an opportunity. The last thing you should do with an opportunity is waste it. If he kept on sitting and crying, he would be there all night. Foxes would creep around him in the dark.

'Do you want that? Or do you want your eyesight back?'

He stood up. He turned round and listened until he was sure the traffic was directly behind him. He slowly rotated, twice more, to be certain. Now he had to locate the little path, facing towards the woods the whole time. To do that, the ground would have to be about two inches from his eyes. That was the furthest he could see with any clarity.

'Get on with it, then, you idiot. Get down on your knees and crawl.'

The trouble was, he didn't know which direction to try first. His instinct told him that he had veered off course to the left. He scuttled, crab-like, to the right.

'You goon. Remember you knocked your glasses and sent them flying. When you went after them, you travelled forwards as well as leftwards. So you need to move back a bit first.'

He stood up, took a few paces back, then dropped to all fours again.

'Come *on*. You have to find the path, but your glasses could be *any*where.'

He moved to the right for ages, but the trees were getting closer together, the vegetation denser. He scurried to the left, feeling all the time with his fingertips. When sunlight dispersed through the branches, he could see it was brighter and watched for anything glinting. When he moved in close enough, he discovered that many things shone in the woods: brand-new leaves, stones with glittery bits in them, white mushrooms, petals cradling raindrops.

The undergrowth became sparser and shorter, until eventually the ground was coarse with yellowish grit.

'Oh look, you've done it. You've actually done it!'

The path began swimming, even from three inches away.

'Stop it, you idiot. You stupid cry-baby.'

He sniffed hard and slapped the tears away. His glasses could be really close now, depending on exactly where he was on the path. He might be further along than earlier. Or he might have to follow it until he reached the point where he had lost them. That was the trouble with being short-sighted. You were so quickly disorientated, so suddenly lost.

'You're not lost. You know where you are. You've found the path. You're on it right now. And that's really something. Don't go and lose it again.'

He took a step backwards, the loose, gritty stuff shifting and scraping under his shoes. He crouched down, wincing as his knees met sharper stones. He fingered the path and the area around it, spreading his arms wide. He repeated the process twenty-three times before he discerned the road closer behind him.

'You were definitely further in than this before you lost them. No, don't blubber. Go forwards now. Don't bother searching the part you've just done. Take twenty-three steps and start again.'

He counted the steps, took off his jumper and tied the sleeves around his knees. It was quite comforting and helped to cushion them a bit. He crawled for a long time, patting every inch of the surrounding ground as well as the path itself. Nothing. The glasses must be caught in the longer grass, beyond reach from here. To find them, he had to leave the path.

'Step to the left-hand side, drop and search. Repeat. Repeat again. Then retrace those steps and you'll be back on the path. Repeat the whole thing on the right-hand side.'

No. He couldn't do this anymore. He was exhausted and filthy. His knees were bleeding through the maroon jumper. His mother had recently knitted it for him. It looked too much like a school jumper. He would have liked a light-blue one. He thought he had asked her, but maybe she forgot.

Stopping confused him again. Had he turned round? He sat down hard. He was on the path, but had no idea which direction he was facing. He squinted, hoping to sharpen his focus, knowing it made no difference.

'You fathead. You're wasting all the chances you've given yourself. You've done all this hard work. Sideways, backwards, forwards. And now you're totally, totally lost. You're so clueless.'

If he sat here, his father would eventually come. He would follow the path and find him and take him home.

'Is that what you want?'

Neil lay face down and scrutinised the path, pivoting gradually around on his stomach. He recognised a stone like a small, grey egg chopped in half. He peered closer to look at its other side. Yes, there it was. A flat brown surface which made the stone look sliced through. If he had already seen the flat part face-on, then assuming he hadn't disturbed the stone in the meantime, all he needed to do now was turn right round.

He pivoted carefully on his stomach and recognised the view of the egg-stone's flat side.

'Well done, you. Good stuff.'

He had a go at his three-steps-left-three-steps-right procedure. It felt stupid at first, until he picked up a kind of rhythm. He quite enjoyed it, in the limited way you enjoy something which takes you back to square one. And in his case, with no guarantee it would actually do that.

He kept going. He stopped dead whenever he heard rustling or cracking. He imagined foxes staring from the undergrowth or bad men who liked to spirit children away. After a while, he touched a bloated clump of thistles growing out of the path and swelling across the ground.

'Oh my gosh, you *know* this. You've touched it. Was it before you swatted your glasses out of reach, or after? When? Come *on*.'

He tried to think straight while keeping hold of his bearings.

'Look, get a grip. The thistle needs to straggle over the right-hand side of the path. If it goes to the left, then you've turned round and you're the wrong way.'

He sat down with the thistle between his legs and growing over the correct side of the path.

'Whatever you do, stay facing this way. Now *think*.'

The odds landed in favour of encountering the thistle before swiping his glasses. He had panicked so much that getting stung would have been the last straw. He would have blubbed his head off, he knew it. He definitely didn't remember being all that bothered by the thistle. He was too intent on the search.

If, at this point, the glasses were not far away, how long after the thistle before he batted them into the long grass? He had no idea. He crawled on a few yards and noticed a tuft of grass in the middle of the path.

'You rested your knee on that. When you were in a state. It felt cool and nice. The glasses went astray between the thistle and the tuft. Simple as that.'

He turned round and picked up his previous rhythm. Three paces each way, his face deep in the long grass. He parted fronds of bracken. He peered between tree roots snaking through sticky mud. He knelt by a huge oak and examined the moist cushions of moss at its base. And there they were, arms open wide, lenses staring up at him. Grubby and a bit scratched, but not broken.

'Stop it. Don't cry. You're too happy to cry.'

He rubbed them clean on his shirt and put them back on. It always amazed him that there was no delay while his eyes adjusted. Without warning, the world thrust itself back into sharp focus.

'Okay, clever clogs, get on with it.'

He followed the path, confident he was heading in the right direction. This was way too easy. All he needed to do was keep walking. He had to climb over a stile, but the path was still there on the other side. It petered out when he came to a stream. He followed the stream instead. The grass was trampled down next to it, which created its own path of sorts. There was nowhere else to walk anyway. There were thick banks of trees either side. The real path was bound to reappear.

Up ahead he could make out a wooden post. Attached to it was a notice in a transparent folder. He ran towards it. *Danger*, it said. *Watch Out*. It was in his father's writing.

Years later, shortly after his mother and sister left, Neil's English teacher, Miss Farrow, set the class the task of writing a piece of creative non-fiction for homework. The theme was 'An Unforgettable Place'. You could write about a holiday, a school trip, your grandparents' house. Anywhere you would never forget. The location itself might be the most memorable thing, Miss Farrow said, but what would bring the piece to life would be the emotions it evoked.

Neil normally did his homework the night before it was due. This time he dashed home from the bus stop. He made a cup of tea, pouring the water before it boiled, and went straight to his room. He set himself the challenge of finishing the piece before his father came in from work at half-past six. This gave him two and a half hours, a third of the time he had spent in the woods.

He wrote about his father leaving him at the entrance. He described the cool moss, the earthy smell, the echo of wings clapping, the absence of sky. He left out his emotions. Miss Farrow had said they should emerge from the writing.

'Don't tell me you felt happy, sad or spellbound,' she said. 'Let your descriptions of Tenby or Majorca or your back garden lead me into another place. A place inside you, where I will understand how you felt.'

Neil let his tea turn cold. He wrote about the methodical process which successfully guided him to his lost glasses. He explained how the path led him deeper into the wood and over the stile to the stream. How the path disappeared, but his father had left him a note.

Neil's pen stopped working. The nib was scratching up the paper. He unscrewed the barrel and took out the empty cartridge. He had to squeeze the new one to encourage the ink to flow. He scrawled on some rough paper for a while. It was the type of pen which had to get at least twenty blots out of its system. It had belonged to his father: a communist pen. The nib was splitting down the middle. It gave every word its own shadow. He had to ditch it and continue in biro.

While his tea grew a skin, he wrote about what happened after he saw the sign. He wondered if Miss Farrow would say, 'You weren't meant to write a story, Neil. The brief was creative non-fiction. Everyone knows a place they will always remember.'

He kept going. In the end he had to use three biros: black, blue and green. Miss Farrow probably wouldn't even read it. She would say Neil Fischer's unforgettable place was a terrible mess.

Neil spun round. There was nothing dangerous. Only the endless trees and the thin, rocky stream. He sat on the grass, listening to the weak trickle of water. He kept staring at the sign, as if that would make the answer appear.

'You twit. The sign wouldn't make sense if you could already see the danger, would it? It's a warning of whatever's up ahead.'

He got up and walked slowly on. He trod carefully, in case there were snakes. They wouldn't be dangerous, though. They would only be grass snakes.

On his sixth birthday, his father had set up a treasure hunt in the park. The clues took ages to find. They led Neil in an enormous circle, all the way back to the start. The 'treasure' was spending the rest of the day there, with his father watching him play. He imagined people from school turning up and shouting, 'Surprise!' But no one had been invited. His mother arrived with a picnic at teatime and set it out on the grass. After the sandwiches and biscuits, he had to keep playing until it was almost dark. He was sick of the swings and slide by then.

Neil trudged on. His feet were blistered and his legs ached. The makeshift path narrowed and the banks either side grew steeper. Neil forgot to be careful and tripped. There was no warning. No time to save himself. His glasses stayed on, but pressed painfully into his face.

He sat up and looked behind him. There were no large stones, no low branches that had caught him out, but there was a length of thin wire stretched between the trees either side of the water.

'No, don't cry. You ruddy well should have spotted that.'

He stood against the wire. It touched his shins at midpoint. 'See. It's high enough above the grass.'

He walked back a short distance. A sign tacked high on a tree said, *Look down.*

'There you go, stupid. You missed the warning. It's your own fault.'

The one comfort was that he must be going the right way. He slowed his pace in case he missed any more signs. Also because he was hurting all over. Where the stream finally tapered to a dribble, a tall mass of bracken crowded in. He couldn't fight through it. It probably went on for miles.

It was hard to make out, but a steep, jagged trail rose through the bank of trees to his left. It was barely a path at all, but he was overjoyed to see anything that might be a way to somewhere.

He had to clutch hold of branches to haul himself up. By the time he reached the top, he was gasping like an old man. The trail took him deeper into the wood. All the trees met overhead. The sky did not exist anymore.

Eventually, the path split into two. He stopped. He swivelled about, gravel crunching beneath his shoes.

'Go on. Just pick one.'

Instinct told him that turning right would take him back to the stream. He set off on the path to the left. He sang hymns and whistled television theme tunes to keep himself company. He drank his bottle of water and ate his ham sandwich, wedging the greaseproof paper into the backs of his shoes, where his blisters were weeping.

He kept seeing something glistening to his right.

'You prize moron. Your instinct's rubbish. You've only gone and looped back to the stream.'

He walked all the way back to the fork and this time turned right.

'Don't make a big deal of it. At least it's the only choice left.'

The path was a sloppy mud track. He squelched around a slight bend and saw another sign: *Where should you always look?*

'Ahead. Got to be.'

But that couldn't be right all the time. He had just proved it. Sometimes you need to double back. Maybe changing direction was a kind of looking ahead.

'Oh, how do I know? I'm too tired for more puzzles. Let's stick with looking ahead.'

He walked on, convinced someone was stalking him, waiting to leap out from the trees.

'Don't be daft. Just keep going.'

After a few minutes, it felt too easy. If his father could set up a tripwire, what else might he do?

'Got it. Look *down*. If I'd been looking at the ground, I'd have seen the wire, wouldn't I?'

Half an hour later, he saw it: a circular expanse of wet leaves on the path. There were millions of dead leaves all over the place, but these looked too neat, too deliberate. He squatted down and pushed them aside. Beneath them his father had dug a hole in the mud.

Neil sat on the edge and dangled his legs into it. He stretched one foot down until the tip of his shoe touched the base. If he had not spotted it, he would have fallen in up to his waist.

'Not bad. You were caught by the wire. But the hole didn't get you. Well done.'

He kept going. His blisters stung, but he didn't care. 'Nice try, Dad,' he would say. Or, 'Make your camouflage less obvious next time.'

He probably wouldn't say any of that. His father was not the type you bantered with.

'But *you'll* know you were on the ball,' he told himself. 'For some of it anyway.'

The path brought him out of the woods near the town. He knew the way home from there. Seven and a half hours after he was dropped off, Neil arrived home.

Miss Farrow asked Neil to stay behind after the lesson. She drew a chair up to her desk so he could sit beside her.

'Sorry about the different colour biro and everything, Miss. I had to get it all down.'

'Let's set that aside for now, Neil. Now, did your father really leave you alone for an entire day in the woods?'

'I wasn't writing about him. It was about how I found my way out.'

'But he did leave you?'

He saw something greedy in her, a desire for something to feast on. She was eyeing him like a butcher. 'It was a fun thing, Miss. It was like a sort of treasure hunt.'

'But there wasn't any treasure, was there?'

'There didn't need to be. It was fun. Honestly.'

She continued to stare at him. Her perfume was nauseating.

'How did it feel to be left all alone?'

'I was all right.'

'Weren't you terribly lonely?'

'I had myself.'

She rearranged the gathers in her skirt. 'Neil, I must ask you. Is this true, or have you made it all up?'

He looked down at his shoes. Even after all this time, there were still dark patches, permanent now, on the skin of his heels. 'Yeah,' he said. 'Of course I did.'

'I thought so. Well, write a new piece and rein in your imagination this time.'

He wrote about a seaside holiday he was too young to remember well. He left out the part he did remember, the part about the cliffs.

*

When Neil arrived home from the woods, his father said, 'You should have stayed by the entrance when I dropped you off.'

'But you drove away.'

'And after five minutes I drove straight back. You should have trusted me not to leave you there all day.'

'So why didn't you get out of the car and come after me?'

'I did. I stayed well back with my binoculars.'

'You were there the whole time?'

'Of course.'

'Why set traps and put up the signs if I was supposed to wait at the entrance for you to come back?'

'Because I knew you wouldn't stay at the entrance. I knew you wouldn't do the right thing.'

Thomas sets off to the farm before dawn the next day. He is working extra hours for the harvest. Silke fetches the chainsaw and Neil carries it to the tree. Silke pulls a handcart for the branches.

'We won't get them all in there.'

'Not all at once,' she says.

'I could get the car and pile a load in the boot.'

'Yes, good. And I have neighbours who will take them for firewood.'

'Thomas will notice the tree has gone.'

'Yes, but the job will be done.'

The celery strand still nags between Neil's teeth. His tongue can't ease it out and he forgot to pack any dental floss. It is not the item missing from his case. The floss was never there.

Thomas's tractor is rumbling in the distance. Neil starts up the saw, but switches it off after a minute to listen.

'We are okay,' Silke says. 'I can still hear the tractor.'

'I can't.'

'Calm down and listen.' She takes his hand. 'You are doing the right thing, Herr Fischer. This is your village now. Your tree. And I have given you permission to use this saw.'

'But you should have asked Thom—'

'He has lost the right to my respect.'

'When are you going to tell him you've seen the file?'

She tilts her head towards the tree and raises her eyebrows. Neil sets to work.

After a few minutes, he stops again. 'How will we know when it's about to fall?'

'We will know.'

It takes a long time. Silke urges him to keep going. When he is almost through, a shift happens deep inside the trunk. Something is changing. He stands back. Silke is already reaching for his arm. She tucks her hand into the crook to draw him away.

From inside the trunk there is popping and spitting, like a flame catching a dry log. Then a much louder crack, like the splitting of fireworks as they hit the sky. The trunk explodes, its girth splintering into long, pale strips. As it falls, Neil expects thunder, a massive tremor. But it simply gives way – a slow and stately surrender – until it is sad and naked on the ground.

'Looks even bigger now it's down,' Neil says, wiping his brow on his sleeve.

'Let's cut it up quickly.'

The tractor is still chugging along. Neil hears it as soon as he turns off the saw. He smiles at so much progress made so early in the day. He works on the trunk and Silke uses secateurs on the slimmer branches. The sun warms their backs the whole time. She takes the handcart to her neighbours, while Neil goes back for the car. He lines the boot and the back seat with plastic bags to protect his upholstery and loads up.

Before driving off, he has a quick look at the drains. He has no idea what he is looking for, but he takes photographs and makes a note to ask a specialist to check them. It will be worth the cost if it stops the school sinking. Maybe he could convert it into a house for himself.

Silke comes back with her empty cart for more wood. They pause for a breather first and he asks her again. 'When will you tell Thomas?'

'Maybe never.'

'Why?'

'Because the truth is making me powerful. If I tell him, he will ruin me all over again. I was a prisoner, Herr Fischer, but when they released me, I was still a prisoner. I lived in fear of my own voice, my reflection, my shadow. But now I am angry and it makes me strong. It makes me free. If Thomas finds out that I know, I might lose this courage.'

'Why?'

'His guilt would surface. He would need me even more. And this would become his story instead of mine.'

They look across to the distant fields. The tractor is at a standstill.

When Jack Claridge was released, Neil met him for a farewell drink in the Hatherley Arms at the end of their street.

'So where are you off to, then?'

'Not saying, mate. Nothing personal. Fresh start and all that.'

'What about Jessie? Aren't you still together?'

Jack pulled open his bag of crisps. 'Water under the bridge, mate. She wanted to, but like I said, I need to reboot.'

Neil put his glass down. 'But wasn't it all for Jessie?'

'All what?'

Jack drank the last third of his pint in a couple of gulps. He had one of those throats that did not need to keep swallowing. The beer poured effortlessly down. Neil picked up his glass. The damp beermat stuck to it briefly.

'Gotta get going,' Jack said, pushing back his chair. 'Nah, you stay and finish your drink. Got a ton of stuff to do before I head off. All the best, mate.'

Neil stayed in the Hatherley Arms for another hour. He wanted to pin down the reason Jack had beaten up Davey Ashdown. There had always been a reason, surely. Not one that could ever justify the violence, of course, but one that would give it a kind of logic. Or if not logic, then at least a context. Jack had been furious with the way Davey treated Jessie. He was... how did he put it... *seriously narked*. That was it. He was seriously narked.

But nothing about him being narked was ever mentioned in the news reports. They referred only to the savage beating meted out to the quiet, unassuming young man who happened to be passing – a young man who had only a tenuous connection with the perpetrator.

Neil had assumed Jessie asked to be kept out of it. But now, after meeting like mates in the pub, even Jack himself had not referred to the reason. He had only talked about the future, about his fresh start.

Neil had seen the assault that put Jack behind bars. But Jack had not mentioned the context of it, the logic behind it – whatever it ought to be called. Not even when Neil brought Jessie into the conversation. Yet this was the last time they would meet – Jack's final chance to bring up his justification to someone who was there that night.

So, there was never a reason. Jack had merely invented something for Neil to believe, then went to prison to shed his guilt. He had paid the price in exchange for a new beginning. And now the score was settled, he had no need to live with it anymore.

Neil walked into town before heading home. It was a late summer evening and everyone else was just setting out. The coconut scent of sun lotion kept wafting past.

He knew now that he had fallen for Jack's story, desperate to believe it. He had granted validity to a lie Jack didn't even recall.

Now Neil had to start living with the truth, with the shame of looking on while someone he loved was beaten to death.

The following week he resigned from Starbucks. He needed more time alone. His properties generated enough to keep him ticking over. There was nothing to spend his money on anyway.

It made him laugh that people spent weekends in shops, brandishing their credit cards and struggling home with twenty-odd carrier bags. What was it all for? Clothes to wear to restaurants, clubs and pubs, he supposed: places where they would spend even more of their money. Then they worked their socks off all week so that, come the weekend, they could do it all again. He didn't know how they consumed all that alcohol without their livers packing up. And what about all that late-night junk food? Perhaps that was the reason for the gym memberships they forked out for. Maybe life was all about damage reversal. Didn't any of them ever wish they could stay at home in their scruffs, enjoying their own company, the way he did?

On Sundays, he still visits Davey Ashdown's grave. The headstone is made of black marble which glitters in the sun. Neil kneels in front of it and asks Davey to forgive him for looking on, for stopping in the middle of the road. He asks his friend to forgive him for what he chose to believe afterwards, for applying Jack's flimsy bit of fiction to the sadistic act.

Neil has not yet asked to be forgiven for the infinitesimally small moment during the beating when he felt gratification. It was fleeting, but it was there.

Thomas comes back late. Neil has already gone to bed, affected by the sun. His head is still boiling hot. His back aches from wielding the saw. He tries to get comfortable, but the mattress is damp, the sheet clammy and ruckled. His one indulgence at home is a clean sheet on the bed every day.

Silke is still downstairs, but she had hoped to be in bed before Thomas turned up. Neil left her setting out bread and butter on the table in case he wanted something to eat. She was not bothering with the cheese and cold meat, the seed cake or the apricot yoghurt he likes.

'He can get that himself,' she said when Neil went upstairs.

Thomas is shouting.

Neil sits up, trying to listen. He gets out of bed, his back protesting. He opens the door a crack. He has to work hard to translate the heated words.

'You have been giving people firewood,' Thomas is yelling.

'So?' Silke says. 'I enjoyed delivering it.'

Neil imagines her crossing her arms, keeping the table between them.

'It's mine,' Thomas shouts. 'And because you are busy giving away my firewood, there is nothing to eat. Why have you done nothing in the house today? Look at the mess. The washing is still outside. The eggs are not collected.'

'Because I have been chopping wood. And delivering it.'

He must have thrown something at the wall, a chair perhaps. Sweat gathers between Neil's shoulder blades.

Thomas raps something, a spoon maybe, on the table. 'Why are you trying to do my job?'

'I am not. And please stop throwing and banging things.'

'But why? Please, why?'

'Because sometimes I want to do something different. And today I wanted to cut down a tree and chop it to pieces.'

'You cut down a tree?'

'You have not noticed? Strange. I thought you noticed everything.'

'What fucking tree?'

A crash roars through the house. Something smashes on the stone floor.

Silke's voice does not waver. 'The tree which is making our school slide away,' she says. 'It had to go.'

'The village doesn't need a school.'

'But it needs firewood.'

Neil pads to the bathroom. He slowly closes the door, holding the handle up to stabilise and quieten the loose hinges, letting it drop gently into place. The bathroom reeks of the TCP Thomas gargles with every morning. Neil pushes the stool under the handle and turns the key.

Chapter Ten

'I had the owner's permission to fell the tree,' Silke says. 'The saw is back in its place. I will not need it again. I distributed the logs to help our community. They were not yours to cut and sell. Again, I had the owner's permission.'

'You are not capable.' Thomas spits out each word separately. He is sweating and his eyes are bulging.

'Yet suddenly I am.'

'It's Fischer, isn't it?' He slams his fist on the ironing board. It yelps and collapses. 'Why are you letting him? Why are you protecting him?'

Silke walks over to the ironing board, keeping it between her and Thomas. 'I did this on my own. And he is not in need of protection.'

Thomas picks up the iron and hurls it at the wall. His face is wet. It may not be sweat. He pushes the board aside and grasps her painfully tight.

'I warned you. I warned everyone. Allow this man in and our lives will not belong to us. Everything will change.'

Silke presses hard with her elbows, digging them in to push him away. 'Sweep up the broken china,' she tells him. 'And put the table back while I collect the eggs.'

The sleeping hens make disgruntled squawks at the disturbance. Silke feels about in the straw, soothed by the soft rustling, the discovery of each warm shell.

She expected Thomas would be unsettled by this new Silke. Since the old East Germany was relegated to history, he has feared anything or anyone new. His hostility to the West, his fear of the evils of capitalist society, has intensified over the years. They had all been encouraged to fear it. The Wall would prevent another world war, they were told. It would keep them all safe. The national song instructed them to let their paths by peace be lighted, so no mother would mourn her son again.

'And yet,' she tells a grey hen with one eye open, 'I did not once suspect him of betraying me.'

The grey hen keeps her eye open, encouraging Silke to continue stroking her. 'You like me to talk about loyalty, do you? Well, all I can tell you is that most of us were loyal on the surface. We protected our thoughts from the authorities. We ground our feelings to dust and some of it survived, as dust does. Perhaps even the Stasi held onto a few particles.'

She takes out an egg encased in sticky straw and lays it in her basket. It is hard to imagine the Stasi as ordinary people. They studied academic papers about how to crush the human soul. Once you know how to do that, your ordinary self might be permanently lost.

She places another egg in the basket. A snail attached to it emerges slightly from his shell. Her essay on the robber crab explained how he toughens up enough to discard the shells he once stole for protection. He develops lungs and leaves his tough, early life in the sea. He adapts to life on land and can live for decades. He can even climb. He grows enormous and powerful. Every year, he sheds his armour and digs a protective burrow until he regrows. He retreats when necessary for survival and resurfaces when strong again.

'He is quite a star,' she tells the grey hen.

The essay and all her notes are in her file. They questioned her about every word of it, no doubt imagining it to contain some secret code. After fifteen hours on a hard chair with her hands ordered to remain tucked beneath her, she began to believe it did.

'Just think,' she says, stroking the hen's soft feathers. 'The Stasi have been defunct for a long time now. Which probably surprises them, even after all these years. They are so obsolete their offices are now a museum. So why do I still sleep bolt upright?'

She shines her torch on the eggs. She has probably found them all. She is tired now and thinks of her bed. She goes back to the kitchen. Thomas is not there. He has righted the table and set it for breakfast. He has picked up the shattered china and made attempts to glue the pieces together.

She knocks an egg against the edge of the table and breaks it into the bowl. She lifts it up and watches a thin, yellowish trail seep from the cracks in the base.

'I don't think this will do, Thomas.'

He is moving about upstairs. He will be unfolding her nightdress, laying it flat and smooth on her pillow. She goes up. He is already in bed, smoking a cigarette. She takes her nightdress and goes across the landing to her old room.

It has filled up with junk, as well as chunks of ceiling plaster. She throws everything from the bed onto the floor until she reveals the faded velour headboard, the grey quilted eiderdown, the school timetable still taped to the wall. Everything is mildewed and smells of decay. The damp sheets and pillows are unusable. She rummages in the chest of drawers and finds a spare blanket. It still smells of life before.

Thomas is hammering on the bathroom door, rattling the handle, calling her name. She scrambles through the junk and hurries across the landing.

'I am not in there, Thomas. It must be Herr Fischer. Stop disturbing him.'

'Why aren't you in our room?'

'Because I am in mine.'

'But you—'

'I am happy on my own. Goodnight.'

She knocks gently on the bathroom door and says, 'The disturbance is over.'

As she lies in her bed, wrapped in the blanket and with her folded towel for a pillow, her heart beats exceptionally slowly. She has read that this happens when you are unusually happy. Or it might be the other way round. Whichever it is, this has not happened for a long time. After her release, her emotions were barely functioning. Disuse had ground them down. But she is happy now. It was not Martin who betrayed her.

Chapter Eleven

The following Friday afternoon, Neil and Silke walk to the school. Neil sits on the tree stump. It is not as flat and comfortable as he was hoping for. Silke has phoned a drainage company and two men are checking things out, but Neil is already convinced the building is leaning less.

'Nonsense,' Silke says, pouring coffee from a flask. 'It has only been a few days. We may have stopped it sinking any deeper, but it will never be level.'

Neil sips his coffee. 'Come on, it definitely looks better. It does to me.'

Silke screws the top onto the flask. 'Not to me. In my opinion, it will always lean. And it is good, isn't it, to preserve the past? The bullet holes in the old buildings of Berlin are not filled in. To me, that is endearing.'

Neil takes pictures with his phone, sighing at how they come out. 'It's the light,' he says. 'It's all wrong. The sky is too overcast. It's probably this phone, actually. I ought to replace it soon.'

Silke takes the phone from his hand. 'You don't need pictures. This is yours to look at every day.'

He tries to see what is endearing about the building. Once the rendering is chiselled off, the windows updated, he supposes it might look more presentable.

'All prepared for the meeting?' Silke asks, passing him a biscuit.

'Not in the slightest. I've tried to write my speech about fifty times.'

'Why is it so hard?'

He tips out his coffee dregs. 'Basically, I haven't much to say. I'd rather keep having a wander, soak up the feel of the place, work on my costings. I might have to postpone the meeting, actually.'

'Herr Fischer, you've postponed it three times.'

Neil stands up and brushes off the back of his trousers. A splinter snags his hand and embeds in his palm. 'The thing is, I might own this village, but I'm not sure I'm the right person to be in charge of it. It's not like owning a house and doing it up to suit yourself.'

They wander down the slope towards the school. Neil searches in his mac pockets for gloves. Silke warms her hands on the heat left in the flask.

'You could do a good job,' she says, touching his sleeve. 'You have to believe in yourself.'

'The trouble is, even though my father grew up here, I can't sense him at all. Can't imagine him playing in this field or singing hymns in the classroom.'

'Not hymns, Herr Fischer. Not here. We sang patriotic songs.'

'Okay, songs, then. There you go. I didn't even know that about him. Anyway, I don't feel I can be his representative.'

'There are one or two people here who can remember Peter Fischer, but his family... well, they all left when he was young.'

'Yes,' Neil says. 'He moved to Berlin in 1960.' He has tried to picture his father as a child. Perhaps he will ask the elderly residents for their memories.

Silke stops walking. She slips her hand into the crook of his elbow. 'Whatever you say, I think you are the right person. I believe you want to do your best for us.'

Neil smiles. He tries to remember anyone ever showing faith in him. He is unable to speak, even to say thank you.

They pause to watch the men at work.

'Have you been inside yet?' Silke asks him.

'I don't want to, really. I'd rather keep checking on the structure.'

'The toilets would surprise you. Close together in a row in the middle of the room. No cubicles. Nothing private. We were not encouraged to think of the individual. From a young age we understood we were part of a collective.'

Neil wonders what he will do with the row of toilets. If their condition is sound, he could sell them to cover the cost of the drainage men. Maybe they could take them today, in lieu of payment.

Silke squeezes his arm. 'Herr Fischer, could I have a lift to the station again on Sunday? I need another day in Berlin while Thomas is at the farm.'

'Of course.'

Neil is already looking forward to the drive, to the chatting. He might offer to take her all the way to Berlin if she chips in a bit for petrol.

The drainage men are loading their van. One of them walks across to Neil and Silke. He says the drains are in reasonable condition, with no blockages.

'Then it was all down to the tree,' Neil says as the men drive away.

'We must hope so.'

'How do you mean?'

'Well, we can never know, can we, what other reasons there might be? It is unseen, whatever damage the tree roots have done, or not done.'

Last year Neil grew tired of being upstairs by himself all the time. It was possible, he supposed, that his father was also lonely downstairs. He might be too proud to ask for Neil's company.

Neil sat on his bed, trying to find the courage to go down and say, 'Fancy a coffee?' Or perhaps he would come straight to the point with, 'I get it, Dad, you can't forgive me for what happened to Davey Ashdown, but I miss you.'

The trouble was, if his father rebuffed him, Neil would feel worse. He could try asking him about his childhood. It might be safer to talk about the distant past. He was ten when he moved to Berlin and the Wall went up a year later. It might not be wise to talk about that. Or maybe that was the issue. Perhaps if he coaxed him to open up about the Wall sickness again, he might welcome it. Years ago, he talked about it all the time. He should have kept talking.

Neil found some pictures online of Berlin in the sixties. With his laptop open, he left his room. His legs were shaking. He almost fell down the last few stairs.

In the lounge doorway, he cleared his throat and said, 'Dad, please can we look at these pictures?'

The room reeked of hard-boiled eggs. The shells were piled high in a bowl on the coffee table. His father was sitting on a hard chair in the middle of the room. He was emaciated, his sweater clinging to his ribcage. He did not look up, nor answer Neil's question.

'Dad, are you all right? Look, it's almost lunchtime. Shall I make us a sandwich?'

'I am tired,' his father said.

'My bread's only a couple of days old and I've got a bit of ham.'

'I am tired.'

'You could have a lie-down first and I'll put the sandwiches in the fridge for when you're awake.'

His father stood up and walked towards Neil. He closed the door in his face.

Neil returns to the tree stump and tries to work on his speech again. It is vital to have every word written down. An audience will make him tongue-tied, a bag of nerves. If it is unreasonable to postpone again, he has hardly any time left. He is not used to deadlines, only self-imposed ones. Being ordered to have this meeting and give this speech makes him feel even less like the owner.

Gudrun would come up with all kinds of ideas. He keeps trying to understand why he was so keen to drop her off. He could have brought her here to the village. Or taken her all the way to Berlin and stayed there with her for a day or two.

He searches for the name Gudrun and one of its meanings is 'wise'. He looks up articles about speech-making, but none of them explain how to address your village. He considers making the point that this village is not his home, but since it is theirs, he will tread carefully. He types this into his phone. After tapping in the full stop, he is stuck, confused by the notion of home – whether it is where you come from, or where you are going.

After his father closed the door, Neil went back upstairs, his laptop still open. He sat on the bed, in the dip he had just left, and lit a cigarette. He was not a smoker, but whenever his father was out, he pinched a few from the many packets left strewn about downstairs. The trouble was, his father retired five years ago and rarely left the house anymore. Neil's stockpile was growing stale.

Neil scrolled through the pictures on his screen while he smoked, tapping the ash into the foil dish he had saved from an individual fruit pie. There were families waving at each other from opposite sides of the Wall. There was a soldier from the East leaping over the barbed wire into the West just before the bricks went up. There was a bride in the East whose mother stood on a stepladder in the West.

Neil searched for articles about Wall sickness. He read several carefully, but there was one he read three times. The writer explained that living behind a wall makes you afraid of what lies beyond it. The communist agenda in East Germany was to encourage mistrust of the West: the Wall kept the enemy out. This agenda was well-served by the detrimental psychological effects of being walled in. A walled-in life makes you downcast, more inclined to conform. And conforming eventually makes you feel well-protected and valued. So when the wall falls, you are cast adrift, exposed to your fears.

As time goes on, you try to tread the line between reflection on your sheltered past and thankfulness for freedom. Not to forget, but also not to look back. But this is a balancing act which can sometimes intensify your sickness. You waver between finding happiness and clinging to the disease which defines you.

Neil's second cigarette smouldered in the foil tray. Word for word, this was how his father had described his sickness.

Neil was far too young to understand it the first time. He asked his mother to explain, but she couldn't make it clearer. He knew it didn't sound like any illness he had heard of. His teacher had taken leave for cancer treatment and came back with no hair. His cousin had multiple sclerosis, which made him limp. An aunt had something which made one side of her face droop. He was aware that some illnesses didn't show. He had seen sad people on television who took pills to cheer themselves up, or were ill from too much wine, but couldn't stop drinking it.

When he was older, he asked to have it explained again. His father repeated the same words as before. Neil recognised 'mistrust of the West', 'detrimental psychological effects', 'walled-in life'.

A few months later, Neil heard him talk about it to his mother after a strained Sunday lunch. His father had thrown the dish of boiled potatoes into the garden because they were still hard in the middle.

'The birds can eat them. They will not be wasted.'

'We could still have eaten them, for God's sake,' his mother said. 'The edges were fine.'

'The roast potatoes are also not properly cooked,' his father said, reaching for the bowl. 'I have said before: they need longer in the oven.'

'I gave them longer. That enormous joint of pork was using all the ruddy heat.'

The roast potatoes joined the boiled on the lawn. Neil's mother tried to protect the carrots and sprouts. Kersten was crying and Neil helped her down from the table. He held her hand and they went into the lounge together. He turned the television on. While Kersten was occupied, he went to the hall and listened to the row in the kitchen, hoping the trifle could be saved.

His mother was saying she didn't ask for much. A normal life, a normal Sunday lunch. Were they too much to expect? When you spent all bloody morning in the kitchen, all you wanted was for everyone to enjoy their meal in peace. And most people would be too kind and polite to chuck the potatoes someone had slaved over into the garden. Even if they were ruddy well rock-hard all the way through.

His father said he could not help it if he was not normal. He was a sick man and she had always known it. Kindness and politeness did not come easily to him. He had to think about them first.

'You don't think very hard, then,' Neil's mother said.

No, he agreed. He didn't. He was not a thinker.

She supposed 'they' had bashed it all out of him.

Yes, he supposed she was right.

He then described his sickness in exactly the same words as he had twice described it to Neil. Not a syllable was different. In every detail it matched the article Neil was reading now. But his father's name and age did not match those of the person who had written it.

Neil gives up on his speech and walks back to the house. The meeting is set for five. It's probably too late now to postpone it again. He will have to blame his poor command of the language for keeping it short. He wonders if that will raise a smile and decides it won't, but knows he will end up saying it anyway.

Passing the farm, he stops to take a picture of the silo. He wishes he could show it to Gudrun. He has read about artists painting murals on disused silos, swinging about in a little basket on a cherry picker twenty metres high. He could imagine her doing that, something wild and daring.

Some people might describe it as a blot on the landscape. They would see it as invasive, hideous perhaps. For Neil it has a mesmeric self-importance.

Some people would be scared of it. There is probably a name for a phobia of tall structures, the fear they will fall on you. His ex was scared of walking under a viaduct. She could picture herself lying beneath a mountain of rubble.

Neil looks at the pictures he has taken. Against the bright sky, the silo looks incredible and exciting, the soundest structure in the village.

He arrives at the community hall a few minutes early. A foul smell of sea lettuce drifts from the marsh through the broken windows. He goes up the steps to the dusty stage. It groans as he walks towards the middle. He looks at the empty chairs and hopes the audience will not expect him to be entertaining.

Thomas is patrolling the gritty wooden floor at the back. He keeps up a rhythm, a set number of paces back and forth before changing direction. He stares at Neil the whole time, like an abandoned dog waiting for his master to give a command.

Silke is in the kitchen, cutting slices of streusel. Neil checks his phone. Ten past five and no sign of anyone yet. He was hoping they would turn up in ones and twos, and exchange pleasantries with him. Now he just hopes they will come. At five thirty, they all arrive at once.

They go straight to the chairs and sit down, with the exception of Thomas. They are not talking among themselves. They are all looking at Neil. He smiles at everyone, hoping he is not coming across as desperate to be liked. No one smiles back.

He wonders how many of them were informers: the old woman in the front row who looks as if she is chewing a wasp, for example, and her round-faced husband in his fawn windcheater zipped to the neck. If the Stasi had doubted Windcheater's loyalty to the party, they would have ordered Wasp to report all his movements. Secret meetings, whispered phone calls. One day they would have turned up at dawn and taken him away. And even now, years after his release from prison, when Wasp passes Windcheater the vegetables at the dinner table, he wonders about her. And she watches her husband carving the meat and asks herself if he knows.

Watching Thomas pace up and down, Neil feels something for him – for his fear of the enemy he believed was 'over there', and his fear of the authorities intent on keeping him safe. To be kept safe, he had to comply. To comply, he had to betray.

Everyone is waiting for Neil to speak. He has no idea what to say and they know it. He feels stripped bare. His throat is painfully dry. From the kitchen comes the clink of Silke's knife.

He swallows hard, then says he is grateful to them for coming. He adds that his command of the language is poor and this will keep his speech short. He is sure they will be thankful for that. No one raises a smile. They are all in late middle age or elderly. They probably think him an upstart, strutting about like the lord of the manor. All he has done so far is cut down a tree and get Silke to dish out a few logs.

In rapidly deteriorating German, he tells them he is willing and able to carry out simple repairs. He tries to make it clear that he will get round to roofs and render in good time, depending on the extent of the work and the costs. He skips most of his notes because they seem to circle his speech back to his own inadequacies.

'So, to conclude, you mustn't worry that I will be breathing down your necks' – he pauses in case they laugh – 'because I have my home and my work in England as well. But I will do my best to support you. Most of all, I would like you to look upon me as approachable and useful. I don't want to frighten you with any sweeping changes. Most of all, I came here to be your friend.'

Windcheater stands up and waves a list of things that are wrong with his house. A woman behind him does the same. Everyone else follows suit. There is silence, apart from the collective whispering of paper.

'Please, stay for coffee,' Neil asks. But they all head for the exit. Thomas collects the lists as they file out.

Neil clatters down the steps and hurries to the door. He wants them to see him take their lists from Thomas.

'Rest assured I will read them all carefully and make notes, make more lists,' he calls out, realising after the door closes that he has said this in English.

Thomas follows them all. Neil goes to find Silke in the kitchen.

'It isn't your fault they rushed off,' she says, wrapping the cake in paper serviettes. 'They are going to the Friday bonfire. You should go, Herr Fischer. You might find everyone friendlier there.'

When he arrives, a group of men are building the fire on the scorched area of grass. Neil picks up a couple of logs and drops them on, but an old man glares at him and tosses them back onto the stack.

'Sorry,' Neil says. 'Didn't realise there was a protocol. I'll watch and learn.'

The men arrange the firewood with silent precision, then stand in a solemn circle while an elderly woman lights it. Some of the residents are taking plastic cups of wine from a picnic table. Neil would like a drink, but is anxious not to violate another rule. He speed-walks past the table without a pause, closing his hand over the nearest cup. He pulls his sleeve down to conceal it and moves briskly away.

An elderly couple in green jerkins are barbecuing burgers and slicing bread rolls. A handful of younger people arrive from the town. Neil is quickly surrounded and takes a few awkward sips from his cup. There is a magic about it: faces lit up by the flames, the crackling warmth, the blistering meat.

'What can you do for my parents?' asks a young woman in a white dress. 'They are getting so old and I worry about them.'

'My grandmother can't use her bathroom,' a man in shorts tells him. 'I think there are issues with the plumbing.'

'We try to help, but we live in Berlin now,' say a couple with a grey poodle.

They want to know how things are going, how the future lies.

'I have all this,' Neil says, showing them the list on his phone. 'And I'm going to compile a spreadsheet. I can't start work until I know the full extent and urgency of the various problems.'

'In the town there are excellent companies for this kind of work,' says an earnest young man with a long chin.

'I need to look at costs first. Work out my budget.'

'We will send you names.'

A young woman with pink hair asks him questions about England. She is planning to travel by minibus with friends next summer and London is on their itinerary. Also Cornwall for surfing, Glastonbury Festival, the Lakes and Edinburgh.

'I haven't been to all of them. Well, none, actually. I've been to the seaside, of course.'

'In Cornwall?'

'Littlehampton.'

She has not heard of it. Has he visited the Tower of London, the Houses of Parliament, Buckingham Palace? He says he has been to London Zoo on a school trip.

'And here in Germany, do you find it difficult to drive on the right side of the road?'

'It was tricky at first. But I drew an arrow on a piece of paper and taped it to the dashboard to remind me.'

All the young people nod their approval.

The man with the chin says, 'My friends and I are also going on a tour. We want to meet our friends from Facebook. Maybe also give a ride to hitch-hikers, make new contacts.'

Neil drains his cup. 'That sounds exciting.'

'Do you stop for hitch-hikers?'

'I prefer to concentrate on the signs, make sure I don't get lost. You never know what you're letting yourself in for.'

The chin man moves away to join the others. The woman in the white dress asks Neil to help with the steaks. When he tries to turn them, they keep sticking to the grill. He manages to release one, but it comes away in pieces, badly burnt underneath. The woman holds out her hand for the spatula. She says she will take over.

'Did you meet any interesting people on your drive through Germany?' she asks.

'I heard conversations,' Neil says, wincing as hot fat splashes his arm. 'There was once a young woman chatting to her uncle. She was getting married soon. They seemed warm and kind. I felt I knew them – or would have liked to.'

'And why did you not?'

'I don't know. The English are kind of reserved. We want to make friends, but we're afraid of seeming forward. Perhaps we're more comfortable being strangers.'

'Yet you listen to other people's conversations.'

'Yes, we listen.'

'You listen while wanting to join in.'

'I do, yes.'

People gather for their meat. Arms reach across Neil, holding out plates. He moves away and finds an elderly woman standing alone. He asks if she remembers his father. She hands him her walking stick and takes a tube of lip balm out of her handbag. She slowly runs it over her lips, staring at him as if the question distresses her. At last she recalls a little boy, watchful and solitary. His parents were taken away in the middle of the night and he was adopted. He left the village and never came back.

'The young always move on,' she says, retrieving her stick. 'You should do the same.'

She must be confused. His father never said anything about anyone being taken away in the night.

Neil goes over to the fire. It is fierce now. The scorching air above the flames distorts and shifts the trees and buildings. It makes him feel sick and disorientated. He must have squeezed his cup too hard. It has split, the dregs leaking onto his hand. He turns away and walks towards a chair, but someone else sits there. More people arrive from the town and surround him. Someone brings him a burger. It turns cold in his hands while he fields more questions about the village. He is frightened of making promises he cannot keep. Someone asks if he will leave England permanently and live in Marschwald.

He imagines selling his father's house, investing the money in the village, fulfilling everyone's needs and making friends for life. But he is tied to the Sunday visits to Davey Ashdown's grave, unable to escape what happened. He will always be part of that.

Jack Claridge has served his time and left it all behind. Neil used to believe he would do the same. When he was driving here, he wondered if perhaps in this village, he might unfetter the past.

The chin man brings Neil a new cup of wine. As he drinks it and makes half-baked promises, as blackened coils of onion drop from his bread roll, the bonfire roars and the flames leap higher, lighting up Gudrun. She is standing in the shadows with Thomas. She is looking at Neil and shaking her head.

Chapter Twelve

As the evening winds down, Thomas mooches off alone. Silke walks back to the house with Neil. She is tired and he says she should use the bathroom first. She leaves the slices of streusel on the table in case Thomas comes in hungry. The serviette is clinging to the little packages, patches of moisture seeping through.

In the bathroom, she takes off her blouse and skirt. Barefoot on the cold lino and shivering in her thin petticoat, she turns the tap enough to release a trickle into the washbasin and takes her flannel off its hook. She watches the water soften its stiff corners and creep towards the middle. She wrings the flannel out and rubs the bar of soap over it. She washes her face and neck, her shoulders and arms, her legs and feet.

She has not had a bath in all these years. She sits on the stool and imagines Martin running one for her. He pours in scented bath foam. In the bath rack he places a soft sponge and pink soap in the shape of a rose.

She kneels on the cork mat and spreads her flannel over the side of the bath. She picks up the rusty plug from the corner of the bath. It has lost its chain. She lets it drop into the plughole. She touches the hot tap, twists it slightly. The tap head shudders. The water is brownish, as if it is infected. It could make her ill.

'No,' she says. 'That isn't true.'

Not true. Not true. She told herself this many times in prison. Every day the guard took her to stand inside a cell fitted with pipes which pumped water inside. If she kept refusing to give up her secrets, she would be locked in there, already sleep deprived, with no chair.

Every morning she thought, 'Today will be the day.'

She had to stand in the doorway while the guard demonstrated how steadily the water would stream in. It was not clean water. It contained faecal matter. She would stand in there for hours while it deepened. If she fell asleep, she would drown.

He talked about the water in a hushed, reverential tone – the way her mother had read to her when she was a child – until she could hear its quiet lap against the concrete walls.

Whenever she turned in her sleep at night and the metal plate in the door shot open for the barked order – 'Flat on your back, hands out' – she wondered if the water-filled cell would be more bearable than this. And throughout the long, empty day, she knew without doubt that drowning would be better than non-existence. She battled with herself to accept that a dry cell, however bleak, was a luxury she must try to appreciate, if she wanted to survive.

When the guard did not leave her there and took her back to her own cell, she trembled with gratitude for his mercy. There was a grace to it. Someone cared about her. She still existed beyond her prisoner number. She was not without worth.

By the next morning she knew he did not care. He led her again to the water room. He was trying to break her. But for the duration of the silent walk through the corridors back to her own cell, she believed she was still human, and so was he.

She was in prison for four and a half years. Without warning, she was released and allowed to return to her studies at the university. She walked out in frayed jeans and a jersey with holes in the elbows. They did not belong to her. A few of her possessions had been moved to a tiny flat on the seventeenth floor of a tower block, a huge, concrete slab. She lived there alone. Thomas had finished university and gone back to Marschwald to chop wood. He wrote that he would not feel safe coming to visit her in East Berlin.

At the end of her first week, she came home from a lecture and began writing an essay. After the first three words, she stopped. Her pen was filled with black ink instead of her usual blue.

The following week, she went into the kitchenette to fry a potato. The potato was already peeled. The next morning, she woke late because her alarm clock was set for eight instead of seven. A week later, the jumble of socks in her drawer were all paired together, neatly rolled, one inside the other.

She went to the doctor and he gave her pills, which he said would stop her imagining things. She swallowed them, but could no longer sleep. She woke up within minutes of dozing off, convinced all the breathable air was being sucked out of the apartment. She told the doctor about it and he said she must keep taking the medication. They would eventually have the desired effect. She must follow the instructions on the bottle. One pill, three times a day. She repeated the instruction all the way back to the flat.

When she checked, the label said two, twice a day. She returned to the doctor. She was always given an immediate appointment. He examined the bottle and said, 'You have failed to listen. It is two pills, three times a day. You must learn to obey instructions, otherwise you will never set your life in order.'

When she looked at the label later, it was blank.

A few days after that, she came home to a rat sitting on her table, eating the remains of her breakfast. She ran out, shouting for help. When a neighbour accompanied her back to the flat, the rat had gone. The crust of bread it had been chewing was still there, intact.

She went to Café Danika every day at different times, convinced Martin would be sitting at their old table. He would not have defected without her. Once they were back together, all this confusion would stop. Her mind would be at peace.

Her patience eventually paid off. One day he was there in the corner, with his usual glass of Vita Cola.

'Oh, thank God.'

She ran across the café, bumping into tables, clumsy and unco-ordinated since the pills. She almost sent his drink flying.

He did not return her smile. 'Do I know you?'

He stared at her as if she were demented. It made her laugh. Of course he knew her. And she knew him. She knew the way his hair curled on his shirt collar, the small chip in one of his front teeth, the slight depression in his chin.

'It's me. Silke.'

He stood up. 'Sorry, I have no idea who you are.'

He snatched his jacket off the back of the chair, picked up his drink and went to a table on the other side of the café. She followed him.

'Please stop bothering me.'

'But I'm Silke,' she whispered.

'I'm afraid you're wrong. You're a stranger.'

As he continued to stare at her, the hollow in his chin became a shadow, a trick of the light, then vanished.

The destabilisation process was fully activated. What had been set in motion was now unstoppable. Her soul was dissolving.

She did not feel well enough for lectures, but kept trying to study. She moved her desk into the passage, watching the door. Her head would droop and she soon woke to the telephone ringing. A voice asked for Herr Schmidt or Frau Kühn. Thirty, forty times a day. Herr Schmidt, Frau Kühn. Herr Schmidt, Frau Kühn.

When she had to leave the apartment for groceries, she came back to something different. Dents had appeared in the lino where her desk usually stood. It had moved two centimetres to the right. She was afraid to move it back, even though it juddered against the radiator when she was writing.

She ran out of sugar and went out to buy more. When she opened the glass door of her kitchen cupboard to put it away, a full packet was already on the shelf.

She dropped off to sleep while writing a letter to her parents and woke up to find it sealed in an envelope. She posted the letter, but it never arrived.

She took up smoking. She kept the packet in the same place, on the middle shelf of the kitchen cupboard. It never moved from there, but one day it was a different brand.

There was never any sign of a break-in. Nothing was ever stolen.

Every day she said to the mirror, 'The years in prison have made you paranoid. You sleepwalk. You are forgetful. You are lonely. You are heartbroken. You have to pull yourself together.'

She ran out of pills, but could not face going back to the doctor. Two days after she took the last one, a new bottle was posted through her letterbox. She sat on the couch, the bottle in her hand. After an hour she unscrewed the top and tipped them onto the rug. She put on her shoes and stamped until she had ground them all to powder. She fell asleep for the rest of the day and woke feeling better, clearer, angry.

The next day she waited outside the apartment building with a notebook. Sleet was falling. She stood under a tree, a flask of weak coffee on the ground between her feet. She scribbled descriptions of the people going in: a man in a short raincoat, a woman in an orange headscarf, another with tight curls. She noted the time they entered and left. She knew only a few of the residents by sight, but they tended to stay longer than visitors. She decided to draw a star beside any who stayed less than an hour, two stars for less than half an hour, three for those who were in and out in minutes.

There were no stars.

When it was growing dark and the sleet unrelenting, she went back to her apartment and inspected every inch. Nothing had changed. Nothing had moved.

She was outside with her notebook again the next day, her breath a cloud of white vapour in the cold air.

'Look at me,' she said quietly. 'I will see you.'

Again, no stars.

Back in the flat, her knives and forks had changed places in the cutlery tray.

She went out again, this time simply to walk. It was impossible to avoid the Wall, although people tried. You could choose all kinds of long, convoluted routes through the city, but it found you. On Potsdamer Platz, Silke stood still and stared at it. The world came to an end here. This was it. No further.

Armed guards patrolled this concrete beast, while the Stasi monitored the wall in your head. They were in her flat now, gloved hands leafing through her notebook. They were with her now: behind her, somewhere to her left or her right. They were in the café, at the university, the doctor's surgery – a step behind, a step ahead.

She took her time walking back. She would give them an endless, freezing day. And while they trailed her, someone else was trailing them. They had to watch each other, as well as watching their prey. And most of all they watched themselves. Exterior eyes, interior eyes – always and everywhere. There was no one person, no entity in charge, who was not being watched while watching over them all. They had done away with God.

When Silke finally arrived at the flat, nothing was out of place. She slept well that night and woke at seven with an urgent longing to get back to her studies.

She ate a slice of bread for breakfast and prepared her bag for the day. The first lecture was at ten o'clock. She worked on the essay before setting off and collected her post in the entrance hall on the way out. There was a letter from the university.

She opened it straight away. It was short and shameless. She no longer had her place.

She was unable to get a job, not even something basic. Interviews would seem to go well, but she would hear nothing further. In desperation, she started telephoning to ask if they had forgotten her. In a polite, but pitying tone, the receptionists would explain that her application was not on file. Her name did not appear on their notes. There was no record of the interview. She reapplied for each position several times. The outcome was the same. She did not exist.

She had to leave the city and return home.

/

Her bath is almost full. She ripples the surface with her fingertips. How easy life must have been for the Stasi men since the Wall came down. She has read that many became private investigators and insurance salesmen – jobs that did not exist here before reunification. Apparently, some of them sell houses for a profit: quite an about-turn. They had all walked away from the collapse of their communist ethos, brushing off its dust without stain.

When they were still Stasi men, they felt no compassion for her. They were not trained or paid to feel compassion. Their training manual taught them how to undermine individual self-worth, create bewilderment and frustration, shoot nerves to pieces, and leave a person too scared and unsettled to dare reject the state again. Yet it was her own brother who had handed her over.

She takes her hand out of the water and examines her pruned fingers. She wonders how long it will take for them to look normal. She gathers her clothes and goes into her room. She will ask Herr Fischer to remove the plug for her.

Chapter Thirteen

In the morning, Thomas refuses to speak to Neil and is curt with Silke.

'How do you think people felt after the meeting?' Neil asks him.

Thomas spoons yoghurt over a bowl of plums, as if Neil has not spoken.

'I've looked at their lists,' Neil says. 'There's a lot to be done. I'm not sure I...'

Thomas is not in his usual place at the table. He has chosen to sit on the chair which scrapes. He pushes it back hard. Silke winces. She pushes her plate of toast away. He takes no notice and carries his breakfast up to the bathroom.

'Are you all right?' Neil asks Silke.

'I will be fine.'

'He told me not to sit on that chair. Is it because of the noise? Does it bother you?'

'It used to. Now, not so much.'

'He did it on purpose.'

'We all do everything on purpose.'

'But he knows you hate the noise.'

'Yes, but he is angry with me for taking his saw and giving away firewood.'

'You have far more reason to be angry with him.'

She gets up from the table and starts the washing up. Neil is finding his rye bread hard going. A caraway seed is trapped in his back teeth and the length of thread he pulled out from his coat lining as makeshift floss is in the bathroom.

Neil goes up to his room. He has not slept. He kept thinking about the meeting last night: the lack of response, the absence of warmth, the long, impossible lists. They all took their cue from Thomas and his ridiculous pacing.

He tips out the contents of his suitcase and spreads them over the bed, lining them up in size order, then colours, then order of importance. He stares at them, the tick of his father's travel alarm clock shuddering through the silence. At last he realises what is missing: an epaulette from his father's military service days, left for him with the letter Neil has yet to open. He cannot remember the epaulette in detail, only that it was stiff, grey and soldierly.

The bathroom door crashes back against the wall. Neil hurries out to the landing.

Thomas is wearing only a towel round his waist. He has a magnificent build. His head almost touches the ceiling.

'I seem to have lost something,' Neil says. 'Any chance you've seen it?'

Thomas strides past, forcing Neil to step aside. Neil's fists clench. His heartbeat is wild, violent. 'Maybe,' he says, watching Thomas slow down. 'Maybe someone has taken it.'

Thomas turns and walks towards him. 'Careful what you say,' he hisses, barely moving his mouth.

Flattening himself against the wall, Neil says, 'Your sister went to Berlin the other day. And now she knows.'

For his mock English GCSE, Neil had to write about a hero. The task was to define what a hero actually was and choose someone who, in his opinion, had achieved hero status. In her pre-exam pep talk, Miss Farrow had advised the class not to settle for the first idea that sprang to mind. The same one was bound to occur to everybody and your own work would not stand out as original, especially if others captured it better than you. In fact, she said, you should probably discard your first ten thoughts.

Neil wrote a brief introduction. He defined a hero as someone so perfect they made you feel inadequate about yourself. He put his pen down and sifted through the obvious candidates: Jesus, da Vinci, Martin Luther King, Nelson Mandela, Bob Geldof. It was easy to find ten. Edith Cavell, Dalai Lama, Neil Armstrong, Florence Nightingale, Marie Curie. After that he was stuck.

Jack Claridge would be writing about Kurt Cobain. Jessie Lynch would pick Denise Lewis. Neil did not have a personal hero. He needed to find a second set of ten and pick from those.

He tried hard, but had a mental block. It happened sometimes. His mind would slowly turn blank, as if a blackout blind were unrolling, sealing off every particle of light.

'Think of the first ten again,' he whispered to himself. 'You have to pick one soon or the time will be up.'

All around him, pens were scratching away in the exam booklets. Pages were turning. Neil was gripped by panic.

'For God's sake, pick Jesus. Or what about Edith? She's not all that obvious, is she?'

What did he know about Edith Cavell? Who was she? A nurse in the war? Yes, that was it. Which war? The First? He wasn't sure. She was definitely a hero, but the details kept escaping. You were supposed to put in a few dates as well. And the place where the heroic feat was carried out. And what the heroic feat actually was.

He scribbled down his first ten heroes – crossing out Miss Cavell – in the margin of the booklet. He tapped his pen beside each one. His memory caught hold of a fact here and there, but they slithered away.

'Just think of one more person. One more that isn't in your first ten. You only need one, for God's sake.'

Trying to focus on one alone forced hundreds of famous faces into his head. They all had long curly wigs and stern expressions, like people on banknotes. They seemed good and learned and wise. But he didn't have a clue who they were.

One girl was asking for extra paper. Another was sitting back and reading through her work. The invigilator kept jangling keys in his trouser pocket. People sighed whenever he did it, but nothing stopped them filling their booklets.

Neil lined up his pencil and pen. He twisted his bottle of water around so the label was facing front. He unfolded his tissue and blew his nose. He straightened his booklet, then angled it. He tried alternate nostril breathing, but it made him more agitated, as if his veins were in crisis from oxygen overload.

'Come on, get started. *Now.* Don't look up, don't take a break. Write about anyone. What you don't know, you'll have to make up.'

His pen hovered over the paper. Who was it going to be? The faces drifted back into his head, staring and mocking. Hard little eyes sank deep into their sockets, cheekbones were honed razor-sharp, lips pressed together, thin and cruel. They were way too old, too far back in history. That was the problem here. He needed someone more recent.

Twenty minutes remained. No name stayed with him for more than a second. No face emerged from the crowd. He opened the booklet and wrote down his original list of ten under the heading *Obvious*. He followed it with the names of ten people at school who were exceptionally bright or sporty, under *People with Gifts I Don't Have*. Then he wrote a list of ten popular students who were *Universally Loved for Being Naturally Perfect*.

He continued with *Cats in My Neighbourhood*, *Action Figures of My Childhood* and *Best* Blue Peter *Presenters in My Lifetime*. He only had time for two *Celebrities Kind Enough to Speak to Me*. These were Stephen Fry, who had signed his latest book for

Neil in WHSmith, and a poet whose name escaped him, but Neil had once made him an espresso in Starbucks. It was just as well the exam was over, because those were the only two he had met, and the poet barely counted.

While he waited for the booklets to be collected, dozens of heroes floated easily into his mind: names, faces, details and dates. Some were quite obscure and would have earnt him originality points. They had all turned up too late. He was already dreading the results. His father was obsessed with exams and would quiz him for hours. He would have a field day with this one.

When Neil broke the news that he had failed, his father sulked for hours. It was clear he was desperate to get into a state about it, but Neil knew it was impossible for a sulker to emerge easily from their sulk – like a hermit crab who has squeezed into a tight-fitting shell and has to put up with being uncomfortable until he works out how to shrug it off.

Neil's father eased his shell off a bit after dinner, while they were having a rare session of washing up. He kept his eyes on the spotless plate he kept scrubbing and told Neil in a quiet, disappointed voice that he could not understand why he had struggled with the hero question.

'I didn't struggle with it. I just answered it in my own way.'

'Which is not what you were asked to do.'

'It was. They said to give my own opinion. It's not my fault if they don't agree with it.'

'How did you define a hero?'

Neil bundled a handful of cutlery into the tea towel. It jangled like the invigilator's keys. 'Can't remember now. Something like… A hero is a very, very… I don't know… a very brave person.'

His father dropped the plate back into the water. 'Wrong. Try again.'

'I can't change what I put. That's what I came up with. End of story.'

'You did not think about it enough.'

Neil tipped the cutlery into the drawer, jumbling knives and forks in together. 'For God's sake, I don't know. A hero is someone who's done something incredible and amazing.'

'Not really.'

'Well, sorry, but that's what I think.'

'But you could not pass the exam with these thoughts. So you must be wrong.'

Neil threw the tea towel at its hook. It flopped to the floor. 'Okay. A hero is someone you look up to?'

'No.'

'Someone with special skills?'

'No.'

'I give up, Dad.'

'You give up?'

'Of course I bloody give up. That's what you want, isn't it?'

His father poured the dirty water out of the bowl. When it had gurgled down the plughole, he said, 'A hero does what he is compelled to do. He never thinks about the consequences for himself, about whether it is a good thing for him or not.'

'That's what I just said.'

'You did not. And pick up that tea towel.'

Neil was incapable of picking up the tea towel. He was powerless to think or speak. He could barely see. He could only feel. He wrenched the bowl out of his father's hands and threw it across the kitchen. He shouted and swore.

Afterwards he could never remember exactly what he said. Something about never being the son his father had wanted. And even if he could understand what kind of son he was supposed to be, he knew he would never live up to it. They were words which could probably be forgiven, but their fury never forgotten.

His father ran, virtually galloped, to his bedroom. Neil followed. He found him crouching on the floor, the other side of the bed. He was trying to crawl underneath. Instead, he curled up small, his arms wrapped around his head.

Neil walked away. He went to his room and tried to blot out the image of his father terrified by his own son. Every day since, even though Neil pleads with it to go, the regret is there. Every day, he wishes he had just picked up the ruddy tea towel.

Thomas steps closer. Neil presses his back tight to the wall. His palms press against the clammy wallpaper. He closes his eyes. The floorboards creak as if they are splitting apart.

He mustn't let himself regret telling the truth. He has a position of responsibility here, for Christ's sake. He came to the village to make things better. It doesn't have to stop at painting and decorating. He doesn't always have to stand by.

The creaking stops. Thomas's breath, hot and sour, is close to Neil's face.

'Wait. Thomas, please listen. Look, the Wall destroyed my father's mind. I never saw him happy. I understand how hard it was to live—'

Neil is on the floor. Pain sears through his face. He gasps for breath. His glasses have gone. He can see nothing at all.

'Leave him, leave him,' Silke yells, running up the stairs.

Neil whispers, 'I can't see.'

Now he is lying in his bed. Cool water is trickling into his eyes, into his hair.

'Open your eyes,' Silke keeps saying. 'Open them.'

Gudrun is in the room. He recognises the soft flap of her sandals. He can smell the contents of her backpack, something for all emergencies: tissues, balm, soft sweets. She can make time slow down.

'I have a sister,' he says. 'I would never betray her.'

'What if your own life depended on it?' Gudrun says.

She is sitting on the bed. She has brought in the pungent smell of the marsh. He shivers violently.

'I have opened the window, Neil. The sharp air is good for you. It will make everything clear.'

He wrinkles his nose. 'The smell, though. It's terrible.'

'I had a hot shower this morning. And used my deo.'

'No, it's not you.'

'I know,' she says. He can hear her smiling. 'It is only the marsh, Neil. Bacteria are feeding on the rotting vegetation. It makes the vapour you can smell.'

'I can't bear it.'

'But it's such a good thing. Completely natural. Dead plants and creatures are our heroes. They make the raw matter for new life in the spring.'

The smell is suffocating. He can taste the decay as if he is sinking beneath the earth. Putrid soil is filling his nostrils, his mouth.

'Neil, open your eyes.'

'No. I still won't be able to see.'

'Why not find out?'

Gudrun is unwrapping a tube. The room fills with the smell of peppermint. Her arms are sliding into sleeves, lifting high to free her hair from under her collar. Her jacket crackles with static.

'Open your eyes, Neil.'

'No, I'm happy listening.'

'You are not listening. You are only hearing things.'

The window closes. He breathes clear, minty air. 'I only told the truth,' he says. 'I didn't want to cause trouble.'

Gudrun is walking to the door, zipping up her jacket. 'You have not answered my question yet. Would you betray your sister if your own life depended on it?'

She leaves, closing the door before he can answer. He is tired of thinking. His head is throbbing, his left eye aching. His cheek is burning with pain. The fried-meat smell in Silke's hair wafts over him.

'Can you open your eyes, Herr Fischer?'

'I had to tell him, Silke.'

'Yet it was not your story to tell.'

'I'm here to help.'

'But not to help yourself to something which doesn't belong to you.'

She bathes his eyes with more cool water and dabs them dry with a towel. She makes him sit up and swallow two aspirins with a gulp of water.

'Can you open them now?'

'No.'

'Open one. Here are your glasses.'

The frame weighs heavily on his damaged cheekbone. He winces, but it is a relief to have his glasses back. His right eye is less sore than the left. He opens it a little and awkwardly blinks.

'Yes, it's all right. I can see.'

'Now the other one.'

He gingerly touches his left eye. The lid is badly swollen. It is puffy underneath and tacky with drying blood. It hurts to open it. He can only manage it in small stages.

'Everything's hazy.'

'Wait, you still have blood in there.'

'It feels more like grit or grain. Tons of it.'

Silke wipes it again and there is a small improvement.

'Still not seeing well, Herr Fischer?'

'Not with this eye. All these little lights keep flickering. Where is Thomas?'

'He has gone to work.'

'I can't stay here anymore, Silke.'

'Please stay. Or you can live in the school. It has the kitchen and toilets. You could camp in the hall.'

'Thomas will come and get me there.'

'I have taken photographs of your poor face. I told him I will show them to the police if he goes near you again. I think he is ashamed. He will leave you in peace now.'

'Has he apologised to you?'

'In his own way.'

She plumps the meagre pillows and goes downstairs to make tea. She brings it to him on a tray, together with a piece of the cake with the damned seeds. Eating is far too painful. Although his jaw is intact, it feels too tender.

'I didn't realise how much of the face moves when you eat.'

'Then take smaller bites. I thought English people had good manners. You put food in your mouth as if you are shovelling coal in a steam train.'

He almost laughs, but stops himself. It would be agonising.

'Herr Fischer, I hate to ask, but you promised me a lift to the station tomorrow.'

'I can still take you. I'll drive you all the way to Berlin.'

'That's not necessary.'

'It is. I really don't think I can trust Thomas. I'll stay in a hotel and have a think about the future of things here.'

'It was never going to be easy.'

'No, but I wasn't expecting to be beaten to a pulp.'

'It's not as bad as it looks. One black eye, one purple eye, a gash on your cheek where it struck a splinter in the floor.'

'I think it's at least a broken cheekbone and partial blindness.'

'The swelling will go down. And you will see more clearly.'

She takes off his glasses. The room blurs again. 'Go to sleep now,' she says. 'You must have a rest today.'

He has not taken a day off for a long time. Living by himself makes it harder to loaf about. He has plenty of opportunity to do that in the evenings and at weekends. If he had a day off, he would need to give it structure and deadlines. It would end up the same as a working day. It would be unbearable to lounge about in bed. Night-time is bad enough, lying there alone with his thoughts.

He closes his eyes and stays in bed all day. In the evening, Silke brings him soup and a soft milk pudding. It is not unpleasant, being looked after. He remembers the sweet taste of warm milk when he was poorly, the melamine cup with Mickey Mouse on it, his mother's cool hand on his forehead.

The next morning he drives Silke to Berlin. His eyesight seems better, but he keeps seeing red and green lights, smaller than a pinprick, flashing and fading. He hopes it will pass if he keeps blinking, if he focuses on the road.

Silke is perfectly still in the car. She has not brought any snacks or drinks. She looks straight ahead. Nothing like Gudrun: fidgeting, delving in her backpack, sliding off her sandals.

'Are you sure you want to drive all the way?' Silke says. 'You might not be well enough.'

'The alternative is staying behind with your brother around.'

'He will be helping with the harvest. And he is unlikely to punch you again.'

'Thank you for the reassurance, but I would like to be in the city. I'm not achieving much in the village.'

'You don't always have to achieve things.'

'But there's all those lists.'

'We are patient in our village. We will give you time.'

His head aches, but being on the move might help. He opens the window a fraction and the air roars in.

'I managed to avoid Thomas this morning,' he says. 'How was he?'

'He was quiet. Last night he laid his head on my lap like a child and wept.'

'Did he apologise for betraying you?'

'He finds it too hard to talk about.'

'*He* finds it too hard? He wasn't locked up.'

'But prison is a state of mind. The facility where they locked me up was so secret it had no official status. It did not exist. Not publicly. On a map of East Berlin, you would not see it. There was no need. The whole of East Germany was one enormous prison. The Wall keeping the enemy out was actually keeping us in.'

The intervals between the flashing lights become shorter. Neil has to keep blinking them away. He stops for petrol. When he goes into the shop to pay, the chocolate display distracts him. Maybe he is hungry. It could be as simple as that. The dizzying variety of bars puts him on edge. The strip light flickering on the foil wrappers hurts his eyes. He reaches up for a block of Ritter Sport on the top shelf. The sudden movement makes him feel faint. He grips the edge of the shelf, not daring to move.

'Careful,' says a woman. 'You're about to fall.'

He waits for the blood to rush back to his head. The woman is beside him, her perfume sharp and fruity.

'I'm fine,' he says.

She collects his Ritter Sport. She is wearing a silk headscarf patterned with ears of corn or wheat. He watches them come into focus. They are pin-sharp for a second, then they distort and blur.

'Careful,' she says. 'You are going to pass out.'

She grips his elbow. A man in a squeaky tan jacket takes his other arm. They guide him to a chair by the till. He is conscious of the queue observing him. He would feel better if they could all leave him alone. He needs to sit in the car. Silke is waiting. He needs the boost from the chocolate.

Someone hands him a bottle of water. He misses his mouth the first time. Having an audience puts him off his stride.

'All under control,' he says, raising his thumb. 'Thank you.'

The queue dies down. Neil gets up slowly and pays for his

petrol. The headscarf woman has bought the chocolate for him. She is waiting with it at the door.

He puts his hand in his pocket. 'That's really kind, but let me give you the money—'

She holds up her hands to stop him. 'It is done now,' she says. 'You need to take it easy.'

'I will, thanks. I'll sit in the car and eat this before I get going.'

As he walks away, she says, 'Don't go back.'

He might have misheard. He is not translating so well today.

In the car, he lets half the bar of chocolate melt in his mouth and feels better. He offers Silke a square, but she refuses. She is too excited, she says.

'So, what are you planning today?' he asks, switching on the engine.

'I am going to visit an old friend.'

'Does she live in Berlin, or are you just meeting up there?'

'He lives there. I have not made an appointment. I have read his jogging blog, every post since 2012. He goes running in the park every morning.'

'And you are hoping to catch him?'

'I will catch him. I know the park. I know his schedule.'

'The joys of the internet, eh.'

'Indeed.'

After fifteen minutes, Neil stops again. He goes into a shop for a can of Coke. Something in it always used to help his mother's migraines: the caffeine perhaps, or just its sparkling nature. Whatever it was, he has an overpowering need for it now. When his mother was suffering, he poured the Coke into a glass and sat quietly next to her. The only sound in the room was the eruption of bubbles, then their long sigh before they disappeared.

He glances at a display of postcards. He wishes he could send one to his mother, but she has no idea he is here. He is going to wait until he can show her a set of before and after photos. He wants her to marvel at the contrast. He has shown her pictures of the properties he has developed, but restoring an entire village is out of the ordinary. He imagines presenting the finished project to her. She will be amazed by the school when he has transformed it into a house three times the size of The Lewis.

When he comes out with the Coke, the woman in the wheat-sheaf headscarf is standing by the bins. She gives him a fond look, the way his mother did when he was still young enough to be collected from school. He recalls the intense relief of seeing her at the end of his first day. She crouched down in the playground and held her arms out wide, as if she had been waiting all day to watch him run towards her.

The headscarf woman clicks her tongue when he passes her. It makes a soft, tapping sound. He drinks the Coke as he walks to the car. He can't wait to feel it doing him good. The gas swells in his stomach all the way to Berlin. He wishes he were alone so he could let some belches rip.

The approaching city makes him feel better. The TV Tower is unnerving, its slender shaft jabbing the sky, way above everything else. Near the top, the sunlight paints a cross-shaped reflection on its huge sphere.

'They used to call it the Pope's revenge,' Silke says. 'It was West Berlin's joke. You know, since communism renounces God.'

Neil is annoyed that she explained the joke. Maybe he was looking a bit gormless and she assumed he didn't get it. Admittedly, he has barely spoken for miles. It is hard to make conversation with lights flashing, with your head reeling.

After Neil parks the car, Silke insists on writing her phone number on a slip of paper. She pushes it into his pocket.

'You are not well,' she says. 'You might need me.'

After she hurries off, he wants to find the Tower. There is no need to make any effort. It finds him. It stalks him everywhere.

He sits down in Alexanderplatz to read about it on his phone: how it was built to be the foremost symbol of the communist state and its superiority over the West. He doesn't want to read about it anymore. He needs to be in the lift that will rocket him 200 metres in forty seconds.

It is nothing like being in a rocket. It feels the same as any other lift. Not that he has ever been in a rocket, but he imagines you would feel a great soaring inside, the reverse of falling.

The view from the sphere is enormous. The windows tilt downwards and glitter all around him. He puts his hands on the glass. He tries to admire the vista, but can only see himself falling out. He glances round, wondering if other people are thinking the same. When he takes his hands away, they leave prints behind which instantly vanish.

He walks around the sphere, trying not to look out, feeling hot and nauseous.

'Why did you come up here when you're afraid of heights?' Gudrun asks.

She is taking photographs like everyone else. People block his view of her, pointing out landmarks to their friends, needing to be the first to see them. Parents want to educate their children, build memories. Neil looks for Gudrun again. She has gone.

He walks around the sphere twice more. He sees the top of her head in the crowd and follows it, but it blends with other heads until they all look the same. Eventually, he sees her face. She turns towards him and smiles. She raises her phone and it flashes over and over again. She takes more pictures of Neil than of the panorama spread out below.

'Stop,' he says. 'That's enough.'

She lowers the phone, but it is not Gudrun. His eyes are still dazzled, but he knows it is not her. He must have turned round again and faced the wrong direction. He has lost her now.

When he can see more clearly, he goes back to the window. He is not normally afraid of heights. He will feel better if he can work out which direction he is facing. He is looking at Alexanderplatz. Is that south? He can't decide. He needs to sit down, recover his bearings.

He goes into the restaurant, where breakfast is still being served. The waiter is displeased that Neil has not booked a table, but finds him a space and leaves him with the menu. It feels good to have something to focus on, a choice to make. It is a relief knowing the waiter will come back.

Neil settles for granola with fruit and yoghurt. He prefers the idea of smoked salmon, but the granola is practically half the price.

He is drinking his coffee and beginning to relax when he realises the view from the window has changed. He looks away, watching the waiter, who is busy serving other customers. It reassures Neil to know he is nearby, to be sitting at one of his tables. He will come to Neil soon.

A leaflet about the tower is tucked between the condiments and serviettes. Neil takes a look and decides he was probably right about facing south on the observation deck. Halfway through his breakfast, he feels ready to re-examine the view from the window. It has changed again.

The waiter says, 'Are you all right, sir?'

Neil has knocked his cup over. The tablecloth is saturated.

'I'm sorry. It's the view out there. It's...'

'Yes, some people say it disturbs them,' the waiter says, peeling the cloth from the table. 'The rotation.'

Neil checks the leaflet. A revolving restaurant. He should have realised. He had let it unnerve him when logic should have made it obvious.

When he was fourteen and struggling to complete an 800-metre run, logic warned him to pace himself, maybe even walk it whenever the PE teacher's back was turned. But he had not paid logic any attention.

The teacher had warned them for ages they would all have to try. Neil's father was excited about the race. It was stupid of Neil to have mentioned it, but it was like having a stubborn splinter. Your finger keeps pressing it, knowing it will hurt, but you need to check if it is still there.

After dashing through the first 200 metres, Neil was scared there was something wrong with his lungs. Maybe he lacked the same breathing capacity as the others. Despite the frost on the ground and a cold fog descending, he was prickling with sweat. Gradually, everyone jogged past him, even the boy with the club foot.

Neil thought he would die on the track. He sank heavily onto the grit. It was sparkling as though sprinkled with salt crystals. His lungs were heaving. He didn't have a stitch in his side. His whole body was a stitch.

'Can't,' he panted when the PE teacher blew his whistle and motioned for him to keep going. 'I give up.'

He had to tell his father the truth because he would only find out at parents' evening. He was the kind of parent who booked appointments with every single teacher. He frogmarched Neil to the park, measured out 800 metres and told him to run it. Whenever Neil stopped, he yelled at him to keep going. In the end, a man in a yellow tabard with a whistle hanging round his neck said, 'I'd leave the lad alone if I was you. He's had more than enough.'

The man might have been a council official or a dog walker. But the whistle and tabard did the trick. His father was a pushover for officialdom. He agreed enough was enough and they went home. Neil was never sure if this was a triumph.

Neil descends in the lift, the leftover granola clumped in a serviette in his pocket. He walks through the city centre. His right forearm, still scorched from the open car window, keeps tingling in the sun. When he stops for a rest, he notices that his feet are scarlet between the straps of his sandals. He walks on, screwing up his eyes against the bright reflections from the tall, glassy buildings. In the end he has to look down. He follows the line of cobblestones set in the ground, where the Wall used to be.

He finds the street where his father once lived in an apartment block. He has seen internet pictures of the row of raw concrete towers, but they have gone now. There are no brutal façades left. They have all been torn down. He walks away. All that is left from that time is the crockery his father brought with him to England: an orange melamine bowl and some mushroom-coloured plates.

He ought to book a hotel. He can drive Silke to the village when she is ready, then come back here and have a decent shower. Afterwards he will go out in the cool of the evening and walk his father's streets, on his side of the Wall. He will imagine the shadow it cast and stand inside it.

Neil sits at the last empty table outside a café. He orders coffee and cake. At the next table there is an elderly man, bent double and wearing thick glasses. A rough-haired mongrel with clouded eyes sits at his feet. A young woman wearing a pink straw hat runs up and greets the man with a hug. She is his niece. She puts down her shopping and drags a chair close to him.

They order the same cake as Neil: a dense sponge with stewed apple beneath and a crisp, sugary topping. The whipped cream on top is slightly sweetened and ice-cold. The niece says she is getting married and they talk about love. Her uncle says it shines out of her. After sixty years of marriage, he is now a widower, but he is never lonely. He tells her no one is lonely once they have been loved.

'Hello, son,' the uncle says in English.

Neil looks across, in case the man is speaking to him. It is unclear which way he is looking. His eyes are so far away behind the lenses.

The uncle stands up, gripping the edge of the table for support. The niece pushes his chair away with her foot. It slides into place beside Neil. She helps the old man to sit there. He places a battered box carefully on the table.

'From the old days,' he says to Neil, tapping the box. 'Good East German design, built to last.'

Together they take off the lid. Inside is a tin train set. The brightly coloured locomotive is called Tornado. Happy passengers and a stout ticket collector are painted onto the windows.

Neil and the uncle spread out the sections of circular track, then clip them together. At first Neil is worried there is not enough space, but it fits perfectly, as if the table is growing to accommodate it.

The niece hands them another box, full of tin houses. Some are large and grand, with window boxes full of flowers. Others are small and plain, glued together to form terraces. There are also wooden trees and bushes, a blue paper brook, a wooden factory with a tall chimney, its bricks neatly inked, and tiny aeroplanes attached to the top of wire stands, as if soaring overhead.

'We have too much,' Neil says. 'We haven't enough room.'

'Let us try,' says the old man.

They create two housing estates in opposite corners, surrounded by woods. The airborne planes soar above, a group of taller trees masking the wires.

'This is brilliant,' Neil says. 'You've thought of everything.'

Inside the circle of track, a forest of firs grows. They unfold the brook and lay it in a clearing. The final item in the box is a little wooden figure. The uncle places it deep in the middle of the vegetation.

'This little boy has to catch the train. Will you help him find his way?'

'But we didn't make him a path.'

'Would you like to create one?'

Neil hesitates. 'I don't know if I'll get it right.'

Uncle takes a large key out of his pocket. 'Take your time. When you are ready, I will wind up the engine.'

'I'll only mess everything up. I don't know how to find the right way.'

'Don't worry. There are no clear-cut solutions.'

They have worked so painstakingly. The trees are densely clustered. You can't put a pin between them. Neil is afraid of knocking things over, losing the child.

The old man puts the key down. 'May we work on this together?'

'Yes, please. I really don't know where to start.'

'Neither do I. Let us think.'

Neil is unable to imagine the path, not wanting the shared quandary to end.

Eventually, Uncle says, 'Perhaps there is only one way.'

'What's that?'

'We could do it tree by tree.'

'Okay, let's start close to the boy and keep going in the general direction of the station.'

They take it in turns, extracting one tree at a time.

'Where shall we put them now?' Neil asks. 'I'd like to use them all.'

Together they discover how neatly the felled trees fit into one of the carriages. They take it in turns to slot them inside. Each tree settles among the others with a small, satisfying thud.

'Okay, so this train carries goods as well as passengers,' Neil says. 'Is that okay, do you think?'

'Certainly it is. Conifers and commuters.'

'Maybe it's almost Christmas.'

'Indeed.'

When the carriage is full, Uncle and Neil discover that the missing trees have created a gently curving trail. Uncle asks Neil to trace it with his finger. Nothing falls. Nothing is dislodged. Neil moves the little boy along the path and he catches the train in time.

'Bravo,' says Uncle. 'He is lost no longer.'

'I can't see him,' Neil says, as the train gathers speed. 'He's fallen out.'

Uncle hands Neil his glasses. 'Try these.'

They weigh less than Neil expected. They bring colours alive and sharpen outlines. Neil spots the bundle of firs, the ticket collector's round face and the little boy in his green jersey and yellow cap.

'I can see him now,' he says, his eyes following the train.

'Well done, son.'

When the train slows down, Neil is desperate to keep it going. Uncle gives him the key, reminding him to be careful. It is important not to overwind.

The train sets off. It speeds up. It spins so fast the colours bleed. They give Neil a blinding headache. He can't make anything out. He has to take the glasses off. Everything close to him is mud-brown and blurred. Everything at a distance is clear.

The old man is a long way down the street, hobbling along with the young woman. She is holding two boxes tied with white ribbons and printed with *Bridal Boutique*. The rough-haired dog walks between them. He turns his head and looks at Neil with clouded eyes. In his mouth is a blue-and-yellow rubber toy in the shape of a train. A waitress is running after the man, holding up the pair of glasses he has left behind.

People swarm past: a frenzied buzz, a blast of radio, conversations in eclipse. Neil strains to keep the old man in view. If the waitress doesn't catch him up, he will come back to the café. Any moment he might appear, making his way back to the table.

Neil's sight returns slowly to normal. He can no longer see into the distance. The man, the woman and the waitress are all swallowed by the crowd. The cream on his cake has melted. A film has developed on his cold coffee. The train has gone. The little boy is lost again.

Chapter Fourteen

Silke returns to the park. She steps across the line of cobblestones into what was once called West Berlin. She crosses it back into what was known as East Berlin. She is the same woman whichever side she stands. She has always been the same.

She sits on the gigantic bench where last time she felt so small. This time she feels mighty. She is wearing relaxed jeans and a T-shirt. Her shoes are old and soft, the insoles moulded to the shape of her feet. She stretches out her legs and observes every duck swimming on the pond, every dog straining at the leash, all the prams, bicycles and people on the path, the walkers and runners, every scrap of paper and tissue blown by the wind. Opposite the park is Café Danika, where Martin passed her so many notes.

She remembers the day she felt unwell and Martin gave her the serviette she slipped into her bag. Thomas was in the café, talking to the bearded man in a short raincoat.

In their flat, as soon as Thomas had left, she tipped out her bag. The serviette was not there. She went out again and waited for the same bus to come back. The driver said she was welcome to search for litter if she liked. She could pick it all up and save him a job.

All the passengers stared at her crouching and peering under seats. One man – a bearded man in a short coat – did not stare. 'Engels' was busy behind his newspaper.

'Engels': surveillance of object leaving apartment soon after return.

15.44 hours: object waits at bus stop. Studies drivers of two buses arriving at 15.58 hours and 16.11 hours. Object does not board.

16.17 hours: object boards bus.

16.18 hours: object asks to search for item dropped earlier. Object finds nothing of interest. Sits on third seat from the front, left side, head lowered. Bites fingernails.

16.51 hours: object alights at Café Danika. Walks unsteadily inside. Appears unwell. Searches floor under table six. Goes outside, searches covered eating area. Picks up crumpled serviette in back corner by bin. Expression of relief. Also a smile.

On the serviette was an imprint of her lipstick, a terrible dark red, with bits of leaf and dirt attached. The scribbled message was not there. She had found only one layer, the underside. The top piece lies in her Stasi file, smoothed out and taped neatly in place.

At the time, she had no suspicions about Thomas being in the café, or the unexpected bear hug he gave her because she was poorly, his hands unavoidably cradling the bag slung over her shoulder. In those times, it was reasonable for people to doubt everyone, even their own brother, but Silke had always trusted him.

She chose to believe the wind had blown the serviette out of her bag when she left the café. The wind had also separated the two layers and let the one with the note drift away.

She convinced herself the scribble would mean nothing to anyone else. The group never wrote names. Only a coded date for the next meeting. Everything would be fine. It was nothing to worry about.

21.00 hours: 'Schmetterling': search of object's dustbin.

21.06 hours: search produces single layer of paper serviette inside plastic bag, consistent with prior communication from 'Mustang'. Item bears message similar to previous examples collected. Code equally unsophisticated.

Silke catches herself wondering if Thomas guessed she would go looking for the serviette. Maybe he planted the blank layer to warn her the group were being watched. She would love this version to be correct. She laughs at herself. She laughs so heartily that people begin to stare at the crazy country bumpkin let loose in the city to cackle on the crazy bench. Their gaping mouths make her laugh even more. Let them look. Let everyone look at her now. She has nothing to hide and every reason to be amused. She is still trying to be loyal to Thomas, for God's sake. She is quite the comedian. Outrageously sentimental. Her file would be half as thick without 'Mustang'.

She wipes her eyes and crumples the damp tissue in her hands, laughing again that grown men with whimsical code names could steal, hide, retrieve and photograph a scruffy paper serviette. How insignificant such a flimsy scrap would be at any other time.

A man in a red tracksuit is jogging along the path on the other side of the pond. She sits straighter, leans forward. Martin is thickset now, but looks like a man determined to control his girth. When he sprints round to her side of the pond, her body clenches. His breathing is loud, the rhythm fast. He has been running for forty minutes. He will pause soon, a few metres from her bench. He will stretch his muscles and drink water from the bottle strapped to the small of his back.

She watches him boldly. He notices. She also watches his thoughts, their entire process. He is intrigued at first, until her intensity begins to needle him. When she refuses to waver, he battles to work it out, to slot her into a place in his current life. When this fails, he tries his immediate past. Finally, his deeper memories heave themselves up to the surface. They shove everything else aside. Throughout the mission he bends each leg in turn behind him, heel thumping buttock, to ensure his hamstrings are kept warm. He also ensures he is hydrated. It aggravates him a little, this unexpected pause. His flow is not usually interrupted.

She walks over to him. 'As you have deduced, Martin, I am Silke. Come on, if you pretend not to know me, you will only humiliate yourself. So how are you?'

He pretends he recognised her straight away. He apologises for the delay in greeting her. He is engrossed, he says, in his daily routine. He makes a vague gesture at the gadget on his wrist monitoring his heart rate. She nods politely, already an expert on his fitness campaign.

She watches him notice her poor teeth, her thin hair, her weight gain. Not in a judgemental way, she thinks. Changes in old friends are fascinating. In turn, she notes he has kept his hair and teeth, but – despite his activity tracker – he has lost the raw energy of youth.

He is making comparisons, observing how much more she has aged. He finds it satisfying and she can hardly blame him. He is following protocol for the sudden renewal of old acquaintanceship. And in his eyes at least, it is only acquaintanceship. She is someone forgotten, now hastily brought to mind. She wonders which memories, if any, are floating to the surface, and how they might differ from hers.

He tells her about his career in marketing. None of it means much to her, but she nods occasionally to show respect for his decades of success. 'Career' is not a word that was known in the communist state. He talks about his managerial position and refers to his 'team', using the English word where once he would have said 'Kollektiv'.

'And how are you?' he asks at last, the faint crease between his eyebrows deepening.

He did not disappear in a bread van. The frown line may be deep, but it is not evidence of his own suffering. It is there because he is afraid to know about hers.

Martin was always direct, intense. His eyes never used to leave her face. Today he looks down at his expensive training shoes.

'Shall we sit?' she asks.

He hesitates. Sitting is not part of his schedule. He is already late for the next lap.

'Of course,' he says, looking up again. The frown is still there.

She leans back, but he perches on the edge, his palms deliberately light on his thighs, fingers tapping. She says nothing. It is up to Martin now.

'How were things... for you?' he says at last.

'After I disappeared, you mean?'

His hands grip his legs. 'Yes. After that.'

'Did you know where I was?'

'No one knew where people went.'

A sudden wind gusts through the trees. It lifts his hair and reveals a bald spot which had been carefully concealed.

'I was in prison for four and a half years,' Silke says. 'Afterwards they gave me back my place at the university. Then they took it away again. I never had a career, as you call it. I went back to the village I came from. Back to the only life I had left. Only this time without prospects.'

He sighs, as if in pain. 'I guessed something like that.'

The wind dies. His hair rearranges itself. His hand goes there, checking the strands are in position.

'Was it... bad?'

'Even if I told you every detail, you could only imagine.'

He shakes his head. It signifies both yes and no, or neither. It is the only possible response.

'And the escape?' she asks.

He leans forward, hands braced around his knees. He does not reply.

'I imagine it went extremely well. The way you talk about your job – sorry, your career – it seems you have been doing this marketing for many years. Not only since reunification.'

'Yes, it went well. In the West, I was able to reinvent myself, as they say.'

'I am pleased for you, Martin.'

'I couldn't contact you. I couldn't risk—'

'Of course. I understand that. When someone risks death to be free, they are unlikely to turn back and risk it again.'

He turns to her at last. He takes a packet of cigarettes out of his pocket and offers one to her.

'No, thank you. These days I only smoke when I have finished something.'

He lights one for himself.

'Do the followers of your blog know about this despicable habit?' she asks with a smile.

He exhales with a grin. 'I never mention it.'

'Then my lips are sealed,' she says. 'As always.'

She enquires about his life outside his career. He is far more comfortable talking about his thirty-year marriage and three children. Family life consumes most of his spare time, but he enjoys every moment. He and his wife have taken up ballroom dancing. He likes playing football with his sons. His daughter accompanies him for the weekly shop in the supermarket.

'I still call it the *"Konsum"*,' Silke says.

He smiles at the old word which links them. This is good enough for Silke, this recognition of their old life. She came here for that.

'Right,' he says, finishing the cigarette. He has already glanced three times at his watch.

'Yes, you must continue on your way.'

But he does not stand up. He twists round to face her. His face is contorted, as if he is having a heart attack.

'Martin?'

'I have to tell you something, but you will despise me.'

'Will that matter?'

'Yes. It will be a loss.'

She waits while he lights another cigarette.

'Before we approached you,' he says, 'your brother Thomas joined our team for a short time.'

'Team?'

'I mean the escape group. After he backed out, we were concerned he could become an informer.'

Silke touches his hand. It feels soft and womanly, not like her work-roughened knuckles. 'I read my file cover to cover. I know he betrayed me.'

Martin's fingers flinch. 'We believed Thomas would never betray us if you joined the group. You became... you became our insurance against capture.'

A patch of sweat on his chest is spreading.

'Go on.'

'I was asked to... to get close to you. To make sure you stayed loyal to us. We didn't imagine Thomas would inform on you, ever. But he informed on you first. We were watching you, day and night. Once we realised they had come for you, we fled. We had it all arranged. The escape was automatically brought forward. We entered our tunnel before dawn. The military were firing shots into the hole, but missed us all. We used you all along, Silke. The whole team used you to protect ourselves.'

She sits still for a minute. Slowly, he takes out his phone and prises a business card from its cover. He places the card between them on the bench. 'If you ever need anything... If I can ever make amends...'

He needs a tissue. She drops one in his lap, a rather grubby one smeared with her lipstick, from the day she came to see her file. She does not say goodbye. She does not pick up the business card. She takes the cigarette from his fingers and walks away.

Chapter Fifteen

Silke calls Neil to say she is ready to leave and will meet him in the car park.

'Already?'

'Yes, all done. Looking forward to your company, Herr Fischer.'

'Are you sure you're all right to find the car?'

'I'm nearly there.'

He was expecting her to need longer. He wants to look at a few hotels, check which are the best value for money. He stares at his phone, wondering whether to call her back and say he could do with another hour. No, he should take her home first. He can sort out the hotel later. No one has looked forward to his company before.

He has been walking since he left the café. He cannot work out the right direction for the car park. Whenever he turns a corner, he is in someone's way. He tries a street which looks familiar and passes a store selling paint. The window display features a white gloss claiming to cover imperfections in one coat. It is reduced in price and he considers buying several tins. Most of the window frames in the village are rotting, but once winter comes, a coat of paint will hold things together. Spring will be the best time to consider the carpentry work, ponder the possibility of replacement. In the meantime, a bit of freshening up might boost morale.

No, painting is out of the question. He is definitely going home soon. A day or two in Berlin, then back to England to work out the future of the village. The prospect scares him, though: living alone in his father's house. Maybe he will sell it and move in with his mother. Kersten's room is free. And if she ever comes to stay, he will make do with a sleeping bag on her floor. They can catch up, chat late into the night. They missed out on all that, the sharing of teenage angst, the big dreams.

And the long drive appeals. He needs the endless motorway, the enclosed space, the inch of wind roaring through the window. He will pick up Gudrun again, on her way home. He can think straight with her.

Neil walks on, but comes to a dead end. He turns round and goes back. In the next street he is desperate for another can of Coke. He spots a small grocery shop, but the door is stuck. After pushing it a few times, a young woman passing by says, 'It's closed.'

The strip light is on inside, flickering rapidly. Hundreds of flies are caught inside. He cannot see a Closed sign. He needs to fathom out how she knows the shop is not open. He turns round to ask, but she is a long way away now, her rucksack bumping on her back.

'Am I going the right way?' he asks a woman pushing her husband in a wheelchair.

'The right way for...?'

He shows her his ticket printed with the name of the car park.

'No, you are going the wrong way.'

She gives Neil directions and watches intently while he tries to repeat them. She offers to walk part of the way with him.

'Yes, please,' Neil says. He is not sure if he is speaking in English or German, but it doesn't matter. She seems to understand.

After a few minutes, the woman stops. She leans over the back of the wheelchair and has a word with her husband. She helps him out and guides him to a bench.

'Come,' she says to Neil. 'Sit. Please.'

He feels better in the wheelchair. No one can jostle him. No one even looks at him.

The woman leans over him and asks if he is on holiday, shouting the question into his ear.

'No, I've inherited a village in the east. But I don't know quite what to do with it.'

'I would think they want your money more than your presence and plans.'

'Probably. I was hoping to make friends.'

'Listen, you have no idea what they have gone through,' she says, forcing the chair through the queue at a kebab kiosk. 'You understand what *die Wende* means, don't you?'

'Yes, the reunification of Germany, the fall of the Wall.'

'That's what it means to you,' she says, bulldozing the wheelchair through a cluster of tourists. 'They are not used to outside influence. They were persuaded for too many years to fear it.'

'I don't want to influence anyone or make them afraid. I haven't stepped on any toes.'

'Then why did you come?'

'My father grew up there. He left it to me.'

'And you feel a connection?'

'I think so.'

'What did your father do for a living?'

'After reunification he moved to England and became an estate agent.'

'Why did he move?'

'My mother is English. He met her here, the night the Wall fell.'

'He was living here at the time?'

'Yes, an apartment in East Berlin.'

Neil once asked what it was like. It sounded exciting, an apartment in a big city. His father said it was tiny and all muted colours. The furniture was plain and functional, the shelf units cheap and plasticky, the yellow wallpaper glued directly onto the concrete walls. Its huge, loud pattern clashed with the floral lino. The doors seemed to be made from cardboard.

'And what did your father do for a living in East Berlin?' the woman asks, propelling him through the crowds again.

'After his military service, I don't know. He went into office work of some sort.'

They pass a shop window filled with dolls staring at Neil, as if in shock. Their bright-red mouths gape open. The doll in the middle has a varnished face and startled eyes. Its stiff hand taps on the glass. It tries to speak to Neil. It keeps tapping. As the wheelchair rolls on, Neil twists round. The dolls turn their heads, their horrified eyes watching him go.

They pass a shop window filled with crystal glasses. When his mother left, Neil found a wine glass in the sink. The faint imprint of her lipstick was clinging to the rim. He carried it up to his room, but his father was on the stairs and took it from him. He threw it down into the hall and it smashed against the wall. The pieces fell onto the telephone, into Neil's shoes, into the space where the suitcases had stood. Neil fetched the dustpan and brush. While he swept up the splinters, the sunlight turned them into diamonds. Most of the glass was shattered to smithereens, but Neil kept a larger piece. On it were her lips, still intact, as if the glass had been uncrackable there.

The woman pauses at a shop with a large window where plastic chickens stand on paper grass. She buys eggs and wants Neil to look after the cardboard tray on his lap. He keeps trying to count them. There are six rows holding six eggs in each, but every time the total comes to thirty-three.

'It should be thirty-six,' he tells the woman.

'Okay,' she says.

*

There were thirty-three recipes in the book he and his mother made together. When he was learning to write, he sat in the kitchen while she baked cakes. She told him the ingredients and he listed them in the book, followed by the method in numbered steps. She helped with the spelling and the abbreviations for tea-spoons and tablespoons.

'These recipes are all in my head,' she said. 'This is the first time they've been written down.'

'So where did you get them from?' he asked.

'Nowhere. I just used my imagination.'

'Why didn't you borrow a book from the library?'

'I don't care for instructions much. I invented them when I was a student. I was too shy for parties and clubs, so I stayed in and baked instead, late at night. When the other students came back from the pub, they crowded into the kitchen because of the lovely smell. It was the easiest way to make friends.'

Neil never told her they were terrible cakes. The one with chopped dates tasted of penicillin. His father refused to eat them. He said the other students must have been paralytic not to notice how bad they were.

Recipe number thirty-three was not for a cake. It was for Rooster Food. Neil chose the name. He wrote it in capitals with a red felt pen instead of biro to show it was different from all the others. They had inherited three hens and a cockerel from a neigh-bour who died suddenly. Neil and his mother carried the coop home between them.

'Instead of buying more food from the pet shop, shall we make up a recipe?' Neil's mother suggested. 'It looks just like my muesli to me.'

Her muesli had not turned out well. The spelt and barley and rice flakes were meant to be lightly toasted in the oven. But she never trusted pale colours. Apparently, things were not properly cooked until they were dark and bitter. In the end, Neil borrowed a library book about chickens and made a list. They went to the health-food shop and bought various cereals, nuts and fruit. He would never forget the soft rush of grains and flakes tumbling into the bucket – the pared almonds, crumbly hazelnuts, pineapple slivers, oats, barley and bran, how it all sifted, both silky and gritty, through their fingers. His mother agreed not to toast any of it and they laughed, their hands brushing together in the bucket.

He counts the eggs on his lap again. He keeps losing track and starting from scratch. It is far from a smooth ride. With every jolt, he loses focus. He can't see any bumps or potholes, but they must be there. In the centre of the city, he loses two eggs. They smash and spill on the cobblestones where the Wall used to be.

'I'm so sorry,' he says. 'Let me clean it up.'

The woman has wet wipes and tissues. They mop up the mess between them, but it is impossible to get rid of the sticky residue. It settles into the crevices of the tiles engraved with *Berliner Mauer 1961–1989.*

Neil pulls another handful of wipes out of the packet.

'Careful,' says the woman.

'I can get into all the gaps if I wrap the wipe round the tip of my finger.'

'Anything could be lodged in there. Animal mess, pigeon droppings, germs. You want to be careful.'

She helps him back into the chair and wipes his hands.

'You should sit on them. So you don't put them near your mouth.'

'They're quite clean now, thank you.'

Christ, Neil thinks. She's an absolute bag of nerves.

He doesn't really need her to wheel him around anymore. He will have to humour her now they have come this far. Once he has his bearings, he will jump out, thank her profusely and be on his way. Silke mustn't see him like this. She needs him to lean on, to take her home to his village.

The wheelchair follows the wayward line of the Wall and Neil feels queasy. The eggs are too much of a burden. There are messages coming through on his phone. He can't read them while he has to keep clutching the cardboard tray.

'You mustn't lose any more,' the woman keeps saying. 'Hold onto what you have left.'

To take his mind off it, he makes fresh plans. If he can find the cheap paint again, he will definitely buy it to stave off any further damage to the windows. He might search for it online when he gets back. He will definitely sort out the ramshackle rendering. Not strip off the old stuff and re-do it, but patch it in. Same with the repointing. Not a full renewal as such. A bit of mortar to fill in the worst cracks. Re-glazing will have to wait. He will need to do a lot of measuring and costing first. But once he is patching and painting, the residents will see that things are being done.

The more he thinks about it, the sense of disappointment – hostility, even – at the meeting could be blamed on a simple breakdown in communication. The residents might have been expecting a cavalcade of vans, a crew of scaffolders, a team of men in white overalls. And if he is being honest about all this, he imagined sipping good coffee in a sunny courtyard with quaint, slightly shabby buildings all round him. He pictured friendly old folk offering to lend their ladders, with strong sons home for the weekend to shin up them while Neil supervised.

He steadies the eggs with one hand and fishes out his phone with the other. He scrolls slowly through his photographs of the village and zooms in on the walls. Perhaps in close-up he will see more of the decay. But the magnified detail is disorientating. He could be looking at the surface of the moon. The image fades. His phone makes a dying sound. He puts it away and looks up. Finally, he understands where he is.

'Stop,' he tells the woman.

He is out of the wheelchair before she applies the brake. He leaves some money with the eggs on the seat.

'Stop,' the woman says.

He takes no notice.

'You are not there yet,' she calls.

He raises his arm to acknowledge her, but does not turn round.

He keeps walking towards the sign for the multi-storey car park. He is fairly sure he needs the fourth floor. In the lift he is overcome with relief. After all this, he might spend the night in the village, then go to Berlin tomorrow for a few days. He would like to walk the length of the Wall and imagine its immensity, alongside and above.

If he orders the materials today, they might have arrived by the time he returns to the village and he will get on with the painting, rendering and repointing. He can also check on the progress of the subsidence. In a week or two, he will have secured the village for winter. He could drop in again before Christmas and show them his plans for spring.

He emerges on the fourth floor and walks carefully along the rows. There is a chill in the air, a shock after the warmth below. He wishes he could have a cigarette and smiles at himself. He only ever wants to smoke when it is forbidden. He pulls the packet out of his pocket, scattering clumps of granola, ready to light up in the car. He can't find his lighter. He stands still and hunts in all his pockets. At last, not in the correct pocket, he puts his hand on it. He takes it out, but it feels too light. The lid is missing and the gold case is empty.

He rummages in the linings and finds the lid, then a little tube, tiny screws, plates and rivets, the wick and flint wheel, a few minuscule hinge pins. He must have sat on it awkwardly.

Maybe the woman made it happen, pushing him so firmly into the wheelchair. He will mend it later. He will have to add it to his list of jobs as a priority. Hopefully, there will be a box of matches in the glove compartment.

He walks systematically, row by row, watching left and right. His car has gone. He is sweating and ice cold. He goes down to the third floor, then up to the fifth. His car is not there. He tries to phone Silke, but he has run out of charge. It hurts to breathe.

He shows his ticket to a man waiting for the lift.

'That's not your ticket,' the man says.

It is the piece of paper with Silke's number written on it. Neil finds the ticket, but the man says he is at the wrong car park. He is a long way away.

'You should call a taxi. You look exhausted.'

Neil is gasping for breath. He has been running, he tries to explain. He is not used to it. He has a friend waiting. And his phone is dead.

The man gives Neil a lift to the correct car park. His car is large, clean and tidy. It smells of fresh toast. He agrees it can be stressful visiting a big city. You forget where you have parked because there is so much else to think about. He has read online about someone who left his car in a side street and it took over a week to find it. He had to ask Twitter to help him.

'These days, if you want to know something, all you have to do is tap a few words into your phone.'

'Absolutely,' Neil says.

'People come swarming to help. The whole world knows about you.'

The man lends Neil his phone and he calls Silke. She says she is fine. It must be annoying for her with nothing to do except stand about waiting. He will definitely stay the night in the village. He will help her cook the dinner.

When Neil gets into his car, he treads on something which splits. Plastic splinters grate beneath his feet. Something waxy collapses, releasing the scent of cherries. He has to sit quietly for a while, his hands too cold to hold the wheel. He asks Silke to find the matches and sits back to smoke his cigarette.

'You were lost?' she says.

'Not lost as such. I was thinking about paint. Then a woman insisted on taking me to the wrong place. And I expected your appointment to take longer.'

'I understand, Herr Fischer. You thought you had more time.'

Chapter Sixteen

After a few kilometres, Silke takes over the wheel. Herr Fischer is not in a fit state. He is concerned that she is not insured to drive his car, but she is too tired to worry about such things. She needs to get back to the village. She has so much to do.

'My old friend Martin is suffering in the same way as Thomas,' she tells Herr Fischer as she presses hard on the accelerator.

Herr Fischer is gripping his seat. His foot presses an imaginary brake. 'This Martin betrayed you too? I should tell them to go to hell for what they put you through.'

'Yes, but the difference is, I have set my pain aside. I did nothing to deserve it. They will always wrestle with guilt. I wrestle with nothing. It is Thomas who wakes in the night, Thomas who needs me to comfort him. Yes, I can't bear water. I loathe the scrape of metal. But doesn't everyone have dislikes? Spiders, heights, mice?'

Herr Fischer is quiet for a moment, then says, 'I hate the little holes in crumpets. Can't go near them.'

She increases the speed. 'Crumpets? What are crumpets?'

'I don't fancy talking about them. Sorry.'

'I will look them up later. But you know, aversions should not be the backbone of anyone's life. Guilt is different. It is the mainstay of Thomas's and Martin's existence. No matter what they hide behind – a marketing career or a tractor – it will always be there. It drives everything.'

Herr Fischer lets go of the seat to light a cigarette. 'Was Thomas exploited, do you think? The Stasi may have threatened him in some way, given him an impossible choice. Not that I'm defending him.'

'We were all used, Herr Fischer: the Stasi, their informers, all regular citizens. We were all watched, intimidated. If the state wanted to break you, it broke you. It spread rumours that wrecked marriages. It shut healthy people away, certified them insane and fed them drugs. Everyone was incarcerated. Even the Stasi.'

She is driving too fast. The marsh is blanketed in mist. The sky is pencil-grey, filled with rain.

'But you survived,' Herr Fischer says. 'You've left it behind. You've held onto yourself. Come on, you're miles away from all that now. So why don't you ease off the speed?'

She keeps her foot down. It feels heavy on the pedal. The brake lights in front are bright.

Herr Fischer scrabbles for the grab handle and shouts, 'You're bloody close.'

'I am, Herr Fischer. I am extremely close.'

If she does not ease off, the wreckage will not be the kind you would walk away from. She has two options: slow down or keep going, and a millisecond to choose between them.

Her foot moves to the brake. She will not make it.

In the mirror, she checks the adjacent lane. Visibility is poor, but there is a small gap. It might be enough. No, she is sure it is enough.

Herr Fischer is yelling her name. She is not panicking. It is good to hear Silke, Silke, Silke.

She makes the manoeuvre.

One driver hoots his horn. Others follow suit in a wild, syncopated fanfare. Silke weaves into the space.

The hooting continues. No longer mass panic, more an angry salutation. It is a good noise. It is all for her, for her courage.

'Christ,' Herr Fischer says, after letting out a long sigh. 'I thought that was it. I thought we'd had it.'

She smiles as she indicates to exit the motorway. 'No, we are still here, Neil. We are safe now.'

'It was bloody close. You've been dicing with death for miles.'

'Yes, but I kept my eyes open. There was always a way out.'

She drives on. At the outskirts to the village, Neil shuts his window.

'The marsh is pungent today,' he says, lighting a cigarette, filling the car with his smoke. 'Christ, I can still smell it.'

'You get used to it.'

He fans the air with his hand. 'If only there was a way to avoid it, though.'

'Think of it like this. It is there to let you know where you are.'

'A signpost would suffice.'

'The strength of the odour lets you know where the ground is unsettled.'

He grunts and concentrates on his cigarette.

'Why is there an old potato in your car, Neil?'

'It's a mystical being.'

'It is also festering.'

Back at the house, Silke sets the table with cooked meats, pale cheese in long, waxy slices, dark, bitter bread and a plain cake. Neil is pale, still shaken. She invites him to sit at the table and hands him an old radio and a screwdriver.

'It will only tune into one channel. Can you make it work?'

He looks at it for a long time, swivelling it round, peering at the back, twisting knobs.

'Perhaps you need to take the back off.'

Eventually, he unscrews it and fiddles about inside. Thomas comes in and tramps straight upstairs.

'Come here,' he says over his shoulder to Silke. 'I have something to tell you. In private.'

She takes out the bread knife and makes a start on the loaf.

'Come here,' Thomas shouts from the landing.

The knife saws through the crust.

'Silke, *now.*'

She cuts a few slices. Thomas thumps down to the kitchen. He glares at her, hands on his hips.

She turns to face him, the knife in her hand.

'I will come when you can talk the way one human should to another.'

A screw from the radio drops on the floor. It rolls into a deep crack in the lino.

'What's he doing with that?'

'I have asked him to fix the defective channels.'

'We are an entire village that needs fixing. Why waste time on that old thing?'

'Because I would like my radio to work again.'

'I need to talk to you upstairs.'

'Then ask me politely if I can spare a minute.'

She picks up a salami, chops through one end, through the plastic coating. The anger in Thomas is changing. Silke senses discomfort when he sighs, maybe even fear.

'Please will you come upstairs so I can speak to you?'

She puts the knife down. She takes the wrapper off the block of butter and sits it on a small plate. She wipes her hands on her apron and walks past Neil, who is prising the screw out of the fissure, the screwdriver still in one hand. She walks past Thomas, up to his room.

Thomas follows her in, pulling the door to. He smells of fresh hay and old sweat. He whispers, 'I have a letter that was in Neil Fischer's room. It was sealed in an envelope. I steamed it open.'

'That is shameful, that is—'

'Yes, all right. In a minute you won't be fretting about my shame.'

'It is not yours to open,' she hisses.

'Yes, yes. But Neil Fischer has intruded on our lives, infiltrated our home, withheld proper plans for our village. He has achieved nothing and impressed no one. The residents asked me to find out what I could. Renate wants details. She is worried he could tear her farm down if he wants. Build a theme park, a zoo—'

'Don't be ridiculous.'

Her voice is low, gravel-hard. It shocks them both.

'Anyway, my point is this. We have no idea what he is planning for us. We are all in his hands and I dislike it.'

'You have made that quite obvious.'

'Everyone dislikes it. They distrust him. He is trying to make you his friend, get you on his side.'

'Why would a letter addressed to him tell us anything about his plans?'

Thomas folds his arms, plants his legs wide apart. 'It does not tell us about his plans. It tells us something else.'

Silke refuses to show interest in the letter. She has no intention of losing the friend she has made.

Thomas uncrosses his arms and goes over to the bureau. He tugs open the top drawer. It whines in protest. He pushes aside a pile of his underwear and takes out the letter hidden beneath. The flap of the envelope is crinkled where the steam has dissolved the adhesive. He peels it back and removes two folded sheets of pale-blue paper.

'I don't want to read it, Thomas.'

'But you will hear it.'

'Move aside. Let me past.'

He is like a rock. With his heel, he shoves the door shut behind him. 'It is from Neil Fischer's father.'

Silke claps her hands over her ears. Thomas puts the letter down on the bureau and looks at her. His eyes glitter with pain. He is asking her to remember: there is a time to listen, he once said.

It was late one night in the East Berlin flat. Silke was reading, feet curled beneath her on the hard, brown couch. The cushions she had made were behind her head, on her lap and piled up either side. Thomas was studying at his rickety little desk. They ate and worked and lived in this one small room. They had a tiny bedroom each and shared a bathroom and toilet with ten others in their corridor. Silke was going to miss this life.

She was not going west for luxuries. She had never known how it felt to have plenty. The escape was all about being with Martin. If he fled without her, she would not see him again. Even if she could have known the Wall would fall seven years later, she would not have waited. Seven years was a lifetime.

She would miss Thomas. He was not a lively type. He could be affectionate and occasionally spontaneous, but mostly he was taciturn and far too serious about his studies. On the day they moved in, he refused to let her put up her John Lennon poster, reminding her that John Lennon was considered a subversive figure.

She arched her eyebrows. 'Subversive? Really?'

'Don't mock.'

'But it's just a poster. *I'm* not subversive.'

'I'm not saying you are. But that is how other people will see you.'

'People?'

'Oh, come on, Silke. The Stasi. Their informers.'

'I was going to stick it on the back of my door,' she said. 'Who'll see it there?'

'It only needs one person, the wrong person.'

'But how? On the back of my bedroom door?'

He said no more. He tore the poster to shreds and burnt them in the ashtray. She watched them curl into crisps and disintegrate.

She soon discovered that the city was not somewhere to hide.

You were not anonymous in the crowds. At any moment you could become a number on a file. You never knew when. One of her lecturers disappeared in her first week. No one knew anything and no one asked questions. In Silke's second week, a young woman with tight curls kept finding her in the canteen and sitting beside her, chatting as if she knew Silke already. She asked her all kinds of questions, sometimes general, sometimes more personal. Silke wondered if it was because she had once written to the BBC. On the Friday, she dashed back to the flat for lunch and never returned to the canteen.

A few weeks later, when she became Martin's girlfriend, she felt unassailable. She was told exactly what to do and enjoyed having instructions to follow. She was only a small cog in the machinery of the escape plan, but an important one. Her job was to appear dizzy and light-hearted, to let Martin kiss her at every opportunity, to walk the streets arm in arm with him as if East Berlin was the best city in the world. There was another girl acting the same part with Andreas. She was not in love with him, not like Silke was with Martin, but while acting dumb and dizzy, they could both observe anyone watching too closely.

On the day of the escape, Silke's instructions were to walk to the café at nine o'clock in the morning. She must be on the alert for anyone following her, anyone lurking in a doorway or leaning against a wall. Fifty metres away, she must pause to light a cigarette. It would give her a chance to glance round. She practised in front of her mirror, to make sure she didn't appear furtive.

She was to enter the café and say, 'One Vita Cola, please, and last time my glass was dirty.'

That was the signal. Members of the group would already be sitting there and would know that, so far, the coast was clear. They would leave the café at intervals. Martin would be waiting at a bus stop near the tunnel entrance, which was a hole in the lounge floor of a house twenty metres away. He would fold up his newspaper as a sign it was safe to proceed. How clever and stylish it had seemed then.

Silke was proud of her role. She thought about it often in prison: the last and most vital trip to the café she did not manage to make, the well-rehearsed words she did not get to say.

Thousands of times in her head she silently repeated, 'One Vita Cola, please, and last time my glass was dirty.' It was a way of keeping sane. Since you were not permitted to experience any positive feelings, you made private thoughts as fulfilling as possible, while resisting their emotional pull. It was easier during the day. Her night thoughts were brutal invaders. They tried to shatter every barrier to pain she had constructed.

She used to wonder if the escape plan had gone ahead without her and Martin. If so, did they choose Andreas's girlfriend to give the signal? They would have made her learn a different one. Silke spent entire days sifting through the possibilities. She whittled her thoughts into a shortlist and resisted picking a winner for a long time. Any mental activity with a streak of defiance had to be spun out. Eventually, the victorious line was, 'Coffee, please, and do you have any matches?'

It made her want to laugh. How many months of relentless contemplation to produce this one banal sentence? She had no idea. And now she had to find a new topic. She tried to remember poems and stories, filling in the blanks with her own words. But in the end, it was more compelling to focus on her own life, what it might have been. Empty hours were filled to the brim with fantasies of Martin: the minutiae of their wedding day, their home, their children.

She built a house for them, filled the rooms with furniture, stocked the cupboards with food, drew up a schedule for housework. When it was finished, she started again – the same empty house gradually filling with the same furniture, the same food in the same cupboards. After months of a standard socialist house, she started using her imagination and made it a home with colours and patterns she had only seen in forbidden magazines. And phones no one could tap, rooms no one could bug, kisses no one could see.

But her control kept slipping. It was so hard not to cry. Staring at the wall without blinking was effective at first, but repressed tears were a heavy weight on the heart and weakened her resolve. Instead, she had to settle for something painful to confront – something that had come and gone in an instant. It shocked her so much that she had to prepare herself to face it, like an athlete warming up. She circled around it, going over and over the smallest details of that time, late at night in the East Berlin flat, when she was reading among her cushions and Thomas was studying.

They were eating ham sandwiches. When Thomas leant on his desk, it jiggled. She wondered if it annoyed the people in the flat below, but decided they would have complained by now. She wished she could switch on the radio, but Thomas preferred silence when he was working. She was wearing a shapeless skirt and a green jumper. There were holes in the big toes of her tights. It was the first day of her period and she felt washed-out. By the time her next period arrived, she would be settled in the West with Martin. They would find a flat for two, a bit like this, but with white walls, deep carpets, a soft leather sofa.

Thomas looked across at her and frowned. He asked why she wasn't doing anything. She shrugged.

'You ought to be working harder. It doesn't take long to lag behind. You need to get into a routine.'

'I know what I'm doing.'

'No, your mind isn't on it properly. You should talk to someone at the university. They'll be glad to help you.'

'I'm fine.'

He left his desk and stood in front of her. She resented having to look up at him, like a dog at his feet.

'Silke, you have to take it seriously.'

'I am.'

She pretended to be absorbed with her hair, trying to coil the spikes around her finger.

Thomas knelt on the floor. His eyes were level with hers. 'Remember they are watching.'

She looked away.

'Silke,' he said. 'There is a time to listen.'

He got to his feet. His knees made their usual cracking noises. He sat heavily at his desk, leant over and wedged a piece of paper underneath one of its feet. It stopped the desk rocking. She imagined the collective sigh of relief from below. Before he set to work again, he looked across at Silke and his eyes pleaded with her one last time.

And that was when it came: a white-hot satisfaction. It came because she knew something he didn't. Or believed she did. Something he would condemn far more than her idleness. She felt a bravado which sparked for a moment and was gone, but impossible to un-feel. It was that simple.

Years later, after she left Berlin, she wanted to escape from herself, from the shadow of her youthful arrogance. After reunification, she considered going west at last. But she stayed. She belonged to what had happened.

'Please listen,' Thomas says now, his hand on the letter.

'Wait. Just tell me something. What would they have done to you if you had refused to betray me?'

'They said if I did not cooperate, they would persecute us all too.'

Six months after Silke returned to the village, their mother and father died. They were in the town one Friday, shopping at the market. They were carrying their groceries to the bus stop when a car lost control, Silke and Thomas were told. The packets and tins were all retrieved, slightly damaged, and repacked in their string bag.

'We were all persecuted anyway, Thomas. They killed Mum and Dad—'

'It was an accident.'

'It was all for nothing.'

'It was an accident.'

'If that is what you want to believe.'

'Do you think I can bear to believe anything else?'

He broke down when they buried their parents. They were two harmless people who wanted nothing beyond peace and trusted the state to ensure it. Like Thomas, they believed you had to balance the restrictions of what they called 'a supervised life' against the prospect of another war.

Thomas picks up the letter and Silke tries to leave. He steps aside, but says, 'Please. Please, Silke, this is something you must know. Let's sit down.'

'All right, come to my room, then. I don't like it in here.'

He follows her along the landing. She sits on her bed. She has piled her old cushions on it. They still smell of East Berlin. She pushes them to one end and Thomas sits next to her, his knees cracking. It is time to listen.

Chapter Seventeen

Neil screws the back onto the radio and switches it on. There is only white noise. He has lost the one channel that was working and is too tired to open it up again. It will have to wait.

The table has been set for some time. The bread is drying out, the cheese slices curling at the edges. It is getting dark earlier now. The sun has already vanished. Silke and Thomas have been talking for a long time, although it is quiet up there now.

Neil is starving. It would be rude to help himself to the food, but he slips a piece of bread in his pocket and goes quietly upstairs. He might read for a while, until he hears them go down. He notices Silke's door is shut. He can hear low voices.

There is something on his pillow. He steps inside, closing the door behind him. He goes over to the bed and there it is, the thing that went missing: his father's military epaulette. Thomas probably took it and Silke has replaced it. There is a note with it, on thin blue paper. She is probably apologising for her violent, kleptomaniac brother.

Neil sits on the bed and picks up the letter. The envelope is underneath, badly wrinkled, the ink bleeding. It is not a note from Silke. It is the letter from his father.

Dear Neil,

This is a letter of explanation. You will understand me better, as a man and as a father.

I did not have the Wall sickness which other people suffered. It was not inside my head. Even all these years after it fell, the Wall continues to infiltrate my heart.

I was a Stasi officer for many years. I do not wish to apologise. We have never been defined as criminals. All that happened – the shadowing, the intrusion, the bugging, the arrests, the detentions, the interrogations – none of this was ever wrong in the eyes of the law.

We belonged to an exceptionally proficient secret police agency, our surveillance techniques the most meticulous on earth. Our attention to detail was quite remarkable. It was all done with the cooperation of informers: one in every six ordinary citizens. But the Stasi were also ordinary people. They simply happened to work for the state, in order to keep the party in power. Otherwise, we were the same as anyone else.

We looked tirelessly for what we called negative enemy force. For this, we needed photographs. That was one of my tasks. For capturing people in the street, entering or exiting buildings, I had a camera concealed in my tie. But many of our pictures were not of people. We needed their story, the story of how they lived.

When the object of interest was at work and their house empty, we entered using skeleton keys and wearing gloves. My first job was to take Polaroids of the rooms before anything was examined. This ensured we returned everything to the right places. We left no sign we had ever been there, unless directed to do so.

Our pictures were of the small, daily details. Details identical to my own: the same food, plates, furnishings. You might say the pictures were dull, mundane. Yet they had their own drama. They captured a person's life, while contributing to their downfall.

Another of my specialities was fabricating evidence and spreading rumours. We were told to unearth facts that would discredit a person of interest. And, if necessary, to blend that information with foolproof fictions to cement their dishonour. This was only a matter of several phone calls. These were suffi-cient to destroy the object's reputation in the workplace, or their marriage. Some embezzlement here, an adulterous affair there.

We were not madmen who had lost our way. We knew exactly what we were doing. We studied scholarly works which explained how to destroy people at their core. We had comprehensive training, manuals which made our job clear, the same as a shop manager or a bank manager would have. Instructions for the working day.

It all came under one heading: Zersetzung. *This is not a translatable word. The closest I can manage is 'disintegra-tion'. The total disintegration of a person's spirit.*

My problem is not one I can live with. I am so tired of confronting the past. I have liquidated souls. I have witnessed the suffering. But you may be surprised to learn that none of these are the hardest to bear. What I cannot live with is my inability to accept that it was dishonourable. What is wrong with me is the absence of guilt: if I had that time back again, I would do everything the same.

I had a job. I was given my orders. I was part of an ide-ology designed to strengthen the country. And if anyone was destabilising the system or attempting to escape it, then they were trying to sabotage our endeavours to make it work.

After reunification, I was lost. I was conditioned to have power. I was incapable of tolerating any other way of life. Everything had to be done my way. You already know that. There is no need to tell you how things were. I know I lost my wife and daughter as a result. I despised you when you dis-appointed my expectations. It made me inhuman, yet I could neither change, nor blame myself.

And you, Neil, are the same as me. You allowed your friend to be beaten and kicked to death. In the company of his murderer, you turned your back and ate chips on the way home. I have passed the gene of coldness to you. If you had been alive then, you might have been a fine Stasi officer, or an informer.

This is why I want you to have the village. You can make it better and stronger. Reunification has weakened it, sucked out the younger generation. You can give this village its life back. Repair it. Invest in it. Make it work again, Neil. Do not let it die.

Your father

The letter slides out of Neil's hands to the floor. There is no sound in the house. Birds are singing in the tree outside his window. A streak of light remains in the sky, among the drag of grubby clouds. In the far distance, a tractor chugs through a field.

The epaulette is lying on the bed. Neil takes out his phone. He struggles to type the description into Google. He keeps making mistakes. He doesn't want to accept the *Did you mean...* suggestions. He wants all his words to come out accurately.

Google keeps telling him there are no matches. He is given tips on how to succeed. He realises he is including too much detail. At last he finds some images, but these are adorned with twisted knots like silver wheatsheaves. His father's epaulette is dull in comparison. Neil is making the drab bit of felt far too complicated, elevating it to a superior rank.

He deletes 'thin, wine-red outer edge, thicker pale-grey border'. He requests results for 'grey Stasi epaulette'. And there it is.

He had always thought his father worked in a humdrum office in East Berlin. Maybe the Stasi training was ideal preparation for his estate agency career in the UK. He probably never let his viewers leave a house until they agreed to buy.

His father reinvented himself as a casualty of the regime, when all along he was its facilitator. Neil tries to process this information, but can only weep for the way it makes his own past feel ridiculous. His father's suffering was the only justification Neil has ever had, the only way to vindicate his behaviour. It was the only solid reason why he was a terrible father, but it was false. It was a reason which never existed.

Neil wipes his eyes. He holds the shoulder board, as it seems to be called, against the images on his screen: a perfect match. Now he will be inundated with adverts for military memorabilia. Every day he offers up more intelligence about himself than even the Stasi gathered during decades of surveillance. Big Brother has become Big Data. Did the irony ever occur to his father, or is that why he always refused to have a phone or order anything online?

Neil shuts the shoulder board in a drawer. He reads the letter again. He searches for mistakes, crossings-out, repetitions, tearstains. Anything that will let slip that this was a difficult letter to write. But it is immaculate. No hint of hesitation, no desperation or remorse. People are still 'objects of interest'. If there is anything to detect between the lines, it is pride. His father calls it an explanation. If explanations should uncover the truth, the letter succeeds. The ink is saturated with non-guilt – only despair at its lack.

Even the part about the village, about not letting it die, is a way of clawing back control. It is not about saving this community. It is not about giving Neil's life some meaning. It is about restoring the old state, kicking against reunification.

And of all the thoughts crowding into Neil's mind, the main one is the knowledge that his father was a coward. His explanation was left behind after death, when no one could hold him to account. He found the neatest possible way out. He hanged himself from the rafters in the attic. Not because of the lives he destroyed, but because he felt nothing for them.

Neil goes to the window. The trees are turning: scarlet, copper, russet. Haymaking is now a relentless activity, the machinery working well into evening. The villagers are part of the race against time, helping Renate to get it baled before the weather changes.

Neil imagines working outside with his shirt off, the last of the sun on his back, sweating from hard work rather than panic. He would have welcomed it. But this letter has been opened and Neil has to go.

He is struggling to breathe. He opens the window. The air is sweet with the threat of rain. The chickens are scratching, frantic to unearth all they can before they take shelter. Neil turns away, throws everything into his suitcase and holdall. He slides his toolbox out from under the bed. A spider has woven a web over the clasp.

He picks up the lists the residents gave him and paces about, reading them. There is so much to be done. He puts the lists on the turnip crate and lights a cigarette. He allows his mind to clear, sitting down on the bed until the cigarette is spent. He stubs it out and picks up the papers. They are no longer quivering. This is his work, here in his hands. Here is the foundation of a new routine.

He has missed his plans and rotas. This is what he does best. He takes out his notepad and writes everything down, crossing out page after page as he reshuffles the jobs into order of priority. He cross-checks his schedule with the lists, making sure he has left nothing out. It is a gigantic undertaking. There is no one else who can set it in motion.

If he sells his father's house, he could move into a little terraced place like his mother's. The old biscuit factory has been converted into dozens of Lewises. He would make a profit to invest in the village. He could employ roofers and plasterers and carpenters. He could build a small cluster of affordable new homes to encourage the young people back. Maybe – in time – a shop, a petrol station, a fully refurbished school.

Across the landing, Silke's door creaks open. Neil crumples the lists into his holdall, throws in his notepad. He runs downstairs, his baggage banging against the bannisters. He stumbles on the gravel. Its dust has turned his loafers white. He throws everything into the car and climbs in. It smells bad, of something rotting.

He fumbles with the ignition. Footsteps are crunching in the gravel. Thomas is coming for him. He is carrying a huge, coiled hose. Neil can't remember how to breathe.

He forgot how to breathe once before, in his second term at senior school. At eleven, he already looked like a young man, far more developed than the other boys in his year. Bumfluff was sprouting on his upper lip. His voice was sometimes deep and crackly. He could never imagine anyone wanting to be his friend. Everyone else looked so good together, some in their pairs and others in groups. Even the lankiest or plumpest boys seemed more normal than Neil. His long limbs gave the impression he might be athletic, but he was hopeless at sport. Once people realised that, he was a colossal disappointment.

At one point, he thought he might not stay entirely friendless. There was Tim Foley. Tim was in the year above and he was always alone. In Neil's second term, everyone was told to go to the hall at lunchtime and study Tim Foley's exhibition of meteorological charts. A group of older boys started messing about and knocked Neil into Tim's easels. Tim managed to save one and Neil grappled with two at once. It was the most coordinated movement he had ever made in his life.

Tim said, 'Thanks,' and Neil said, 'Yeah, cheers,' which he had never said before. It made the back of his neck burn.

It was horrifying, the future Tim's climate charts were predicting for the world, but Tim Foley himself had a reassuring presence, like a gentle professor. His faraway eyes were kind. He said scientists were taking notice of the problem and would basically work out how to unclog the sky. Neil visited the charts at break and at lunchtime every day for the entire week of the exhibition.

He decided to invite Tim to tea. Not at the weekend when his father was bound to orchestrate the whole visit. If they sat in the garden, he would drag out the swing-ball set or hammer in the cricket stumps. If they listened to music, he would trail up to Neil's room and sit with them, shaking his head because it was pop instead of classical. He would be the elephant in the room. Neil and Tim would have to keep dodging his swaying trunk, the quiet flap of his ears.

When Neil finally found the courage to ask, Tim said no.

'Sorry. Not ungrateful,' he said. 'It's just I have a ton of work to do.'

Neil said it was fine. He had masses of work as well. At the end of the corridor, he said, 'See you then cheers,' and spent the first half of double French in the toilets.

He sat in a cubicle and thumped his thighs with his fists. It was excruciatingly stupid to be disappointed. But it was the kind of disappointment which crushes you. Not because Tim had said no, but because it was Neil's own fault he did not say yes. He wanted to kick himself for going about it all wrong. What if he could be given that time back? He would handle it so brilliantly.

The other reason he ended up in the toilets when he should have been conjugating irregular verbs was because he needed to revisit all the things he had said and how he had said them. He stripped every word and gesture to the bone, trying to uncover the moment he had fouled up.

He started laughing at himself. It echoed off the tiles, mocking him in every cubicle, urinal and washbasin. He went to the second half of French and claimed he had been in the sickroom with a headache, but the teacher checked. Which meant his absence was unaccounted for during the hour in which someone vandalised Tim Foley's meteorological charts.

The headmaster sent for Neil. He was considering suspension. This was exceptional for a pupil in their second term. Neil felt faint and couldn't take in enough air. He was violently ill over the headmaster's sisal rug and ended up in the sickroom after all.

Tim Foley stepped up and said Neil was the only person to have shown a genuine interest in his climatology exhibits and he did not believe for a moment that he was the guilty party. The headmaster took this into account, but remained unconvinced that Neil had sat in the toilets for the hour in question. He gave him Friday afternoon detention for the rest of term.

There was sustained sniggering from the gang of boys who were almost certainly the culprits. Neil had blotted his copybook now, their smirks said when they silently waylaid him in quiet places. Every time they fancied damaging something, he would be first in line for the blame.

Neil kept his head down and worked hard, hoping to be exemplary, wishing he could be trusted again. But he knew trust was hard to recapture. He knew there would always be someone out to get him.

The car starts. Neil pushes the gearstick into first. He feels for the handbrake. He is about to release it when Gudrun says, 'Driving away like a criminal, are you?'

His fingers rest lightly on the handbrake. He is not a criminal. He has come to rescue a village.

He gets out of the car. He tries to keep his movements slow and fluid. He can smell Thomas.

'Don't come near me,' Neil says.

He repeats it. He keeps his voice low, his tone measured. He maintains eye contact with Thomas. He has never faced anyone down before.

'There is a fire at the farm,' Thomas says. 'Quick, drive.'

He throws the hose onto the backseat. Neil does as he is told. The smoke scalds their throats before they see the flames.

'Renate has allowed a party in a field,' Thomas says. He is breathing loudly and his hands are in fists. 'It is a group of young people from the town. They were using a generator for the music. They packed straw bales around it to deaden the noise.'

Neil parks in the adjoining field, where there is a tap next to a trough. Thomas thinks his hose will just about reach over the hedge. Beyond it a plume of dirty grey smoke is rising. They work together to unspool the hose. Neil fetches his fold-up stepladder from the boot. They climb to the top of the hedge, drop down the other side and run with the hose to the fire.

People are shouting, tossing buckets of water. Others are dragging the unlit straw bales away. Flames are already licking at the car which brought the generator. The bumper is alight before Thomas and Neil can reach it. No water emerges from the hose.

Thomas swears and shakes it. There is only a trickle. Neil runs back along its length and finds a kink. He straightens it, but Thomas shouts, 'Still nothing.'

Neil runs further along and finds three more kinks. He untwists them all, but the first one reappears.

'Let go a minute,' he shouts to Thomas.

Thomas drops the hose and Neil grabs it. He carefully loosens the stubborn kink, making sure he does not reinstate the others.

'Right, go,' he says.

Nothing. Thomas curses again.

The car is well and truly alight. A woman keeps screaming. Someone is phoning the fire brigade to see how much longer they will be. With the village so remote and the lanes narrow, it will be twenty minutes more.

At last the water comes. It dribbles out for a few seconds, then gushes. Thomas blasts the fire from close range, but has to move back from the heat. It is not enough water, not enough power. The flames leap higher.

Sparks fly into a few straw bales which have been hauled aside, close to a barn. They all ignite. Thomas can do nothing to fight it.

More people arrive with hoses, but there are no more taps nearby. People come with buckets. They fill them at the trough in the next field and climb over on Neil's ladder. By the time they have staggered across the field, the buckets are barely half-full.

The firefighters arrive too late to prevent the barn burning down. It is stacked to the rafters with hay. The fire is jubilant, spreading relentlessly from bale to bale. They work for hours to bring the blaze under control, but will have to stay all night. Thomas is told to fetch the tractor and trailer and remove as many bales as possible. The men blast them with water on the ground.

Neil can only stand back with everyone else. The heat haze above the flames is mesmerising him. It used to happen in chemistry lessons. There would be a shimmering around the Bunsen burners. The atmosphere undulated, a distortion which made him calm and sleepy. He wondered if he was the only person who saw this hidden world of the air.

Silke arrives with coffee. She does not offer any to Neil. She passes the flask to others, then watches Thomas shifting the bales and the firemen dousing them.

Eventually, she asks, 'Will you make sure Renate has a new barn?'

'She will have to ask her insurance company,' Neil says. 'And they won't be pleased she allowed people to surround a generator with straw near a barn full of hay.'

'I don't know if she has insurance. People are saying it's your responsibility now.'

Neil cannot imagine the fire and its ramifications are anything to do with him. It is his village, but individuals still have to take responsibility for their own mistakes.

'I'll add it to the list,' he says. 'By the way, it looks as if someone has steamed a letter of mine open.'

'That will be the damp, Herr Fischer. It penetrates everything.'

'It also disappeared from my drawer and turned up on my pillow.'

'Really? Are you sure you didn't take it out yourself? You have been confused since you fell on the landing.'

Thomas has finished moving the hay. He comes over to them, wet and filthy. 'We can drive home now,' he says. 'The firemen are staying. I'll come back at daybreak.'

Neil retrieves his ladder and folds it back into the boot. He takes out a sheet of polythene. Thomas is already in the car. He has to get out while Neil spreads the polythene on the passenger seat.

'There. You can get in now.'

Thomas sits obediently on the polythene. From the backseat, Silke says, 'Herr Fischer tells me he has a letter which appears to have been steamed open.'

Thomas lights a cigarette. 'The damp distorts anything made of paper.'

'Then he will have to rectify the damp.'

'Perhaps he intends to.'

'Or perhaps he will add it to his list.'

'Come on, Silke, have faith. He helped tonight.'

'Thanks,' Neil says. 'Thank you, Thomas.'

Silke goes straight to bed. Thomas finds two bottles of beer and sits at the kitchen table.

'Join me,' he says, uncapping the bottles.

Neil sits down. His throat is raw from the smoke. He and Thomas gulp the beer in a cordial rhythm. Neil is seeing the red and green lights again. Maybe it is an effect of watching the fire. He closes his eyes, hoping to shut them out, or in.

Thomas's head is drooping. His breathing is shallow and regular like a child's. Neil is convinced he has not read the letter. His distrust would not be thawing this easily. Not in a million years would he have clinked bottles with Neil. There is real scope now for friendship. Silke was frosty tonight, but that was down to the shock of the fire and concern for Renate.

Neil is beginning to believe he moved the letter from drawer to pillow himself. He has felt spaced-out since the fall on the landing. As for the damp, he can see from here that the newspapers stacked by the back door are badly buckled. The calendar on the wall is curling at the edges. You could not bring anything vulnerable into this house.

Neil dozes off, aware his tired breaths match the tempo of Thomas's. Later, he wakes to the rough, persistent caw of the heron and sunlight creeping through the crooked blind. Thomas is watching him.

There are eight more beer bottles on the table, all empty.

Chapter Eighteen

Silke does not sleep. An hour before dawn she squashes her belongings into plastic carriers: jeans, a couple of jumpers, the new outfit bought for Berlin, her stupid cushions with their scent of other times. She stuffs them and all the clothes back in the wardrobe. She is tired of memories. Instead, she packs her toothbrush, a bar of soap, her flannel and cold cream. They fit into one small carrier. She picks up a small photograph of her parents' wedding. They look serious, but not unhappy with their supervised life. She removes the picture from its frame and tucks it into her handbag with her phone, a torch, a pair of pinking shears, a small spirit level, a ruler and a roll of masking tape.

When she came home, her parents said nothing about her time in prison. Maybe they thought the house was bugged and doubtless they were right. They handed her full responsibility for the chickens. All their conversations were about laying and worming and grain. Later, in the final weeks of their lives, the focus swung to concealed dangers: rats, red mite, foxes at night.

Silke pads down to the kitchen, the handbag and carrier looped over her arm. She takes no notice of the men asleep at the table. She quietly packs a chunk of cheese and a few slices of bread. She leaves the rest of the loaf on a tray with the butter and a few plums for Thomas and Neil's breakfast. They will imagine she is busy outside or visiting Renate. She will not be missed. Later, of course, when there is no dinner, no sign of her, they will be thrown by the disruption to routine. By then she will have forgotten them.

She has a look at the sleeping hens and finds an egg she did not see yesterday. It is especially large and feels heavy. It will have a double yolk. She leaves it there and says goodbye.

She leaves her stiff, uncomfortable shoes behind. It is a long walk to the station. Perhaps one day Herr Fischer will arrange a bus service. The village has tried for years, but the authorities seem to believe Marschwald no longer exists. Well, the village has Herr Fischer to speak up for it now. Perhaps someone will listen to him, if he chooses to act.

On the way, she visits Renate. The firefighters are packing up and Renate is already busy with the day's work. There is still much to be done in the fields. She has not had time to count the cost of what is lost.

'Where are you going so early?' she asks Silke, nodding at the carrier bag.

'Just out and about. Will you be all right?'

'Of course. No life was lost. Thomas on his way yet?'

'Soon, I think. He fell asleep at the table with Herr Fischer.'

'Ah yes, Herr Fischer. Skilled at straightening hoses, I believe.'

They walk briskly around the yard. Two tractors are manoeuvring into position by the silo, ready to power the machinery which will fill it with grain.

'Your Herr Fischer has made a mistake cutting down that tree,' Renate says, beckoning the tractor drivers to move closer.

'He thought it was causing subsidence,' Silke says.

'Yes, but removing the tree may cause a new problem. A problem he has not foreseen.'

Silke has to shout over the approaching tractors. 'What problem is that?'

'It is called heave. The soil swells because the tree is no longer there to absorb water.'

'So instead of the ground shrinking, it will expand?'

'Exactly. If that happens, it will become unstable. He should have checked first whether he was about to make things worse.'

'I believe he did look it up online. Maybe he skipped that part of the advice.'

Silke wonders how long it will take to reveal its consequences, this unseen shift of the soil. She no longer cares, but she will remember the day she wielded the chainsaw.

Renate whistles for her dog. He bounds up to her, his coat matted with mud. Silke pats his head, surprisingly warm and soft for such a bony creature.

As Silke leaves, she asks the firefighters for a lift. Anywhere near the railway station will do, she tells them. They will pass it, they tell her. They can take her all the way.

The sky is overcast, but one towering cloud has a dazzling edge beneath it. By the time the fire truck reaches the outskirts of town, the sun is creeping out. When they pass the cemetery where her parents are buried, Silke places her hand on the window. After they died, Thomas was the only person left to trust. He was over-protective, determined to keep her under his wing, yet so insecure he could not sleep alone. He was her husband, her child, her custodian. Now he is 'Mustang', a foolish name in a file.

'What do you think of your Herr Fischer, then?' one of the firefighters asks when they stop at the station.

She takes her hand off the window. 'I don't think anything of him.'

'Is he going to do something for your village?'

'I don't know,' she says, watching the outline of her fingers disappear from the glass. 'But he has done something for me.'

One of the men jumps out and walks round to her side. He wants to help her down.

'Thank you,' she says. 'But I can manage.'

She gets out and the man reaches in for her carrier bag.

'Wait,' she tells him. 'I don't need that.'

He glances inside. 'But these are your things.'

'Not anymore. Help yourselves to the food.'

She goes into the station and collects her ticket. There is only half an hour to wait. She sits on a bench with her handbag on her lap, her legs crossed at the ankle. Her tall cloud has followed her, about to release the whole of the sun. The warmth slides over her feet, her ankles, her calves.

Five minutes before her train is due, Silke stands up. She waits for it to appear, tiny in the distance. As it approaches, the track seems to shudder. When the train stops, Silke is directly in front of a carriage door. A young woman in shorts emerges. She has lean, golden legs. As she walks past, Silke turns round and watches her take a tube of sweets from her colourful backpack. She sits on Silke's bench, a wrapped sweet between her teeth, while she searches for her ticket. She stands up and hoists the pack onto her back. She smiles at Silke before heading towards the taxi rank.

'Are you getting on?' enquires a man behind Silke on the platform.

Silke turns back to the train and climbs inside. She finds a seat by a window and catches sight of the cloud, like a mass of synthetic whipped cream, the socialist kind. Shortly before departure, it drifts out of sight. The train jolts and she is on her way.

She is going to Mitte, the heart of Berlin. It was once split in two, the eastern part surrounded on three sides by the Wall. Now Silke has access to everything: the cathedral, Alexanderplatz, the TV Tower, Unter den Linden, the Brandenburg Gate, the Victory Column, the Reichstag. East or West, it is all her city again.

She takes out her phone and looks at the address she has memorised, the address of the furnished flat waiting for her in Mitte. She scrolls through the pictures of the imposing old building with large windows. The flat is tiny, like a box. Everything she needs is in there. Everything she needs beyond it is out there, in her city.

At the park gates, Silke watched Martin pick up his business card and put it away. He got up from the bench like a tired, old man and walked away with his head down. Anyone passing him in his sweaty jogging clothes would assume he had overdone it. At one point he sat down on the grass by the pond. He drew up his feet and rested his arms on his knees. He looked down at the ground, at the small patch of green between his legs. She had shrunk his world to less than the space in her cell.

She had glanced at the card, committed his number to memory. She phoned him a few minutes later and said, 'I need to live alone in the city. A basic flat is all I need. I will get a part-time job, cleaning or waitressing, to pay for essentials. The rest of the time will be for my degree. Only thirty-seven years late.'

Martin said he would call her back. Twenty minutes later, he said, 'I will rent a place for you. It's the least—'

'Don't. Let's talk only about money. That's all we have in common now. You have it and I need it. When I am a lecturer, I will pay you back. That is a promise and you know I mean it.'

'You don't have to pay me—'

'I am free now. I can choose what I do, Martin. Do you agree?'

Martin agreed.

The building is still peppered with bullet holes from the war. It is tired in a majestic way. Silke had imagined concrete stairwells filled with echoes, but there is warm, red carpet on the stairs. The corridors are also carpeted and the doors to the flats are the old, solid kind. Not the sort with a metal bracket which swings them shut with a bang. They even have their own doorstep, their own doormat. This is a private place.

The flat is neat and clean, the décor and furniture pale peach and white. She has not lived with gentle colours before. She touches the smooth walls, the glossy skirting boards, the gleaming mirror. Martin has put bread in the kitchen cupboard, butter and cheese in the fridge, an envelope filled with money on the worktop. She can use it to open a bank account, to begin her life.

The description of the flat mentioned a breakfast bar. This must be the counter with a stool tucked beneath. It is presumably meant for every meal, not just breakfast. It makes sense not to crowd the small space with a table for one. She slides the stool out cautiously. It makes no sound. She turns it upside down. Little felt pads have been stuck to its feet. She told Martin she wanted a quiet place, somewhere that would not feel like a prison cell. It seems he got the message.

She rights the stool and skims it back beneath the breakfast bar. Not a sound. She takes a plate from the crockery cupboard and a knife from the cutlery drawer, and makes herself a sandwich. She pulls out the stool and sits at her bar, watching her city from her window.

When she has finished the sandwich, she goes from room to room with her phone and takes an enormous number of pictures. She photographs the contents of drawers and cupboards, and every item of furniture from different angles. She peers at the surfaces and walls, all bare apart from the mirror. She asked Martin not to provide ornaments, lamps, books, cushions, radio, television or paintings. Again, he has obliged.

She takes the spirit level from her handbag and places it on top of the mirror. It is slightly off-kilter. She leaves it that way. She measures the gap between the sofa and the wall, between the bed and the wall. She fetches the stool and stands on it to shine her torch on the ceilings. She attaches a small strip of white masking tape to one edge of the smoke alarm in the hall.

She repacks her handbag and goes out for the rest of the day. She buys a toothbrush, flannel, eggs, underwear and a pair of jeans. She drinks coffee in a huge department store and watches people choose from the enormous array of food. Some are confident and gather their items quickly; others spend a long time deciding and queuing. She watches people who arrive after her, particularly people who are alone and not constantly scrolling on their phones. She waits for them to leave.

She sits there until late in the afternoon, leaving behind three solo coffee drinkers: a woman in a green dress, a man in a blue suit and red tie, another in a grey jacket and cream shirt. She takes a convoluted route to the exit. They do not appear behind her.

Once outside, she waits near the entrance doors for over an hour.

16.33 hours: woman in green comes out, sees a friend, walks away with her.

16.47 hours: man in blue suit/red tie rushes out, hails taxi.

17.35 hours: man in grey emerges, strides off down the street.

They do not glance at her as they pass, nor look over their shoulder as they go on their way.

Via a long-winded route, pausing every ten minutes to let people behind walk past, Silke returns to the flat. She compares every object and surface in every room with her photographs. No change. She checks inside the drawers and cupboards. All in order. She inspects the walls, ceilings and skirting boards. No dis-coloured patches on the paintwork.

The tiny screws in the light switches are in exactly the same positions. The mirror still tips to the same slight degree. She looks behind it, checking the wall for the slightest imperfection. She reviews the positions of the furniture. No old dents reveal themselves in the carpet. The sofa is still five centimetres from the wall, her bed three centimetres away.

She fetches the stool and stands on it to reach the smoke alarm. The tape is still there, still the same shape – one end straight, the other zigzagged where she cut it with pinking shears. She removes it and measures the length: exactly twenty-two millimetres, as it should be. She opens up the alarm casing, just in case. No foreign object inside.

She lines up her purchases in cupboards and drawers which glide silently open and shut, then cracks three eggs into a blue bowl and makes an omelette. She eats it at the breakfast bar, watching the streets she has walked as a free woman.

After she has washed up, she goes into the bathroom. The bath has a frosted screen and a shower attachment. She inserts the plug and turns on the hot tap. Clear water cascades. She reads the directions on a bottle of rose-pink bath foam. A thin stream is all that is needed. She pours carefully. The fragrance of spring flowers bubbles up.

She will empty the bath in a minute. But one day, she will climb in and lie back in the soft, scented water.

Chapter Nineteen

Neil lifts his head from his arms. He rubs his shoulders and neck. Thomas is blue-grey with stubble, his eyes bloodshot. He is finishing off the beer dregs.

'What time is it?' Neil asks.

Thomas shrugs. 'Past dawn.'

Neil shifts on his chair, trying to ease the stiffness in his back. He would love a cup of tea. He is not in the mood for monosyllabic conversation.

'We should be helping the firemen, shouldn't we?'

Thomas shrugs again. It is not like him to shirk. He is always at work early, either at the farm or chopping wood here in the yard.

'Aren't you meant to be at the farm anyway?'

'Not today.'

Neil's heart sinks a little. 'Silke out with the hens?'

There is no answer. Neil stands up and stretches. His head immediately swims and he has to sit down again.

'My blood pressure,' he says. 'It's a bit low.'

Thomas lights a cigarette. He switches the radio on. Nothing happens.

'I didn't break it,' Neil says. 'I was trying to mend it.'

Thomas gives it a thump. 'Then you failed.'

'You broke my lighter.'

'Prove it.'

'How else did it get broken?'

Thomas blows his smoke at Neil, then says, 'You should take more care.'

Neil gets up slowly and goes to the kettle. The coffee is in a tin with a rusty lid. Neil has no idea how much to put in the ancient-looking glass jug. Maybe it's one spoonful per person and one for the pot. That was how his grandma made tea. There is a plastic spoon with a split handle in the tin. Neil wonders if everything in the village is old and broken, rotting and rusting. They could do with throwing it all on the Friday bonfire and starting again. But first things first. He has his new schedule now. Spoons can wait.

He would like to tell Thomas about his plans, but he is like a bear with a sore head this morning. He would rather tell Silke first anyway. She will definitely approve. He will ask her to help him fix up another meeting so he can make public promises. That way he can't change his mind.

'Would Silke like me to make her some coffee, do you think?'

Thomas holds out his hands in a gesture that implies he doesn't care. 'She's not here,' he says.

Neil fills the kettle. 'She must be outside, collecting the eggs.'

Thomas snorts. 'Hens lay six hours after sunrise. Eggs are collected in the afternoons.'

'Of course, yes. I wasn't thinking.'

He puts the kettle on the stove. Maybe he should treat them to an electric one, as a thank you for having him.

'Is she letting the hens out, then?'

Thomas finishes smoking, then lets out a series of burps. The smell of them reaches Neil at the sink, where he is rinsing cups. He puts them upside down on a tea towel and turns to face Thomas. Perhaps he can stare him out, force him to answer.

Thomas pulls the noisy chair out from the table. His feet thud onto it, still in their work boots. He scratches his bristly chin. He takes out the spray he uses to clear his nose and squirts it up each nostril. He tips his head back and yawns, his jaws clicking. He speaks before the yawn has ended.

'She's not here. Not in the yard. Not in the house.'

'Have you phoned her?'

'No answer.'

Neil looks at the neatly laid tray of breakfast. 'Has she gone to the farm for meat?'

Thomas points at the string bag hanging from a nail on the back of the door.

'She might have gone to help clear up after the fire.'

Thomas points at her wellingtons and galoshes on the doormat.

'Then she must have gone for a walk. What shoes would she wear for that? Where does she keep them?'

It was a mistake to ask two questions. An answer to one is like getting blood out of a stone. Thomas goes over to the corner cupboard and yanks it open. The ironing board and broom fall out. The board whacks him on the nose. He throws it down and stamps on it. He flings the broom across the kitchen. Neil ducks as it flies past him and thumps against the door.

Neil soaks a dishcloth in cold water and wrings it out. 'Here. Put this on it. It brings out the bruise, they say.'

'Who says?'

'No idea. It's just something people say.'

'What people?'

'I really don't know. Let's forget it. It will get lost in translation.'

The kettle is too quiet. Neil taps it lightly. It is stone cold. He has forgotten to light the ring. They really could do with Silke coming back soon.

'Shall I look for her shoes?'

Thomas sits down, gingerly touching his bruise.

'You big girl's blouse,' Neil mutters. He steps over the ironing board to the corner cupboard. 'So what are they like, her usual shoes? This is where she keeps them, I'm assuming?'

Thomas sits down, breathing heavily, the reddening flannel sucking into his face.

'I've found some sandals,' Neil says. 'Brown leather straps.'

'Mine.'

'What about ankle boots – red quilted ones with a sheepskin lining?'

'Mine.'

Eventually, Thomas mumbles something about Silke moving things into her old bedroom. He says the shoes are flat, brown lace-ups. Neil runs up to have a look. The bed is made and the room fairly tidy, apart from a heap of fallen ceiling plaster. He looks everywhere, but finds only the stiff-looking navy pair from the first visit to Berlin. He goes back to the kitchen.

Thomas tries phoning Silke, but there is no reply.

'I'm sure she's all right,' Neil says.

'She had a shock, so...'

Neil waits for Thomas to go on, but he leaves his sentence there.

'You mean, the shock of seeing her file? For what it's worth, I think she's coping well.'

'What you think is worth nothing. You do not know her.'

'Tell me about her, then.'

'She was clever,' Thomas says. 'But also careless, too easily led. I tried to hold her back, you know. I wanted her to be safe.'

'Maybe she was unhappy with the regime. She wanted to do something about it.'

'There are some things you must do nothing about.'

'But you must have been relieved when the Wall fell.'

'It was not all bad here,' Thomas says, lighting a cigarette. 'But after reunification our industries shut down overnight. For the first time, we had a serious unemployment problem. People with a good education suddenly had nothing.'

'At least you were free.'

Thomas tilts his head back and exhales a column of smoke. 'Freedom was a struggle for us. It is hard to live without restrictions, to understand independence. When we were always watched, it made us feel protected.'

'Would Silke agree, do you think?'

'She never discusses it. And I have finished discussing it with you. Come on, we must search.'

They troop out to Neil's car and drive around the lanes. The sky has cleared and the sunlit village looks almost wholesome. Neil pulls up by the marsh.

'We will not find her here,' Thomas says. 'Keep going.'

Neil is tired of Thomas calling all the shots. He gets out and walks a few metres, trying to remember the route that was safe.

Thomas shouts from the car, 'You go too far, my friend. You are near dangerous ground. I don't want to have to rescue you.'

Neil picks his way carefully back to the car, his trouser hems sodden. 'I was only planning to go a bit further,' he says, his loafers slipping on the rubber mat as he steps inside. 'Then I would have turned back.'

Thomas's laugh sounds like a bark. 'You would not have had time. Come on, drive.'

Neil's feet squelch on the pedals.

'Look at you,' says Thomas. 'You are not meant for this.'

Neil insists that they head towards the shops in the nearby town in case she called for a taxi, although Thomas mumbles that she has never done so before.

In the town, they are caught in a traffic jam near the station. The fire engine is a few vehicles ahead in the queue.

'They must have finished, then,' Neil says, drumming his fingers on the steering wheel. His stomach growls with hunger.

Thomas sits up from his slumped position. 'What's that smell?'

'A mouldy potato. I'm keeping it for sentimental reasons.'

'Fucking idiot.'

Thomas winds down the window and shouts to someone he knows. He does not ask if they have seen Silke. He talks the way men do when they see a male friend.

'It doesn't smell as bad as you,' Neil says to himself.

Neil parks by the station. Thomas heads to the butcher and the chemist. Neil goes to the supermarket. He keeps seeing the coloured lights: static green and flashing red. They make it hard to think straight.

In the first aisle, a young woman is offering samples of cheese to taste. Neil goes back to her three times.

'Gudrun?' he says.

She stares at him. He is pleased when she laughs, but she keeps laughing. It turns into a mocking cackle. She is not a young woman anymore. Her face is lined and weather-beaten. Her teeth are worn to stubs. Lipstick is bleeding into the creases around her mouth. He can still hear her laughter when he leaves and all the way back to the car.

The department store and bookshop have just opened their doors for the day. Neil goes inside both shops, but there are no customers. He hurries back to the car. Thomas is already leaning against it, smoking and waiting for him.

'She's gone *some*where in those lace-ups,' Neil says as they drive back to the village. 'Anywhere else you can think of?'

Thomas shakes his head. He tries phoning Silke again. Nothing. He tells Neil to stop at the farm. They both get out of the car.

'You stay here,' Thomas grunts. 'You'll look like an idiot in those shoes.'

'I'll stay on the less muddy bits. I just want to watch them doing whatever they're doing with the silo.'

'They're filling it.'

'Don't you get to help with that?'

'It's a skilled job.'

Thomas goes in search of Renate. Neil can hear the dog barking and the heron calling. He can smell the marsh more than the farm today. The sun seems to strengthen its bitterness.

The farmhouse is smothered in ivy. It has grown so high it is invading the gutter, creeping into the chimney. He looks it up. If you snip the stems with scissors, it will wither. When it grows back, you snip it again. No need to wrench out its roots. That would be hard work.

Thomas is already striding back to the car. 'She was here a while ago. With a plastic bag.'

'Ah, well, that tells us something.'

'Tells us what?'

'That she was going shopping with a plastic bag?'

'It had things inside it already.'

'Blackberries?'

'Wrong shoes for blackberries.'

'You're obsessed with shoes, Thomas.'

It is reassuring that Silke is busy doing something, somewhere. Neil drives them back and makes the coffee at last. He puts the breakfast tray on the table and they eat every crumb. Thomas goes outside to sharpen his axe. Neil copies his lists again in neater handwriting, then types them into his phone.

He walks to the school and takes a photograph. He uses the gridlines to adjust the picture until the tilt is no longer there. He pushes the door open and steps inside. With his practised eye, he can see the potential straight away: an extension for a small canteen, another for a gym, perhaps a mezzanine floor.

There are still curtains hanging in the classroom. They are falling apart, but he can still make out their brown-and-orange patterns. Dusty books with covers featuring Lenin's profile are stacked on the shelves. Hanging crooked on the wall is a huge, vibrant painting of farmworkers gathering in the harvest. The desks are still in rows facing the blackboard. He tries to guess where his father sat. Probably right at the front. He would have been the first to answer questions, clean the blackboard, impress the teacher.

Neil wonders which of the little chairs were empty the day after the Wall fell. He thinks about the shock for those who arrived the next morning to find their friends had gone.

He makes notes: *hire a skip, clear everything out, have a good clean-up*. He walks around the hall, treading carefully at first, then with more confidence. The floor feels reasonably sound. Yes, he thinks, bouncing lightly on a couple of sagging boards, it is generally solid. He looks up. *Possible issues with ceiling*, he notes. *Rewiring also on the cards*. He adds several question marks.

When all the work is done, they could have a party in here to relaunch the school. Young families from the town could come with their children. They could all bring food and he could organise games.

His father devised a game for Neil's fifth birthday. It was an obstacle course in the lounge. He lined up all the most delicate things in the house: a crystal vase, a tall china dog, a delicate lamp, a wooden warrior with a long spear, an enormous lit candle.

'You must jump over these without touching a single one,' he said.

'I don't want to,' Neil told him, his chin trembling.

'He can't,' Neil's mother said. 'He will fall. He will break everything.'

Neil's father said it was important to conquer fear. And it would be fun, he insisted. After Neil had completed it once, he would beg for another go. He would want to repeat it again and again.

'Here,' he said, taking Neil's arm and pulling him closer. 'This will make it more interesting for you.'

He tied a dark woollen scarf around Neil's head.

'No, no. Don't blindfold him,' Neil's mother said.

'Don't get hysterical. It's just part of the game.'

The rough scarf was tied tightly. It prickled Neil's face and stuck to his tears. He froze to the spot. His father picked him up in one arm and carried him.

'You are now at the starting line,' he said. 'Stop whimpering. We will assist you. You must have faith in us.'

Neil's mother was crying. His father told her to calm down, then whispered something Neil could not hear. After a minute he felt them next to him, one each side. His mother tucked her hand under his right arm, his father did the same under his left. Together they guided him along the course.

'Now *leap*,' his father said when it was the right moment to clear an obstacle.

They gripped his arms tighter to help him spring high enough. Neil was terrified he would smash everything and set the carpet alight. But there was no sound of breakage, no heat from any flames.

At the end of the ordeal, his father said, 'Congratulations, you have succeeded! Now I will remove the blindfold. Look back, Neil, and celebrate your big achievement.'

It was rare for his father to be pleased with him. Neil felt a glorious sense of triumph. He was excited to see the frightening obstacles again, to not be frightened this time.

The scarf was removed and Neil looked back. There was nothing there. All the obstacles had been returned to the correct places. Neil's father was laughing so hard he had to sit down. He slapped his knees and guffawed.

'You jumped over fresh air, Neil. Oh God, you should see your face. Hey, don't look so sad. Did you really think we would trust you not to knock everything over? Great fun, eh? What a game. What a game!'

*

As Neil leaves the school, Gudrun is walking down the slope towards him.

'Hi, Neil,' she calls.

She waves briefly, then eases her thumbs under the straps of her backpack, as if it is too heavy now. A plastic shell hangs on a thin, leather cord around her neck. An empty water bottle hangs from the belt of her shorts and taps against her thigh. The bruise on her toenail has disappeared, the trapped blood finally free to recirculate. Her face is smooth and dark gold from the sun and wind.

'I hiked all the way here,' she says, sinking onto the grass. She puffs and pants, hamming it up.

Neil sits beside her. He wishes he could kiss her. He can already taste it.

'I am glad to see you,' she says, smiling until her nose wrinkles.

'Same.'

'It's beautiful here. You're so lucky to own it.'

His hand is suddenly warm. She is holding it between hers. He looks up at the school in the sunlight, the trees turning colour, the enormous sky.

'I'm going to make it better,' he says.

'You have so much work here.'

'I'll manage.'

'Do you know which was your father's house?'

'I'm not sure.'

'It is the house with the yellow door.'

'How do you know?'

'I asked around. An old lady told me all about him. Some of his relatives escaped to the West, so his parents were taken away for questioning. Your father was immediately put on a train to Berlin and adopted by a family loyal to the regime.'

'Did his parents come back to the house with the yellow door?'

'They were never seen again.'

'Why did my father never tell me?'

'Perhaps it was easier to accept his new life and forget what he had lost. No one should hold onto what has gone.'

'I thought you said it was important never to forget.'

'Not if it makes you unsafe.'

They sit there until the clouds bundle together, until the wind brings the stench of the marsh and the heron's screech, until nearly all the light has gone.

Gudrun says, 'I can't stay.'

'Why not?'

'Because you are swamped.'

'It can wait.'

Her smile disappears. 'Take care, Neil.'

Her hands move away. She uncrosses her legs and stands up in one fluid movement.

'Gudrun, please stay. I'll be happier here with you.'

'You will see me again on one condition.'

'What's that?'

'That you close your eyes while I go. And when you open them, you do not close them again.'

'What, never?'

'Not until we meet in England.'

'You're coming to England?'

'If you can get there, I will find you.'

'Of course I'll be there.'

'That is good to know.'

She turns away and he closes his eyes. Even after half an hour, he can still hear the tap of her water bottle against her thigh. She must have changed her mind. She must be walking around him in a circle, smiling at his confusion. He opens his eyes, but she has gone.

He walks up to the road, but she is not there. He passes the house with the yellow door. An old man with thick glasses is crouching on the roof, tapping loose slates with a hammer, making it safe. The tapping follows Neil all the way back to Thomas and Silke's house.

He pauses to watch the chickens. They show a slight interest in him, in case he has something for them. He fetches some bread and crumbles it in his hands. They flock to him, jittery with expectation. He flings the crumbs, forcing them to run in all directions. He did the same the day after his mother left, when his father went out to round up the three hens and the cockerel. He yelled at them to scatter, willed them to hide in the hedge. But his father caught them all. His hand was still bleeding hours after he packed the cockerel into the crate.

Neil goes upstairs to transcribe the notes to his master list, but he is tired. He lies down on the bed with his father's cassette recorder, the first luxury he bought in the West. When Neil was thirteen, his father gave it to him. He said it was something he had wished for when he became a teenager. He left a cassette on Neil's bed before he killed himself. He had recorded all the fairy stories he used to read him at bedtime.

They were the best memories Neil had. Until he was about five, he had felt secure. At bedtime, warm from his bath and his head sinking into his pillow, he listened to his father's stories until his eyes closed. As soon as he started school, the stories stopped. His father said he should read by himself.

After his father died, Neil bought a pack of blank tapes. He wants to record all the good times he can remember. He wants to read them like stories and keep them for the children he might have in the future. He often slots a cassette into the player and presses Record, but his mind stays as blank as the tape.

In the late afternoon, Thomas and Neil walk to the bonfire to ask if anyone has seen Silke. An elderly woman says, 'Yes, I saw her in the fire engine.'

People laugh, as if the woman is not all there. Thomas makes a phone call, its blue-white light harsh on his face.

'It is true. The firemen drove Silke to the station.'

'She must have had another day in Berlin,' Neil says. 'If we go now, we can meet the last train.'

Thomas clasps Neil's shoulder to steer him away. 'She can make her own way home,' he says. 'Goodnight, everyone. Come on, my friend.'

It rains on the way back. Neil's trousers are soon soaked. He has to break into a half-run to keep up with Thomas. The soles of his loafers have worn through now and are letting in bits of grit.

The house is in darkness. It smells different without Silke, as if the air is too still.

After an hour, Neil says, 'I don't want to alarm you, but we should phone the police now.'

'Let's try one more thing. We will ask Renate again. She was busy earlier, but now she may remember something.'

There is no signal, he says, at the farm. They will have to walk over there. Neil sighs. They set out again, his trousers slapping his ankles. The stones in his shoes chafe between his toes. As the light disappears, a fox screams. A female's mating call perhaps. Or a male, claiming his territory.

When they reach the farm, Thomas says, 'Renate is still outside somewhere. I can hear the dog. Mind where you tread in those shoes.'

'The dog is inside, Thomas. I can see him at the window.'

'We will walk round to the back, then. She doesn't like people knocking on the front door.'

Neil sploshes behind him, round to the side where the moon casts a yellowish light on the silo.

'Quite a sight, isn't it?' he says.

Thomas stops, turns round. 'I have a signal,' he says, holding up his phone. 'And a message from Silke.'

'Oh, thank God. What a relief.'

Now this long day can come to an end. He will go back, stuff down a slice of bread or cake or something. Climb into dry pyjamas and get some proper sleep. When he closes his eyes, the red and green lights might disappear.

'What does Silke say?'

'She had a day out. She's left a note in our room. I must have missed it.'

Neil suppresses a sigh. It would be a mistake to show his irritation now they have bonded.

Thomas lights a cigarette, points it at the silo. 'Some beast, isn't it?'

'I love it,' Neil says. 'I could stand here all day. I don't know why, but I can never resist anything monstrous like this. I feel drawn to it.'

He says this in English. It is far too late to translate the magnetic attraction into German. But Thomas is nodding as if he gets the gist. They are on the same wavelength at last.

'Want to climb the ladder and take a look?' Thomas says, shining his torch upwards.

'We can't. No way. Not without asking Renate. And not in the dark.'

'I have worked here for decades. She trusts me. She would not object to us having fun after such a long day. Watch.'

For a big man, Thomas shins lightly up the ladder, his phone between his teeth. He looks into the silo, raising a thumb to let Neil know how thrilling it is up there.

He makes his way down and says, 'See for yourself.'

'I don't know.'

'Be careful. If you fall in, you sink fast.'

'Christ.'

Neil steps onto the ladder.

'My shoes are too slippy,' he says.

'Wait there.'

Thomas disappears. He comes back with a pair of boots he keeps in Renate's porch. They are not a perfect fit, but Neil feels good in them. The soles grip well. They are heavy, though. They weigh his feet down.

Neil climbs steadily to the top of the ladder and steps onto a small platform. He crouches to open the hatch and peers down into the silo. He can see nothing except blackness. The little lights reappear, all flashing red now. He ignores them. He takes out his phone and switches on the torch. Leaning right over the rim of the silo, he shines his light inside, onto the grain far below.

There is a gentle thud on the rungs, like a delayed echo of Neil's climb. He smells Thomas, feels the vibration as his boots thump onto the platform.

When Neil was six, his father picked him up when they were walking on a cliff. He held him out over the edge and said, 'If you are not careful up here, you will fall. You will disappear into the sea.' It only lasted a second. It was his idea of a joke, or a warning.

Neil has imagined the descent ever since: how long it would last and how it might feel. There was no safe way to fall.

'I will raise the alarm in a few hours,' Thomas says behind him. 'Tell them my friend Neil went off to search again. Renate knows you're obsessed with this monster.'

Thomas presses both hands on Neil's back. He pushes hard. He keeps pushing. Neil is falling. Without solid ground beneath him, the wind and waves crashed as if they were inside his ears. Now, as he lands, he hears the same thunderous rush.

The grain yields under his weight, enough to cushion his fall. It only hurts a little. He has avoided hitting the metal sides. It was a clean, straight descent. He is fine. He will laugh about it later.

This is what friends do on a night out. They play practical jokes. Thomas is in high spirits because Silke is coming home at last. Neil wants to call to him. He needs to think of something witty, something clever. It might be best to wait until he gets out. His voice will bounce about, booming inside the metal cylinder. Thomas will not want Renate to hear what they are up to.

From inside the silo, the echo of Thomas climbing down the ladder is deafening. Time goes by. Neil cannot hear him walk away, but knows he has gone.

Neil battles to shift his body upwards. His legs are already locked. He cannot even wriggle his toes. The grain is ice cold and rising fast. It reaches his chest.

He remembers the importance of staying calm, the advantage it gives you. He saved himself in the gravel pit. If he does not panic, he will be fine by the time Thomas comes back.

His phone has gone. He has lost his glasses, but it is dark in here anyway. He packed a spare pair in his suitcase. He can't remember seeing them, but they must be there. Thomas will guide him home. He will help him to find them.

He must stay calm. He concentrates hard on breathing, but the colossal weight packs him tight. His lungs are straining to inflate. Every time he takes a breath, more grain fills his airway.

A weak circle of light flickers on the concrete wall. Inside the light is Gudrun's beautiful face. He can smell the contents of her backpack, something for all emergencies. Gudrun can make time slow down.

'I am glad to see you,' she says, smiling until her nose wrinkles.
'Same.'
The light is already fading.
'I can't stay,' she says.
'Please, we haven't had enough time.'

'I have always been with you, Neil.'

'No, only a few hours. I could count—'

'Never look back. We are always inside time, drifting. Nothing ever goes away.'

'Gudrun, please, let me come with you.'

The light disappears. The grain fills his mouth.

'Close your eyes, Neil.'

There is a sense of release. Panic is impossible now. As he sinks, he discovers that deep down it is airless, but so much warmer.

Acknowledgements

My heartfelt gratitude goes to friends and fellow writers for dispelling self-doubt, to editor Laura Shanahan and the team at Fairlight Books for responding to my novel in the way every writer hopes for, and to my wonderful family for their unfailing encouragement and endless belief. Thank you all so much.

About the Author

Joanna Campbell studied German at university and as a student spent time living in West Germany. She has worked as a teacher of both German and English, and now writes full-time. Her debut novel *Tying Down the Lion* was published in 2015, and her short story collection *When Planets Slip Their Tracks* (2016) was shortlisted for the Edge Hill Prize. She is a prolific short story and flash fiction writer, with pieces published in many anthologies and literary magazines, and has won several awards, including the London Short Story Prize. Her novella *Sybilla* won the 2021 National Flash Fiction Day Novella-in-Flash Award. She lives in Gloucestershire, and when not writing she enjoys painting and playing the piano.

RICHARD SMYTH

The Woodcock

In 1920s England, the coastal town of Gravely is finally enjoying
a fragile peace after the Great War. Jon Lowell, a naturalist
who writes articles on the flora and fauna of the shoreline, and
his wife Harriet lead a simple life, basking in their love for each
other and enjoying the company of Jon's visiting old school friend
David. But when an American whaler arrives in town with his
beautiful red-haired daughters, boasting of his plans to build
a pier and pleasure grounds a half-mile out to sea, unexpected
tensions and temptations arise.

As secrets multiply, Harriet, Jon and David must each ask
themselves, what price is to be paid for pleasure?

*'The bleakness of the coast, the mist, the shifting nature of
the sands all speak of contingency, brutality, deception'*
—*TLS*

*'Smyth's evocation of place and nature ... is imbued with
a compelling sense of closely observed realism'*
—*Literary Review*

SOPHIE VAN LLEWYN

Bottled Goods

When Alina's brother-in-law defects to the West, she and her husband become persons of interest to the secret services, causing both of their careers to come grinding to a halt. As the strain takes its toll on their marriage, Alina turns to her aunt for help – the wife of a communist leader, and a secret practitioner of the old folk ways.

Set in 1970s communist Romania, this novella-in-flash draws upon magic realism to weave a tale of everyday troubles that can't be put down.

'A story to savour, to smile at, to rage against and to weep over'
—Zoe Gilbert, author of *FOLK*

'Stunning ... tense and atmospheric'
—*Mslexia*

ALAN ROBERT CLARK

Valhalla

May of Teck, only daughter of a noble family fallen from grace, has been selected to marry the troublesome Prince Eddy, heir to the British throne. Submitting to the wishes of Queen Victoria and under pressure from her family, young May agrees. But just as a spark of love and devotion arises between the young couple, Prince Eddy dies of influenza. To her horror, May discovers she is instead to be married to the brother, Georgie, a cold and domineering man. But what can she do?

From the author of *The Prince of Mirrors* comes this gripping account of the life of Queen Mary, one of the most formidable queens of Britain.

'This novel took me by surprise. Clark takes an iconic and forbidding figure and transforms her into a passionate, loving and damaged woman. It's a very moving tale he tells'
—Simon Russell Beale

'This is a heart-breaking tale and no mistake. A beautiful and lyrical tale told with deft brilliance'
—John Sessions